MW00771990

DAY
OF THE
DEMON

Trials of a Demon-Hunting Soccer Mom

DAY
OF THE
DEMON

Trials of a Demon-Hunting Soccer Mom

M&O

DEMON-HUNTING SOCCER MOM

Carpe Demon
California Demon
Demons Are Forever
Deja Demon
The Demon You Know (bonus short story)
Demon Ex Machina
Pax Demonica
Day of the Demon
How to Train Your Demon

Praise for the Demon-Hunting Soccer Mom series

"Ninety-nine percent of the wives and moms in the country will identify with this heroine. I mean, like who hasn't had to battle demons between car pools and play dates?" *Jayne Ann Krentz, New York Times bestselling author*

This book, as crammed with events as any suburban mom's calendar, shows you what would happen if Buffy got married and kept her past a secret. It's a hoot." *Charlaine Harris, New York Times bestselling author*

"Kenner scores a direct hit with this offbeat and humorous adventure, which has an engaging cast of characters. Car pools and holy water make an unforgettable mix." *RT Book Reviews*

"Julie Kenner's Demon Hunting Soccer Mom is one of the high water marks in urban fantasy. Kicking evil's ass is just another thing on Kate Connor's to-do list, but she'll manage it with wit and wisdom, and then drive home in her minivan. This series may be more fun than we deserve!" *Christopher Golden, New York Times bestselling author of ARARAT and RED HANDS*

Day of the Demon © 2021 by Julie Kenner

ISBN: 978-1-953572-15-8

Cover Design & Image by Jocelyn Grant

Published by Martini & Olive Books

V-2021-4-27P

I always knew that parenting a teenager would be like living with a demon from hell. The hormonal explosions. The friend drama. The dating drama. The high school drama. All of the little passion plays that make up the theater that is known as adolescence.

I read all the parenting books. I talked with other moms. I watched movies and television shows.

I anticipated everything ... except for the one thing I couldn't possibly have imagined—

My teenager really is a demon.

Okay, maybe that's a slight exaggeration. Technically, she's only part demon, and that from her father's side. And I'm not even sure how much demon is in her, because we don't really know how much was in her father in those years when he was growing up, his body and soul unknowingly entwined with a demon put there by his own parents when he was an infant in a ritual that no parenting book would ever endorse.

And, yes, the fact that our daughter is part demon did save the world just a few days ago—though that little tidbit didn't even make the local news. Not like that's a shock; preventing the apocalypse hardly ever makes CNN.

But none of that changes the fact that something demonic lives inside my strong, beautiful, snarky daughter. Not just lives—*is*. She's not possessed. She's not playing host. That darkness is part of her. That yearning for power and mayhem. That fundamental, hard, cold evil.

I've never seen it in her. It's never come out.

But I know it's there, and that simple reality scares me to death.

Because how do I protect her from something hidden deep inside her?

My name is Kate Connor and I'm a Level Five Demon Hunter.

And right now, my biggest fear is that someday the demon in my daughter will burst forth, and that will be the end of everything. Because even if it meant the apocalypse, how in hell could I kill my child?

CHAPTER 2

"*S*o the kid's got some evil inside her," Eddie said, leaning back in the recliner he'd claimed as his own. He rubbed his stubbly gray beard and made a snorting noise. "Like that's news? She's fifteen. Whoever heard of a fifteen-year-old who wasn't evil?"

"Um, hello?" Allie said. "Sitting right here! And *so* not evil!"

My daughter Allie, the subject of this particular conversation, glared at her great-grandfather. Or, rather, at the man she considered her great-grandfather. Like me, Eddie Lohmann had retired from the Demon-Hunting life. Also like me, he'd been pulled out of retirement and is now back in the thick of it.

I'm a Level Five Demon Hunter, which puts me out in the field. And although he's not officially on the *Forza Scura* payroll, Eddie's stepped up as my *alimenta-*

tore, a sort of mentor-teacher-researcher-coach. And, in Eddie's case, a sometime babysitter and all-time curmudgeon.

Forza Scura is the secret arm of the Vatican created thousands of years ago to train, educate, and organize hunters to fight the demons, vampires, zombies, and other creatures of hell who move secretly through our world. Demons are the most prevalent because they're the ones who can look the most human because, well, they pretty much *are* human.

The thing is, demons are all around us all the time, and I mean that literally. Walk through the world, and you're walking through demons, albeit demons in another dimension. Those of us in *Forza* call it the ether, but it's fair to say it's a kind of limbo, and it's where demons wait, lurking around for the chance to slide into a body that a human doesn't need anymore.

Not that they can take over every dead body. There's a very short window of opportunity, so the demon has to be *right there* and ready, paying attention and on his toes.

But that's not all. Even if the timing is right, the departing soul can still protect the body. It can fight, and most souls do. And the more faith that a person had in this life, the harder it is for the demon to battle its way inside.

Still, quite a few demons make it, and you hear about it every day. A heart attack victim miraculously revived? A drowned swimmer brought back to life?

Maybe that's just exceptional work by the EMS folks, but I usually assume demon. Call me a pessimist, but I figure it's better safe than sorry.

Once a demon is inside a body it could simply stay there for as long as the body lasts, living out its life as a super-strong human. Most don't, though. They're demons, after all, and that means they want to get out and do a little damage. Shake things up and go all evil on the world. Also, most tend to be minions, doing the work of High Demons who have a Serious Agenda. Like, oh, bringing about the end of the world as we know it.

Those demons are easy for a Hunter to spot.

But the others? Well, they manage to blend in. Some slide into regular jobs. They're demons, yes. They're evil, absolutely. But they also just want to be human. I've known demons who ran convenience stores and strip clubs and telemarketing farms. Usually their true nature gets the better of them after a while, but the point is, they're out there.

And now I can't help but think that Allie has something in common with them.

The thought isn't a happy one.

"—just like Father Donnelly said. Right, Kate?"

Eliza's voice pulled me from my reverie. "I'm sorry. What?"

My eighteen-year-old cousin and Allie exchanged exasperated glances.

"Jeez, Mom. Distracted much?"

I didn't answer, because yeah, it was fair to say I was little distracted. Exhausted, too. We'd only arrived back home in San Diablo two hours ago after flying more than fifteen hours from Rome. There wasn't enough coffee in the world to unfog my tired and garbled brain.

"Eliza said that all the stuff inside me's good," Allie plowed on as my husband Stuart, who was sitting beside me on the couch, tightened his grip on my hand. "Just like Father Donnelly said. I've got the essence but not the evil. Strength. And strategy. So, that's all a plus on the hunting end. Right?"

She shifted to look from me to her father, Eric, who was sitting in one of the dining room chairs that we'd pulled into the living room for this impromptu family meeting. "Right?" she said again, and though I couldn't be sure, I thought there was a note of panic in her voice.

"Of course it's all good," Eric said, his body shifted toward the left to favor his working eye. He'd lost the right one in our last battle before going to Rome, and all things considered had adapted remarkably well.

"Right," Allie said. "Okay." I was grateful that Allie was looking at Eric so intently that there is no way she could have noticed how Eddie rolled his eyes, making his caterpillar-like eyebrows twitch.

"You saved the world, didn't you?" Eric added.

"Damn right she did," Eliza said fiercely. "She saved all of us."

At the time Allie had been saving the world, Eliza had been in the hospital, having faced death in the process of trying—and failing—to save her mother, the aunt I'd never known. I glanced at the leather cuffs she now wore on her wrists. They looked like the fashion statement of a badass girl with attitude. And while that description fit Eliza, the real reason for the cuffs was to hide the nasty, jagged scars.

"I'd never freaking kill myself," Eliza had said on our last day in Rome, two weeks after the world hadn't ended. We were on her first outing after the hospital, and she'd wanted to go to the open-air market. I'd understood why when she'd headed toward a display of leather goods and picked out the cuffs, then snapped them around her wrists and had Allie adjust the laces so they were perfectly sized.

"And there is no way I'm letting every clerk at Target think I tried to slit my wrists," she'd added, then thrust up and down as if blocking an attacker. "Plus, they should do good for deflecting knives, right?"

I'd agreed. More than that, I'd even bought a set for both me and Allie, though we don't wear them constantly the way Eliza now does.

Now, Allie scowled from where she was sitting cross-legged on the floor beside Eliza. "I saved the world *because* of what I am." She pulled her knees up and hugged them, her attention tight on Eric. "I'm different, aren't I? From you, I mean. We got it out of you. But with me—"

7

She cut herself off with a frown, then shook her head.

I knew what she was thinking. For years, the demon Eric's parents had put inside him had stayed bound, trapped through a binding ritual performed by the Church. But the binding didn't work the way it should have, and things got out of hand not that long ago. Eric had gone all Jekyll and Hyde, losing it so much that he'd almost hurt Allie, not to mention me.

It's better now; the demon was destroyed and Eric survived. And there weren't any little demonic bits lingering inside him. At least as far as we knew.

"It's different," Eric assured her gently. "I had an actual demon shoved inside of me. That's not you. You've—"

"Got it all through me," she said. "*Infused with the essence of the demon.* Isn't that what Father Donnelly said? I mean, I'm stuck with it. I *am* it. And I just—"

"*Essence*," Eric said. "There's no demon inside of you, waiting to take control."

"Oh, right," Allie snapped. "And you know this because it happens all time. I'm the first, remember? Because your parents wanted to freaking *breed* their way to me, and—"

"Sweetheart," I said gently, because her voice was rising, edging toward hysteria.

She took a deep breath, then tossed her hands out to her sides the way she does when she's overwhelmed by a pile of homework. "You know what? Never mind." She stood. "Can I go?"

"Go?" Eric asked. "Go where?"

"Out. The beach. The mall. Mindy," she finally said, referring to her best friend. "Can I just go out with Mindy?"

Her eyes were still on Eric, and for a moment he said nothing. I could read his face well enough, though, and I knew he wanted to keep her in the house, safe with us. Safe from the outside world. And, hopefully, safe from herself.

Apparently Allie could read his expression, too, because she snapped, "I can take care of myself, you know. And I'm not going to go all demonic at the beach. I promise not to open any portals to hell. You just said there's no demon waiting to pop out. All I want is to get out of here. I want to see Mindy. I want—"

"Of course you can go," Stuart said gently, and the storm I'd seen brewing on Allie's face started to fade.

Eric turned to Stuart, and since I could tell he was about to argue, I held up a hand. "Stuart's right," I said. "Allie and Mindy have a lot of catching up to do. And it's a gorgeous day for the beach."

"I'll come too," Eliza chimed in. She'd been watching the four of us, obviously trying to assess the situation.

"I don't need a babysitter! I'm not going to grow horns!"

Eliza sat back, her hands rising as if in self-defense. "Didn't say you did. But I thought you wanted me to meet Mindy. That's what you said in Rome, right? And I'm dying to go to the beach. I went all the time in San Diego, and I'm having withdrawals. Is there anyplace to rent boards?"

"You surf?" The looming issue of Allie's demonic heritage faded against the shining brilliance of learning to surf. "Will you teach me?"

"Allie," I said. "Remember the last time you were interested in surfing?"

"Well, yeah. But this time, *I'm* the demon."

"Allie!"

"*Kidding.*" She scrunched her shoulders, looking like my little girl. "Honest, Mom, surfing isn't the problem, and you know it."

"Well, it might be *a* problem, but we can have the sports and safety discussion later. Now, I guess you can just go."

"Really? Awesome. Can you drive us?"

"Bus," I said. "Consider the walk to the bus stop part of your surfing training regimen."

Allie rolled her eyes. "Can Eliza drive us?"

I frowned, having forgotten that we had another licensed driver in our midst. At least, I assumed she was licensed. "Can you?"

"Sure," Eliza said. "But my car's still in San Diego."

I nodded, suddenly remembering that Eliza hadn't told us her plans. Was she going back home? Was she staying in San Diablo? Was she moving to Rome to train?

That, however, was a discussion for another time.

"You can borrow the van," Stuart chimed in, when it became obvious that I wasn't going to answer.

"Oh, right. Yeah. The keys to the Odyssey are hanging in the kitchen. Check the gas," I called as they hurried off. "And the tires!"

A whisper of worry cut through me, and I tried to shove it down, telling myself that I was nervous because Allie was being driven around by another teenager. But Allie'd been driven around by her older high school friends for the last year.

No, the real reason for my worry was exactly the same as Allie's. It stemmed from what she was. From what we now knew about her. I was afraid that like every teenager, she'd lose her cool. But unlike every teenager, her explosions of temper might cause real damage.

True, they never had before. Her toddler temper tantrums never opened a portal to hell, and her snits as a teen never summoned an army of vampires to our home. But that was before.

Things were different now. She'd stood at the portal to hell, and her blood had held back the demonic hordes. *Her blood.*

A golden light had filled the chamber then, bathing us all. For all I knew, that day had changed something fundamental inside her. Even if it hadn't, she was growing up. Growing and changing.

As a mom, that made me excited and thrilled and a bit sentimental.

As a Demon Hunter, it terrified me.

Not only because I didn't know how the scary demon bits inside her would ultimately manifest—if they did at all—but also because her grandparents had purposefully bred her in the hopes of creating the ultimate demon-fighting weapon. And I had a feeling that the general demon population wasn't too happy with that.

Mostly I was afraid of the unknown. Afraid for my baby. And frustrated that I didn't have a clue how to help her.

As if he knew what I was thinking, Stuart squeezed my hand. "She's a great kid. It's going to be fine."

I smiled, and for one blissful moment, I let myself believe him.

Then Eddie went and shot my fantasy all to hell by releasing a loud snort. "You got a damn funny view of 'fine,' boy," he said. "Because I'm thinking that things are about to get messier than ever."

"Thanks, Eddie," I said dryly. "Thanks so much."

"Just calling it as I see it, and the truth is, I don't see much."

Eric cocked his head as he listened intently to Eddie. "What do you mean?"

"Just that we don't have the whole picture. And if

Father Donnelly's running the show at *Forza*, you never will."

"Father Corletti is still in charge of *Forza*," I said loyally. Father Corletti had been like a father to me when I'd grown up as an orphan inside *Forza's* dorms.

"Maybe," Eddie said. "But he didn't know about Father D's little Frankenstein plan. The way that traitorous bastard helped get the demon inside of that one," he said pointing to Eric. "Father Corletti didn't even know the truth after you gave birth to Father D's monster."

"Eddie!" There was both shock and anger in my voice.

He waved away my outburst. "Just following the analogy. I couldn't love that girl more if she really were my great-granddaughter, and you know it. I'm just saying that we thought Eric was supposed to be his secret weapon, but really it was Allie."

"But Father Donnelly told us that he didn't realize she had demonic essence inside her," Stuart said, looking between me and Eric. "When we had that meeting in the Vatican before we headed home. That's what he said. He wouldn't lie to us. He's a priest."

"You go right on being a good Catholic boy," Eddie retorted. "But as for me? I never believe a word that man says. And in the end, what does it matter whether he knew or not? The end result is that he got what he wanted. He engineered a new breed of Demon Hunter."

"Eddie's right," Eric said slowly. "Whether he knew

that our daughter would have demonic essence or not, she's what he was trying to accomplish with me. That's why he wanted her to stay behind in Rome. That's why he used words like weapon when he talked about needing her to fight the demons."

My stomach twisted, but I tried to think rationally. To think like a Hunter and not like a mom. And Kate the Demon Hunter knew they were right.

"You said he wasn't happy when you refused to leave her behind to train," Eddie reminded me, his fingers sliding over the hilt of the stiletto we'd brought back as a gift from Rome. "I think that's because he's not telling you something."

"What?" I demanded.

"Don't know. But he's holding something back. I'm betting there's more power in that girl than he's telling you, and we don't know how it's gonna come out."

"Good lord," Stuart said.

Eric said nothing, but his eyes were on me, and I saw the fear in them.

"She's a good kid," I insisted.

"She's a teenager," Eddie countered. "And that means she's gonna go a little wild. Nothing wrong with that. Except that with this one, who the hell knows what wild means?"

I stood up, then started to pace between the living room and the kitchen. I didn't want to hear this. Didn't want to think about it. I wanted to think about all the other things that needed to get done. All the regular mom stuff that had been waiting for me upon our return. Getting ready for the upcoming school year. Taking care of unpacking. Getting back into a workout groove. Grocery shopping. Planning Timmy's third birthday party. Cleaning out the damn garage.

Normal stuff. Life stuff.

And, honestly, I didn't think that was too much to ask. After all, we just closed a gate that was going to release all of hell into the world. So surely the universe owed us a little break.

That was only fair, wasn't it?

CHAPTER 3

*E*ric grabbed his cane and stood up, and on the other side of the room, Stuart did the same. Eddie didn't stand, but he reached for the handle on the side of his recliner and tilted all the way back even while he snagged the remote with his other hand.

All in all, the living room was suddenly full of the vibe of finished business, and that was fine with me. I wanted to call Laura. I wanted to think about toddler presents and pre-school guest lists for my little boy, sound asleep in his room despite the family drama. I wanted to inventory the freezer and the pantry and figure out if we had anything to eat in the house.

I wanted to unpack and do laundry. And I'm ninety percent sure there had never been a time in my life where laundry was actually at the top of my wish list. But I'd just returned from a non-vacationy vacation in Rome, and I confess I was craving a little normalcy.

Or, at least, what passed for normal in most families.

But then Eric spoke, and I slammed headfirst back into reality. "We should talk about training Allie," he said, as I reeled under the force of those words, so heavy with practical, horrible reality. "Kate, I don't suppose you could make a pot of coffee?"

I wanted to protest simply on principle—about training, not about coffee, even though that would be fair since he knew perfectly well how to operate the coffeemaker—but he was right. Even before we'd learned about Allie's demonic essence, Father Corletti suggested we formally train her. He'd even raised the possibility of her moving to Rome in order to live in the *Forza* dorms as I had. At first, the idea had thrilled Allie no end, but after learning about her demonic heritage, she'd stopped begging.

I hated the fact that my daughter had to deal with that burden, but I'd be lying if I didn't admit that the mommy in me melted a bit when she tearfully told me she just wanted to be at home and train with me.

The words had been a relief. She's only fifteen, after all. And while I knew that when she turned eighteen she could make the decision to go on her own, for at least three more years, I could still keep her close. I could make sure she was ready.

Honestly, I didn't trust anyone else to do it.

I nodded, then started for the kitchen. Because Eric

was right. There was a lot to figure out, and coffee was on the agenda.

Stuart's voice pulled me back. "I think this is a conversation that can wait until tomorrow."

I turned, frowning, and saw that Eric's expression matched my own.

"She needs to train," Eric said. "And if Kate and I are going to do that, we need to start working out the details."

I cocked my head. Until now, Eric hadn't specifically said he was going to be part of her training. I'd expected it, actually, but he'd kept quiet during the back and forth at the Vatican. Now, I couldn't help but wonder what he had in mind.

Not long ago, he'd come close to killing both me and Allie when he'd lost himself to a powerful demon. After, he'd packed up and moved to Los Angeles. If he thought that I was going to do some split training schedule where Allie worked with me here during the week and him in LA on the weekends, then we really did have some serious talking to do.

"I'm thinking I can use Cutter's studio," I said, both because it was true and because I wanted to make it clear right off the bat that ultimately I was calling the shots. "After school and then longer weekend sessions there."

"That's workable," Eric began, "but—"

"Tomorrow," Stuart repeated, in the kind of voice that reminded me he was not only an attorney but had once planned on running for public office. His focus was entirely on Eric. "You can come by after Mass, *David*." He emphasized the name, reminding everyone —as if we could forget—that my first husband, Eric Crowe, had died years ago. He might be alive again, but it was in the body of high school chemistry teacher David Long. And David had no claim over me or my family.

A muscle in Eric's jaw twitched, and I stiffened. The demon may have been expelled from him, but all that meant was that he wouldn't fly into a murderous rage or try to raise hell here on earth. Even without the demonic influence, the man had a temper.

Right then, though, he was holding it in, and all I could think about was long fuses and apocalyptic explosions.

"Whatever the devil you're doing," Eddie put in as he ramped up the volume on a *Friends* rerun, "do it in the kitchen. You're screwing with my morning routine."

Eric kept his focus on Stuart. "Fair enough," Eric finally said. "I have things to take care of today, anyway." He shifted to look at me, his expression softening. "We'll talk tomorrow."

I watched him go out the front door, then jerked my head toward the kitchen before turning on my heel and heading that way, hoping that Stuart was following.

Since I wanted both caffeine and something to

occupy my hands, I started to scoop the coffee into the basket. "I thought you two had reached a detente," I said, once I'd poured the water into machine. "So why are you shutting him down?"

"Detente, yes. Best friends, no." He leaned back against the counter, looking both casual and completely in control. "He doesn't live here, Kate."

"Of course he doesn't," I said, starting to realize some of what was driving his reaction. Eric had followed us in his car from the airport to the house. There'd been no discussion, no invitation. It had simply been a given since, after all, there were demony things to talk about.

But I was Stuart's wife, not Eric's. Not anymore. And after already having traversed a rather rocky marital road on which Eric had been one of many stumbling blocks, I could understand that Stuart would want our home to simply be our home for at least one day. A day to decompress. To hang out. To just be a family.

"I get it," I said with a gentle smile. I pulled two coffee cups down and started to fill them even though the coffee maker had barely started brewing. "Eddie's commandeered the living room TV, but we could spend the afternoon in the bedroom watching some-thing. Or not watching something," I added with a suggestive lilt. "Timmy's still zonked from the time change, and Allie will be gone for a least a couple of hours."

"Not a bad idea," he said in the kind of voice that made clear he was only being polite. "But I really need to take care of a few business things."

I blinked, then slowly closed my mouth once I realized it was hanging open. "You're leaving? Right now?"

"It's past ten. I need to go see Bernie before noon."

"Then why the hell did you send Eric off? We need to figure this out. I need to know what—"

"Didn't you tell me you needed to dive in with planning Timmy's birthday party? We have *two* kids, Kate."

I tightened my jaw, the tension in my face reminding me of what I'd just seen in Eric's. Stuart was right—I needed to get the invitations out or we'd have more kids saying no than saying yes. We'd stayed in Italy longer than we'd planned, and as a result there was only a week between the invitations going out and the actual party. And while I might not be a social butterfly, my little boy was not going to be the kid who was outside the pre-school neighborhood loop.

But that didn't mean I needed my husband holding my hand and micromanaging playdates and parties.

I opened my mouth to say exactly that, but then shut it tight again as reality smacked me hard against the face.

This wasn't about Timmy. It wasn't even about Allie.

This was about me and Eric and Stuart and jealousy. A jealousy that I thought had been resolved—or at the very least swept under the rug—when Eric had left town, and Stuart had come home to me.

But things had changed once more. Yes, Eric now lived over an hour away in LA, but he was involved again. I wasn't going to keep him out of Allie's life, not now. Not since he was free of the demon. Not since he was the only person alive who had the slightest sense of what was going on inside of her.

Stuart knew that, of course. And I couldn't blame him for wanting to clearly set the family boundaries. But I also knew damn well that no matter how hard he tried, the lines were going to get blurry.

The thought made my gut twist.

I'd lost Stuart already—not once, but twice. The first time because I'd kept my demon-hunting life secret, and that decision not to trust him—to fool myself into believing that I was somehow protecting him and our marriage—was on me. But the second time ... well, that was on him, and it stemmed from fear, pure and simple. Fear of what I am, not to mention the danger that surrounds me. But he'd come back, choosing to face that danger in order to keep our family together.

His leaving had felt like a betrayal, but his return had been a miracle. He'd seen first hand the destructive power of hell, and he'd watched as his wife—who could barely manage clean laundry and clean dishes on the same weekday—sent one of the most powerful demons in the universe all the way back to hell. He understood the danger he was walking back into, and yet he'd still chosen our family. And that had meant the world to me.

When he'd traveled with us to Rome, he'd promised me that he was back to stay, and in that ancient city, I'd fully regained the trust that had soured when he'd walked away.

But now that we're back in San Diablo—now that he's drawing boundaries and playing testosterone games with Eric—I can't help but wonder if Stuart doesn't really understand just how messy this is going to get.

And that scares me almost as much as the demon lurking inside my daughter.

I was surrounded.

There was no other way to describe it. Wide swatches of color. Dozens of textures. And non-human creatures with enormous eyes and toothy grins hovering all around me.

I was overwhelmed—so afraid I was going to screw this up. That I couldn't pull it off, and then my entire family would end up buried in absolute chaos.

"Kate?" My best friend Laura pressed her hand against my back, silently urging me forward. "Do you have a plan?"

I steeled myself. I could do this. I just had to make the first move.

"Nemo," I finally said, pointing to the colorful *Happy Birthday* banner that featured the little clown fish. I drew a breath, relaxing now that I'd made a decision. "We're going with a Nemo theme."

That Major Life Decision handled, I tossed the package into my cart, along with Dory-covered plates and cups.

"Good choice." Laura grabbed a paper tablecloth featuring a happy, smiling shark. "Timmy loves *Finding Nemo*."

"Unless I should go with SpongeBob?"

Laura waved the thought away. "He's turning three. The gang at Bikini Bottom is really more appropriate for the sophisticated first grade crowd."

Since I couldn't argue with that, I deferred to my bestie's party-planning expertise. "Banner, tablecloth, cups, plasticware. What am I missing?"

"Invitations and napkins," Laura said, efficiently grabbing both. "And are you making the cake or buying it?"

I didn't even bother to answer, just cocked my head and gave her a thousand-yard stare. Laura knows as well as I do that if I tried to make and decorate a cake, all I'd end up with is a messy—or messier—kitchen and a blob of cake-like product that might or might not be edible.

"Right, well, then you don't need the cake-topper.

You can have the bakery at Ralph's do that," she said. "Or I can make it for you if you want."

Laura Dupont is a domestic goddess in addition to being my best friend, and I truly appreciated the offer. But I knew she had her hands full as a single mom to Allie's BFF, Mindy, an almost-sixteen year old who was doing summer musical theater and, therefore, needed almost constant chauffeuring. Even so, my reasons for declining were more personal than benevolent. "If you're going to do me favors, I'd rather hit you up for the kind I can't offload on the local grocery store."

"Or I could do both. I'm talented that way." She narrowed her eyes. "By the way, are you ever going to tell me all of what happened in Rome, or do I have to guess? Or, God forbid, are we now the kind of friends who drink wine together and talk about their kids?"

"We're already that kind of friend," I pointed out.

"True. But our conversation is broader than that. Kids and demons. Wine and weapons. Ours has evolved into an eclectic friendship, and I like it that way. Seriously, Kate," she added, "I get the feeling there's something else going on. Did some demons get free?"

Her brow was furrowed, and I saw genuine concern in her eyes. She already knew some of what happened in Rome because she'd been the lead player on my off-site research team. So Laura knew that the demons had been trying to open a gate to hell. She knew that I'd been knocked for a loop finding out that, though I was an orphan, my mother had a sister. And that sister had a daughter. And my cousin—Eliza—had come all the way to Rome to find me.

Not to mention that Eliza happened to be in the demon hunting biz, too. Albeit not officially on the *Forza* payroll.

Laura knew that it had been a close call—"Seriously, Kate!" she'd said when I'd finally called to tell her all was well. "Do you know how stressful it is hanging out in California knowing the world might end any second?"—but she also knew we'd managed to shut and lock that particular gate. Crisis averted. Demons conquered. World saved. Apocalypse averted.

For the moment, anyway. One thing I've learned over the years is that the world is always about to end. It's a heavy burden, but there's nothing like advance notice of an impending apocalypse to re-order your priorities. I mean, what's a messy kitchen when you're trying to hold back the fires of hell?

Laura knows that a few weeks ago, my family managed to do exactly that. What she didn't know was that it was Allie's blood that closed the gate, and the only reason Allie's blood worked was because she's part demon. Something we hadn't known before that very moment, but considering the horde of demons that had been about to barrel down on us, that disturbing revelation had a definite upside.

I'd been telling myself that I hadn't shared that part of the story because it wasn't the kind of thing you talked about over the phone or in text messages. But that wasn't the entire truth.

No, the sad truth is that I was afraid that my best friend would look at my daughter askance. That she'd start finding excuses to keep Mindy out of Allie's life. That she wouldn't see my beautiful, bright, funny, talented, sarcastic, sometimes pain-in-the-butt daughter as a real person anymore. She'd be tainted. She'd be the enemy.

Or worse, she'd be something to pity.

I worried about all of that. And even as I struggled with that fear, I hated myself for thinking so little of Laura as to even entertain those thoughts.

But which way was I supposed to go? Protect my daughter? Or protect my friendship?

And though I hated being disingenuous with Laura, when I put it like that, there really was no debate. In the end, my kids would always come first.

"—America."

I frowned, completely lost.

Laura rolled her eyes. "Earth to Kate. I said that if you're not sure about Nemo, you could always go with Captain America."

"No," I said firmly, because right then I really just wanted to get home, and I appreciated the fact that Laura obviously understood that I wasn't yet ready to tell her the full story of what happened in Rome. "Nemo is great."

"Speaking of great, Eliza seems like a good kid." She

efficiently snagged a package of Pixar-themed wrapping paper and tossed it in the cart without missing a step as we headed toward checkout.

"She is," I agreed, "though she's had a hard go of it." It hadn't been easy for her in Rome. The demons had been just as aware of her as they'd been of me. "And though I don't know her well yet, I think she'd probably frown on the *kid* thing. She's eighteen. I'm pretty sure eighteen-year-olds get touchy about that. What with the whole right to vote thing."

"Phhhbt. Until they can sit down with us and have a cocktail, they're a kid. For that matter, forget cocktails. I want a college degree on their wall, and a paycheck in their hand. Or a family or a career or both. Oh, hell, Eliza's just going to have to deal with my personal prejudices, because as far as I'm concerned, Mindy's going to be a kid to me forever."

We'd reached the checkout stand, and I kept my head down as I unpacked the cart. Because the truth was, as much as I wished it were true, Allie wasn't a kid to me any more. She'd always be my baby, but my daughter had been forced to grow up. And while I think she'd done a damn fine job of it, I couldn't help but mourn that lost piece of her childhood.

"Hang on," Laura told the cashier after she scanned the last item. "I'm sure I have a coupon in here somewhere." Not that long ago, Laura had spent money without a second thought. After the divorce, she'd become remarkably frugal.

"Don't worry about it," I said. Now that I was back on the *Forza* payroll, I was feeling a little more flush than I'd felt when we were a family of four on a government lawyer's salary.

"No, no. You should use it. It expires soon, and I know I put it in here..."

I was about to tell her it wasn't worth it, when the woman behind me huffed heavily. I glanced toward her and saw a gum-smacking sour-faced woman holding a basket in front of her with a single ugly candle. Weird green swirls inside an ivory column. Definitely not centerpiece material, except maybe for druids conducting some sort of tree-worshipping ceremony. Her eyes were narrowed and her expression was nothing short of a scowl. And, honestly, we'd reached the cashier first, and it wasn't as if we'd been dawdling.

Suddenly, an extra minute to find a coupon seemed like no big deal at all.

"If you can find it, that would be great," I told Laura. "I'm in no hurry."

I didn't look back at SourBitch, but I was certain I felt her eyes boring down on me. And while I'm not remotely psychic, I'm also sure I heard all the nasty names she was calling us loud and clear in my head.

After full minute passed, I almost told Laura to forget it. But just as I was opening my mouth, she whipped her hand out with a flourish and waved the coupon. "Ha! Told you!"

She passed it to the clerk, and I was suddenly the

beneficiary of a whopping ten percent reduction in my bill.

We grabbed the bags and scurried toward the exit, and as I slipped through the automatic glass doors, I glanced back and saw SourBitch looking right back at me, pure malevolence in her eyes.

"What?" Laura whispered.

"Nothing," I said, but it wasn't the truth. Because in reality, I was in the mood to kick a little ass, and I suddenly wondered if SourBitch wasn't a full-blown demon from hell, and I'd just walked away from the perfect opportunity.

CHAPTER 4

"She *was* chewing gum," I added, as I shut the door to the hall closet where I'd just stashed all of the birthday paraphernalia, well away from prying eyes. I'd brought up the possibility in the car that SourBitch had been a demon. Not that I would have whipped out my stiletto and stabbed her in the eye right then and there. Discount stores tend to frown on that kind of thing. "And that candle? Could any creature with a soul pick out a candle that ugly?"

"I think she was just bitchy," Laura said as she leaned against the wall. "Not that long ago, you were knee-deep in demons and saving the world, so of course you're seeing them around every corner. But you and yours just stopped the apocalypse. Like, the Big One. Demons aren't going to shoot you dirty looks and get on your bad side. You're a badass Demon Hunter."

"Damn right, I am." We shared a grin. "You're probably right," I conceded. "Just because I got attacked near a fruit stand in Rome doesn't mean I'll get jumped in a checkout line."

"My point exactly." She gestured to the door. "Do you want me to get out of your hair so you can unpack?"

"How about you stay for a glass of wine? Unless it's too early. My internal clock is still messed up." I glanced at my watch and saw that it wasn't even four yet, but that meant it was late in Rome, and I was starting to feel draggy.

Laura and I had run a variety of errands in addition to party shopping, plus we'd grabbed lunch at Luigi's Pizzeria. "So you can tell me all about the sights and shopping and food of Rome in the proper atmosphere," Laura had said.

We'd had some wine then, so I figured why stop now? "I have to bathe the kiddo, so you'll be drinking on a porcelain throne, but—"

"—when have we ever stood on ceremony?" she finished with a grin. "And besides, that'll make me queen for the evening. So that's a bonus. Especially if you have something white and chilled. Assuming Eddie didn't drink us dry." I had yet to do a thorough inventory of the kitchen, and I was actively avoiding thinking about going to the grocery store to refill our larder. As far as I'm concerned, a nest of bloodthirsty vampires beats my local Ralph's any day of the week.

Laura followed me into the living room as we headed to the kitchen. That's where I found Timmy, wearing only Captain America undies on the floor in front of Eddie's recliner, his toy doctor bag wide open. Boo Bear, the bedraggled blue bear that had been his favorite lovey since he was an infant, was splayed out on a small green blanket, the "stitches" from a recent repair apparent in the matted fake fur. My future surgeon was bent over, his little back arched as he listened to the bear's heart through a plastic stethoscope.

"How's the patient?" I asked.

He hadn't heard me come in, and now he looked up with the kind of grin that made my mommy-heart squeeze. "A-Ok, Mommy!" He frowned down at the bear, then back up at me. "He needed a shot. Grandpa, too!"

I turned, looking back to where Eddie napped in the recliner.

"World's best babysitter," I quipped, shooting a grin Laura's direction.

"I heard that," Eddie grumbled. "Just resting my eyes. Little stinker watched an entire *Barney* DVD. A man can only take so much purple."

True enough.

I gave Timmy a five-minute warning for bath time, then told him to go pick out two toys for the tub. While he did that—"Walk, don't run on the stairs, young man!"—I rummaged in our tiny wine fridge for a bottle of white while Laura pulled down two plastic sippy cups and took off the lids. No glass allowed in the bathroom, and apparently my bestie knew that rule as well as my kids.

"You're brave to bathe him before dinner," Laura said as we both made our way up the stairs.

"We're overdue," I confessed. "Between dealing with Eliza in the hospital, changing our return flight, and what felt like days in the air—in coach with a toddler, no less—it's been awhile since my little guy's been well-scrubbed."

"Still…" I could hear the pending doom in her voice.

"I know," I said, because she was right. Pre-dinner toddler baths were a dangerous thing. "Stuart's bringing home dinner since our cupboard is stocked only with what Eddie considers food, and he knows not to get anything too messy." Despite my general loathing of the place, I'd fully intended to hit the grocery store today, but in what I assumed was his way of apologizing for the Eric kerfuffle, Stuart had texted and offered to pick something up for dinner.

Since Eddie hadn't joined us in Rome, we're stocked up on basics like coffee and milk and orange juice. But the man lives on frozen dinners, Kraft Mac & Cheese, Eggs waffles, and pizza delivery, so there was no way that his idea of a well-stocked kitchen was going to result in a dinner for five. True, I could have defrosted something from the garage freezer or raided the pantry out there of its bulk canned goods from Costco, but I'd gratefully latched on to Stuart's offer. Then I'd mentally shifted my grocery store run to tomorrow's To-Do list and done a little happy dance around the bedroom where I'd been unpacking.

"You're okay with hanging out?" I asked as I perched on the side of the tub and started fiddling with the temperature. "No hot date?"

"Not tonight," Laura said.

I looked up from where I was pouring Mr. Bubbles into the stream. "Everything okay? I mean, it's Saturday night. You and Cutter aren't—"

"It's all good," she assured me. "He even took me for a weekend in Santa Barbara while you were gone— after you saved the world, though, because I was on-call as Research Girl," she added.

"Timmy!" I called, then turned back to Laura. "And yet no date tonight?"

"He's in LA. Some sort of martial arts conference thing. For studio owners. Not a competition, so I don't have to be there to cheer him on."

I met Cutter soon after my first San Diablo demon attacked me. I realized I needed to get back in shape and refresh my atrophied fighting skills. I'd found him in the martial arts studio in the shopping center at the entrance to our subdivision. A former Navy SEAL, Cutter's got the skills along with romance cover model good looks. And though he'd been curious about why I could match him—let's face it, most stay-at-home-moms couldn't have—he hadn't pushed me for answers.

He's in the know now, though, and I'm glad to have him be part of my ever-expanding circle of confidence. I'm even more glad that he's with Laura, who'd been emotionally slammed when she learned that her now-ex husband had been cheating.

"Ducky and boat, Momma!" Timmy raced naked from his bedroom, thrusting the toys at me. I handed them to Laura before helping him into the tub.

"You're going to be the cleanest boy in San Diablo," I told him, in reply to which he thrust up a fist and said, "*Super clean!*"

"If only that applied outside of the tub," I said, shooting a sideways glance to Laura, who passed the toys back to me. I handed Timmy the plastic purple duck, then settled his favorite red boat on top of the water. "All yours," I told him, then shifted my little plastic stool so I was looking more directly at Laura, my back against the wall and my fingers slowly stirring up the water as Timmy hummed to himself.

I took a sip of my wine, then returned to the topic of the hour. "So you two are really getting serious, then? Santa Barbara. That's pretty romantic."

"A bit," she said, her cheeks actually turning pink. "But we're taking it slow." She cocked her head. "What about you and Stuart? Things still back on track?"

"Also good," I said, though I turned my face away,

ostensibly to soap up Timmy's back as I continued speaking. "He stepped up to the plate coming back home, and then in Rome, too." All of which was true, although I'd be lying if I didn't admit that the fact that he left with Timmy in the first place still hurt, even though I understand why he did.

Sort of.

When I'm feeling generous.

As for this friction with Eric? Well, that was all just alpha male territory claiming, right? And when you got right down to it, wasn't it good that Stuart wanted to claim home and hearth again?

"I'm hearing a but...?" Laura pressed, as Timmy took the cloth from me and started in on his underarms before slapping his hands on the water's surface to make the boat and duck bob into each other.

I wiped some of the errant splashes off my face. "No buts," I assured her, even though there were definitely a few buts. "Softer, kiddo. Mommy doesn't need a bath."

"It'll be fine," Laura said, proving why she's my bestie. "He knows he screwed up by walking away. And he knows that your ex pretty much saved the world. You can't expect them to launch into a bromance. You get that right?"

"I do. Of course I do." I battled back a wallop of guilt. I'd told her about the Stuart-Eric showdown this morning, true. But Laura doesn't have the full story of what happened in Rome. She knew that a gate to hell had been about to open. And she knew that we'd managed to lock it tight.

She also knew—because I hadn't been thinking clearly when I called to share the good news that the world wasn't ending—that the secret to closing the gate had been the blood of a hybrid. She'd reasonably assumed that meant Eric, and I'd let her cling to that assumption because Allie's my baby just as much as the little guy now splashing in the tub.

Thus began the guilt.

Until now, I'd been keeping Laura in the loop about my demon-hunting adventures. Even though my status as an official *Forza* Demon Hunter is supposed to be a deep, dark secret, I'd been relieved back when she'd stumbled onto the truth. I'd been unceremoniously pulled out of retirement, and I'd desperately needed a confidante. At the time, no one else knew, and it had been like lifting an emotional weight when I told her everything.

Now, I was struggling under a different weight, and once again I wanted to share everything with Laura and lift it right off my chest. But how could I? I want to believe that Laura wouldn't treat Allie differently, or even *think* about her differently. I want to think it—but how can I know for sure?

And even if I were one hundred percent positive, at the end of the day, it's Allie's secret, not mine. And that means that she gets to decide who knows.

"—all of it."

"What? Sorry."

"I said that I really do want to hear about all of it, but if you want to wait that's fine, too. It's just that with everything—and you being all the way across the globe—I haven't even heard the details of how Eliza found you. She seems like a great kid, though."

"She is," I agreed, feeling a bit more guilty as I realized that they hadn't even met until earlier when Eliza and Allie went to Laura's house to get Mindy and head to the beach.

Granted, we only got home this morning, but my guilt isn't limited to one little incident. The truth is, that I should have taken the time to bring Laura up to speed during one of our many phone calls between Rome and San Diablo in the days following the near-apocalypse. But those calls had mostly been quick check-ins, since I'd been running around like a crazy person. Eliza had been in the hospital, Allie had filled entire days training with Marcus Giatti at *Forza, and* Stuart and I had worked hard to squeeze in a few hours of actual vacation.

On top of all of that, we'd each—all of use including Eliza—spent time with Father Corletti individually and as a group for the sole purpose of talking about Allie and what this new revelation meant for both her and our family. I'm not sure if any of us had a major breakthrough—my takeaway was pretty much *love my kid like I've always loved my kid, and expect the teen years to be a tad more dramatic than the version of hell*

I'd been anticipating—but it helped having Father to talk to.

In other words, I'd been both incredibly busy and emotionally drained. Not to mention exhausted. Battling demons takes a lot out of a girl. Add in a series of unexpected familial revelations, and I was craving neighborhood gossip during my calls with Laura, not a deep-dive into my own family's craziness.

So, yeah, maybe my guilt about staying silent from half a world away was misplaced.

Now though…

Well, now I knew that the friendship rules required catching up, even if I did intend to keep a few secrets to myself.

For now, anyway…

"You're telling me she got away?" Laura sat across from me at the kitchen table, her eyes wide with both shock and loyalty. "From *you?* How is that even possible? I've seen you in action."

"Right? I could barely believe it myself, but she grabbed it and sprinted. Beautiful leather. Perfect stitching. And the strap was just the right width, you know?"

"So it doesn't cut into your shoulder," she added, nodding knowingly. "It sounds amazing."

"It was the most perfect shoulder bag ever," I said,

still mourning the loss of the bag that Allie had spotted in one of the leather good stores we'd stumbled across during an afternoon of exploring. "I seriously considered taking her down before she paid—I had my stiletto right there—and she *was* chewing gum. I could have totally justified it as honest confusion..."

"You're a strong woman, Kate."

"The sacrifices we make," I said, and we both nodded sagely, then grinned at each other.

"Harumph." Eddie's snort drifted the short distance from his recliner in the living room. "You two aren't nearly as clever as you think you are."

"We aren't? Are you sure?"

He made a noise that might have been a laugh, and I took another sip of wine.

Across from me, Laura was examining the purse I ended up buying for her without the aid of bloodshed. "As far as I'm concerned, this bag is brilliant," she said. "It's the perfect size, and the leather is so soft I'm tempted to use it as a pillow."

"You haven't looked inside yet," I told her.

Her brow furrowed. "I thought it was empty." She plunked the bag on the tabletop and peered in.

"Interior side pocket," I said, then sat back feeling smug when she gasped.

"Kate," she said, her voice low and a little awed as she pulled out the beautiful glass bottle, about the size of an airplane offering of whiskey, with a tiny gold screw top. "It's lovely."

"Back before my time, the bottles had cork stoppers. Screw tops are more practical. Less spillage."

"Your time?" She held the glass up to the light, tilting it so the liquid inside moved back and forth. "I'm guessing this isn't a sample of Rome's finest grappa?"

"More like the Vatican's finest. You're holding an official *Forza* holy water flask."

"*Oh.*"

I saw her hand tighten around it, and her face took on a reverential glow. "Is that okay? For me to have one? I mean, I'm not officially with *Forza*. Plus, not Catholic."

"Father Corletti himself suggested it."

"He did? Really?"

"Yup. He suggested I get one for myself too."

Her brow furrowed. "You didn't already have one?"

"Broke. Last assignment before I retired, actually." I'd been heartbroken, but as I was leaving *Forza*, it felt symbolic, and I'd never asked to have it replaced. That Father Corletti both knew and suggested it had felt like a blanket of warm fuzzies around my shoulders.

"This is—wow. Thank you."

"You earned it," I said, humbled by how much the gift obviously meant to her. "Honestly, if you'd started a few years earlier, you could have trained as an *alimentatore*."

"Yeah?" She leaned back, her finger tracing the lines of the bottle. "I'm always afraid I'm in the way. I mean, Cutter's helping me with the fighting, but let's get real,

Lara Croft I'm not." She tapped the bottle. "But this—Father Corletti thinking of me like it matters…"

"It does matter," I said, as she trailed off in a shrug.

"You two getting sappy in there?" Eddie called.

"Maybe a little," Laura answered, then lifted her wine as if to toast him.

"Phht. A little bottle? You get a silver stiletto with a flask in the hilt—now that's a gift that matters."

Laura almost choked on her wine, but recovered well. "You're the man, Eddie."

"And don't you be forgetting it."

I polished off the last of my wine, then topped it off, ridiculously pleased that Eddie liked his gift enough to get competitive with Laura. "Mindy got a bottle, too," I told her. "Allie got it from the Vatican gift shop and filled it there. She put it in the inside pocket of the jacket."

"That jacket is gorgeous," Laura said, and I had to agree. We'd bought a far-too-expensive leather jacket for Allie after she saved the world, even though we'd previously told her the jacket was way too pricey and wouldn't be coming home with us.

The store had a second almost identical one, and since Allie begged to get it for Mindy, we'd caved. Because, well … Saved. The. World.

Laura reached across the table and took my hand. "I should know better than to drink in the afternoon because it always makes me emotional, but I just have to say thanks."

I knew she wasn't talking about the gifts, and I could feel that guilt start to bubble up. "Laura, you don't have to—"

"You could have made something up. That first night I mean, when I followed you. Or you could have told me the truth and then told me to stay away. But you pulled me in. You confided in me. And—and well, I get how much pressure you've been under, and it means a lot to me that—oh, hell, you know what I'm saying, right? It's just that I've got your back because you *let* me have your back, and I guess I'm honored. Because your job comes with a lot of secrets, and you've let me in and shared them with me."

She grabbed a napkin and dabbed her eyes. "And now I'm going to smear."

"I love you," I said, because it was true. But the secret I was still keeping sat heavy in my gut. "You're part of the team."

That was true—I really, truly believed it. Even Father Corletti did, taking it upon himself to praise Laura when he could have just as easily told me to discourage her involvement. We were a team. And I couldn't help but wonder if an NFL team would have a shot in hell of winning the Super Bowl if the quarterback kept vital information to himself.

I didn't know the first thing about football, but even I was pretty sure of the answer.

Definitely not.

I frowned.

"What's wrong?" Laura asked, as Eddie snorted in the next room, undoubtedly understanding exactly what I was thinking.

I shook my head, trying to scatter my errant thoughts. "Just wondering if any NFL players are demons. I mean think about that speed. That strength."

Laura squinted at me. "I'd say that your conversational shift surprises me, but honestly, you stopped surprising me long ago."

"Just a random thought," I said, then pointed to her glass. "More?"

"If I do that I'll end up on my couch watching an endless stream of TV for the rest of the evening."

"You say that like it's a bad thing."

"Unfortunately, I promised myself I was going to make a dent in the laundry and plan next week's meals."

The miraculous thing is that she meant it.

"What a coincidence," I said. "That's my plan for the evening, too."

We both had a good laugh at that, since I'm pretty sure that me planning a week's worth of meals really is one of the signs of the apocalypse.

"They'll probably end up at your place first," I said, referring to the kids as we headed to the back door. Unless she happens to arrive in her car, Laura rarely enters and leaves from the front. She and Mindy live one street behind us, and our properties are separated only by a fenced utility easement, gated on both sides for easier access. Between Mindy and Allie and me and Laura, we've created a well-worn path between our two yards. "Remind Allie to text me."

"Will do," Laura promised as I hesitated by the French-style doors that lead into our back yard. I was expecting Eddie to say goodbye, too, but when I turned back toward his recliner, I realized that he and Timmy had both left the living room. I frowned, then heard a thud in the upstairs playroom followed by an "*atta boy*."

"That man pretends to be a curmudgeon better than anyone," Laura says. "But his sweet spots tell the real story."

"True enough." And every time I see my kids interacting with their faux great-grandfather, I say a little prayer of thanks for that day when I found the drugged up and crazy old man in the nursing home and brought him safely home.

"Is it okay if Allie sleeps over?" Laura asked. "Eliza, too, of course. Mindy mentioned they might come back and do a movie marathon. I guess Allie's in withdrawal from lack of TV in English?"

"Sure," I said as Laura tugged open the door, and I followed her onto the patio. "Just tell them—"

Yeaaaarrrrrhhhhooooooowwwwww!!!!!!!!!

The hellish scream was accompanied by a fast moving, furry blob that brushed past my legs and tore into the house.

"What the—"

I ignored Laura, primarily because I'd been knocked

flat on my back by another fast-moving creature, and my sharp, hunterly-attuned senses had already figured that out that I'd been attacked by a demon. The same demon that had scared Kabit, our cat, back into the house.

Now, the demon hovered over me, his putrid breath right in my face and his long, greasy hair brushing my forehead. Even as I mentally kicked myself for not having a weapon—I *really* should know better by now —I physically kicked the demon. Or tried to. He was straddling my hips, and my efforts to spin him over were less than effective, especially since he had his hands around my throat.

I brought my arms in and up in an attempt to break his hold, only to be surprised when he let out an earth shattering howl, slammed his palms onto the top of his head, then lurched up took off running across the yard.

Above me, Laura proudly held up the small bottle of holy water. "This stuff packs a serious—*aaaaaah!*"

I managed a kip-up, bringing me to my feet as another demon—this one of the spry geriatric variety —yanked her close, its bulbous nose wrinkling as it sniffed, then said, "It is not you—you are not the one who is new."

He shoved her aside, and Laura landed with a thud on the gravel as I lunged, grabbing the demon's upper arm so that I could spin it around and shove my finger —*ick*—right through its eye, releasing the demon and sending it back into the ether.

I didn't even wait for now-unoccupied body to hit the ground. Instead, I took off running after the greasy-haired demon, all the while sternly reminding myself to keep a weapon on my person at all times. Either that, or get acrylic nails.

CHAPTER 5

"*M*om?"

Mindy raced toward me, her shrill cry tearing at my heart as I sprinted in her direction.

"She's fine!" I cried, not breaking stride. "Your mom's fine! Allie?"

"Demon!" We passed each other at top speed, my heart tightening even more as I approached the easement and the sound of kicks and grunts.

Oh, God! Allie!

I sprinted the rest of the distance, then plowed through the gate, pausing only long enough to bend over and grab a fallen branch from a nearby tree. Then I hurried down the incline, only to find that I was too late.

It was all over.

And there was my baby girl standing victorious over the body of the greasy-haired demon who'd attacked me, his face scarred from the holy water that had dripped on him and an ivory-handled stiletto protruding from his eye.

"Hey, Mom," she said, her chin trembling a little as she blinked rapidly. "I got him."

"Oh, sweetie!" I raced to her, then pulled her into a tight hug before releasing her and pushing her to arms length so that I could inspect every single inch of her. "Are you hurt?"

She shook her head, taking deep breaths. "I'm okay. Really." Her breath shook as she drew it in. "Honestly," she said, pushing my hands away as I continued to pat her down for hidden injuries, the branch I'd brought as a weapon now shoved into my back pocket. "I'm really fine."

Her voice was clearer now. Stronger. And with a firm nod, she pushed me away. "I'm all right, Mom."

"Holy freaking crap," a small voice murmured from the dark.

I twisted around, grabbing the branch as I did, then found Eliza sprawled on her back, her face hidden by a shadow cast from the line of trees on Laura's side of the easement.

She pushed herself up onto her elbows, bringing her into the light and revealing a metal grating that she'd been leaning against. Access to one of the sewer lines, presumably, since this stretch of city land is essentially a trench that not only allows runoff water to flow, but also provides access to the sewers and whatever other underground utility gizmos and gadgets it takes to keep our city running.

As Eliza climbed to her feet, footsteps pounded toward us. Immediately, all three of us went on alert, ready for the next demonic foe. Then we all relaxed together when Mindy came into view, her breath coming in gasps. "Mom's hiding the other one," she said. She hugged herself, then drew in a breath. "This is really freaky."

Mindy clambered down to us, then nodded toward the body at Allie's feet. "What should do we do with this one?"

"You were freaking incredible," Eliza said, ignoring the question. Her eyes were tight on Allie, but she turned toward me. "Seriously. She was absolutely freaking incredible."

"That's my girl," I said proudly, but my smile was a little bit too tight, because there was something about Eliza's tone that gave me pause.

"It wasn't that big a deal." Allie shrugged, her hands shoved deep into the pockets of her jeans.

"He turned, and you nailed him through the eye. From all the way over there." Eliza gestured vaguely behind her. "One shot, and *bam*. It was awesome."

"Yeah, well, all I did was train while you were laid up in a hospital bed, remember? It's no biggie."

Eliza rolled a shoulder. "Whatever." She nodded toward the demon. "So, Mindy's right. What should we do with him?"

"Drag him home?" Allie suggested.

I grimaced, glancing around for another solution. Our yards might be fenced, but I wasn't keen on hauling a body in the middle of the afternoon. "What about that?" I asked, pointing to the grate against which Eliza had been sprawled.

I hurried that direction as the girls shrugged, then knelt in front of it and found myself squinting into a sewer drain about twenty-four inches in diameter. "We'll hide the body here."

"Hide it?" Allie repeated. "You mean, like to rot?"

I tilted my head and gave her the same stare I use when she leaves wet towels on the bathroom floor. "Your father can deal with it."

Mindy snorted, and we both turned to her. She went pink. "My mom always used to say that when it was something gross. Like cleaning out the disposal." She swallowed, then shrugged as she glanced down. "Now she does all that stuff. Or Cutter does."

"Mindy, honey, I—"

"Um, therapy later?" Eliza said. "Body, remember?"

"Right," Mindy said, before I had a chance to lecture my cousin on being emotionally sensitive. She peered at the grate. "How are we supposed to get it open?"

Eliza had come up behind me and was now bent over in front of the grate. As if to emphasize Mindy's point, she rattled the rusty padlock. "You got bolt cutters in your storage shed?"

The truth was I had no idea if we had bolt cutters or

not, but I made a mental note to add that to my list of household/demon-hunting tools to acquire.

"Even if we did," I admitted "I have no idea where they might be. But how about some wire? Paperclips? Something I can use to pick the lock?"

"You can pick a lock?" That question came from Allie, who seemed to be perking up in the face of the possibility that her mother was trained to do potentially illegal things.

"Theoretically. I haven't had the need since long before you were born."

I shifted my attention to Mindy. "Can you run to your place and bring me back some paperclips? Or bobby pins?" Her house was slightly closer to the easement than ours, being set further back on their lot. And on the off chance that Stuart had come home, I didn't want anyone blowing whatever cover story Laura might have spun.

"Oh! Wait!" Eliza started rummaging in her pockets. "I've got some of those."

I remembered that she'd had her hair pulled up in a messy bun earlier in the day. Now, it hung loose around her shoulders.

After digging in each of her four pockets, she handed me two bobby pins. I went to work bending them, one straight, one hooked so that I could try to work the tumblers. I was seriously out of practice, but fortunately for us, this lock wasn't meant to protect precious artifacts. As far as I could tell, its only purpose served to keep small children from getting lost in the sewage system and then washed out to sea.

Still, rust proved to be a bitter foe. That and the fact that Eliza was so fascinated with what I was doing that she kept moving and blocking my light.

"Come on, Mom," Allie pressed. "We could have gone to Home Depot and bought bolt cutters by now."

A slight exaggeration, I think, considering it had been less than five minutes. But I did understand. We were sitting in the middle of the neighborhood with a dead body. And I don't think any of the neighbors would be convinced if we told them that the man sprawled at the bottom of the easement actually died a long time ago. The only new thing to happen was that the demon that had invaded its body had been evicted.

Nobody but me, Laura, and the girls knew that.

As a Hunter, I'm not overly concerned about the zillions of noncorporeal demons hovering around us in the ether each and every day. Instead, I only come on duty when there's a demonic creature actually walking the earth. And these days, that's limited to walking the earth in San Diablo—or at least Southern California. I may be back on duty, but international travel is no longer part of my job description.

For the most part, I hunt corporeal demons, but I've put down zombies, staked vampires, and decapitated a few werewolves in my day, too. Those demonic forms are relatively rare because, frankly, they tend to stand out. While young vampires do a reasonably good job of

blending in, were-creatures really don't mix well in
society. And zombies? Well, they aren't demons at all.
They're just animated corpses controlled by a demonic
master. Like a disgusting, worm-ridden, remote
control doll.

I bit my lower lip as I continued picking the lock,
diverting my attention only once to scowl at the body,
now nothing more than a human shell, aka a handy
little skin-suit for a previously noncorporeal demon.
Because that, in fact, is what most demons do. They
wait for an opportunity—usually death—and then they
slip into a human body as the previous owner's soul
slips out.

Why? Because most demons want to be human. Or,
at least, they want to experience the pleasures of
humanity. Sights. Sounds. Smells. Sex. Sin. All those S-
words, and a whole lot more.

Some demons want it so badly, that they go the
possession route and hijack a body while the soul is
still there, squashing it down and being all evil and
dominant. But possession isn't subtle, and like high
school freshmen, demons just want to fit in. But a
demon who's possessed a body isn't going to be joining
a wine club or learning to ballroom dance. (Although I
should point out that Eric and I once captured one at a
truly hard core Rave in Istanbul, and he'd blended in
remarkably well. But, well, it was *that* kind of party.)

Most demons eschew the possession route for the
neater prospect of a viable body they can call their

own. Those demons tend to linger about in the ether, often around hospitals, awaiting the moment of death. Why? Because when someone dies, a demon can move in.

You've heard about a doctor who brought someone back to life after he'd flatlined for far too long? Or the guy in a coma they thought had slipped away, but then miraculously woke up?

Yeah, well, that probably wasn't so miraculous after all. Nine times out of ten, that body only looks alive because a demon moved in. The original occupant has left the building. Ladies and gentlemen, there's a new tenant now.

Not that demons can just pop in willy-nilly. Only High Demons can infiltrate the body of the faithful. Souls *fight*, keeping the demon out of the host body until the gap closes and a demon can no longer take root. I don't understand the theology of how it actually happens, but I do know the results. And the bottom line is there's a limited window of opportunity for the demon to move in. And as far as I'm concerned, that's a very good thing since demons do a pretty exceptional job of blending into society. Especially if they just want to hang out and, say, run a Fortune 500 company.

It's the ones who walk the earth because they're doing a High Demon's bidding that are truly gnarly. And lately, that's the kind that's been infesting San Diablo.

For years this town was sleepy. A true demon-free zone.

Recently, there's been an infestation, and the more I squash them, the more they seem to reappear. And unlike roaches, Raid doesn't work. More, I can't call an exterminator. Mostly because I *am* the exterminator.

The problem of course is detecting the demons that are moving around in the world with us, since they can blend almost seamlessly into a community.

I say *almost* because there are always signs. Breath for one thing. Sure, it might be rampant halitosis, but when I see someone popping breath mints like candy my first thought is *demon*.

(I'm careful not to act on that first thought, though, because the unfortunate truth is that dental hygiene among humans really isn't what it should be, and taking out a living, breathing human is what we in the Demon-Hunting trade call a *Very Bad Thing*.)

That's when you turn to other tests. For example, as you'd expect, demons react very unfavorably to holy ground and holy water. Which is why I like to always keep a vial handy. If I'd had any doubts about they guy who'd attacked me—and who I was now shoving into a storm drain—the holy water-induced welts would have confirmed my suspicions.

In other words, this guy was a demon, no doubt about that.

But there's no way in the world I could convince

the San Diablo police if a nosy neighbor decided to cry Civic Duty and call 9-1-1.

Thus, stealth.

Right then, though, I was ready to chuck stealth and race to Home Depot after all, because the padlock just wasn't cooperating. Finally, I said a quick prayer to Saint Baldomerus, the patron saint of locksmiths, then exhaled in relief when—*finally*—the lock snicked open.

"Way to go, Mom!"

I took a moment to bask in the light of teenage approval, then stepped back as Eliza pulled open the grate. The hinges screeched like a demon from hell (trust me on that), and all four of us froze, looking at each other like spooked deer as we waited for one of our adventurous neighbors to venture into the easement to see what was up. Granted that wouldn't be as easy for them —they don't have the gates Laura and I do—but ten-year-old Brian who lives beside us gets into everything. And I really didn't look forward to explaining to his mother why her son found me looming over a dead body.

"Hurry," I hissed, and after much pushing and shoving we finally got the body into the pipe. We shoved it far enough back that no one would notice that there was a body in there unless they were specifically bending over to look. Or, unless they were with the city and actually going into the pipe for a reason. That, however, was a risk we'd have to take.

We closed the grate, and I locked it again. Then I

straightened and glanced around, expecting to see Brian peering down at us, his forehead furrowed under his baseball cap. But there was no Brian, no neighbors, no cops.

So far, so good.

"Girls, grab some brush and cover the grating."

They did as I asked without complaint, which reinforced that this was Serious Stuff. Most fifteen year olds are genetically unable to follow a parent's direction without at least a huff and an eye roll.

"Why'd you lock it?" Allie asked after the grate was well hidden. "Daddy's just going to have to get it open again."

"Your father is more than capable of picking the lock, too," I said. "And I'll tell him to bring bolt cutters. As for getting the body somewhere else..." I trailed off with a shrug.

"Eliza and I can help," Allie said. "He has to, um, take it away, right? He can't just do it here."

I wrinkled my nose. "He'll have to take it away, yes. And we'll offer up whatever help he needs." I just hoped Stuart wasn't home when Eric needed help. Stuart has come to terms with the fact that I kill demons. I don't think he's spent too much time thinking about what happens to the bodies.

It's not something I like to think about either, and I sincerely resent the fact that *Forza* is so stingy about sending a disposal team up from LA when I need one.

"What's Eric supposed to do with it anyway?" Eliza asked.

In response, the rest of us wrinkled our noses.

"Melt them," Allie said. "Gross, but effective." She spoke with the kind of casual, business-like efficiency that made a mother proud. Not to mention nostalgic for the days before she knew any of this.

As she called Eric to tell him the situation, I ran Eliza through Eric's major contribution to demon hunting in San Diablo. Specifically, using the chemistry he'd studied in conjunction with his fascination with rare books to set up his own little demon disposal system.

I'd prefer that the families were able to get the bodies of their loved ones back, but unfortunately, when a demon takes over a human body, the only ways to expel the demon are impaling through the eye or beheading. And both of those methods result in the kind of dead body that would make a cop take notice. (Technically, beheading just removes the head; the demon can still animate the body. But since headless bodies tend to attract unwanted attention, the demons always skeedaddle. Well, nine times out of ten, anyway.)

"Daddy's on his way," Allie said, then shoved her phone into the back pocket of her jeans "Can I stay the night at Mindy's?"

I had to hide a smile. No matter what else had

changed, at least I knew she was still a teenager at heart. A teenager in a world filled with demons.

I frowned. I'd already talked that over with Laura, and a sleepover was already the plan, but that was before the two demons had attacked us in the backyard.

Apparently, Allie picked up on my hesitation, because she sighed in her trademark Teenage Girl Sigh and said, "Come on, Mom. You know we're probably done. I mean, three demons in one day? That's a really high count for a town this small."

Her brow furrowed, and she tilted her head to the side as she added, "Although, we were in Italy for a pretty long time. I know Eddy nailed a few, but I don't think he went patrolling every night the way you and Daddy used to. So I guess there could be more. Maybe a lot more."

Her eyes met mine as she nodded slowly. "I mean, think how many people probably died at Coastal Mists while we were gone. Not all of them could be inhabited, but still…"

I frowned. She wasn't wrong. Death came regularly to the nursing home.

"And there's also—*oh!*" The word was so sharp that for a moment I thought she'd seen another demon. But no, she'd just seen the error of her own ways, because she suddenly stood up straight and started to shake her head. "But I'm sure it's totally safe now. It's not like demons are going to flock to Mindy's house, right?"

She glanced at Mindy, who helpfully said, "Um."

"Because why would there be more in the neighborhood?" Allie continued. "Especially since we just took two out, and that other one's got to be laying low for the rest of the night at least."

I crossed my arms and tilted my head. Then I gave her the Mom Stare.

"*Please.*" She combined prayer hands and puppy dog eyes. "We'll be inside, and Mindy can take care of herself, too. And Aunt Laura has holy water and pepper spray."

"That's right," Mindy chimed in. "Plus, I trained every day with Cutter while you guys were gone, and I—"

I held up a hand. "All right, all right. You can—wait. *Three?*" I looked between the girls. "What do you mean three demons? What other one?"

They looked at each other, and Allie bit her lower lip, always a sign that she was contriving a story.

"Allie..."

She shrugged. "It's no big," she said. "At least, it's not anymore. I mean it all turned out just fine."

"You're not giving me a warm, fuzzy feeling. What happened?"

"Yeah, what did happen?"

I turned around to find Laura walking up behind me, her gaze fixed on Mindy, who swallowed rather dramatically.

"Allie nailed the demon that got away," I explained.

"But I've just learned that there was another demon in the mix somewhere."

"What?" In an expression that must have mimicked mine, she looked at all three girls in turn as well. "What's going on?"

"It really wasn't that big a deal," Eliza said. "We were walking on the boardwalk at the beach—it's a really nice beach here, I have to say. I mean, I love San Diego, but it's so pretty here, and so much less crowded. I really think that you could—"

"Eliza!"

"Sorry, sorry. Anyway, we were walking along and some guy who looked like he'd been living on the streets came up to me. And he asked if I was the one who was new."

"New?" Laura asked, getting there before I did.

"No idea," Eliza said. "But he seemed nice enough. But then—"

"But then we noticed his breath," Allie said. "Because he turned to me and got in really close. Putrid, you know. Like he was rotting from inside. And then he said that he wasn't a threat to me."

"He *what?*"

She nodded. "I know. Weird, right? Like just because I'm new at this, he thinks I'm naive and will trust him and let him get close. *As if.* Then he started to reach for my arm. We were in the middle of everything with all these people around. I mean, I had my stiletto,

63

but I knew I couldn't just poke him in the eye. Not on the boardwalk."

"Right. Go on." I felt ridiculously tense, and swore to myself that I would never let her leave the house again. At the moment, that seemed entirely reasonable.

"Well, he said it again. That he wasn't a threat, I mean. And as he was talking, this other guy rushed up. Really cute. I've seen him around the high school. And he put his hand on my shoulder and stared down the demon. And he said, *not a threat? I bet her mom would disagree*. And then he pulled out a knife and told the scruffy guy to get away from me."

"And the demon left?"

"Yeah, but he kicked the knife out of Jared's hand—he told us his name later—and Jared stumbled backwards, and the demon ran off."

I didn't even know where to begin breaking down this story—or interpreting all of the ramifications. So I focused on potential clues. "What did the demon mean by *new*?"

Allie shook her head. "No idea. But Jared dusted himself off, then said he was sorry that the guy bothered me, and that he hoped to see me around. I wanted him to wait, but he took off."

"New," Laura said. "Maybe a new demon hunter? Allie is pretty new to it all. Or maybe he was looking for Eliza and got them confused."

"But then why not just ask?" Eliza pointed out. "Unless he was afraid he had the wrong group of girls?

But it's not like anyone but us would take him seriously. Ask someone other than us if they're the new demon hunter, and they'd just think they were getting punked, right?"

"But Jared mentioned me," I pointed out, my focus on my baby girl. "He knew who you were, and he knows what your mother is, and presumably the demon knew, too."

"I'm not so sure Jared knew," Eliza said. "I think he just meant that any mother wouldn't like her daughter talking to some creepy guy on the street. Honestly, I'm not even sure Jared knew the grungy guy was a demon. He might have just thought we were being harassed and pulled a knife to scare him away."

"Well, I thought he was talking about Aunt Kate," Mindy said. "I mean, we were threatened by a demon, so I just figured he was talking about the local demon hunter."

"Well, we're not figuring it out right now," Allie said. "So can we *please* get back to the point?"

"The point?" Laura asked, clearly as confused as I was.

"Duh. Can we sleep over at Mindy's?"

I swallowed a burst of laughter as I shot a sideways glance to Laura. I could tell from her expression that she was thinking exactly the same thing as me—*at least some things never change.*

"Yes," I said, glancing at Laura for confirmation. "But you stay inside, and you stay careful. I don't care if you see your dad out the window, you do not come outside again until morning. Understand me young lady?"

"Totally."

"And tomorrow we're all going to Mass in the morning—so be home by nine—then we're going to go by Cutter's studio."

"Cutter's still in LA, Kate," Laura said.

"We're all going to go to Cutter's studio, and Laura is going to let us in with her key, and we're going to practice training, and then next week starting when Cutter gets back, the three of you are having regular training every day after school." That, at least, was the plan. We'd see if it actually came to fruition.

"I'm not in school anymore," Eliza said.

I tilted my head, and she held up her hands. "But happy to train whenever you want."

"Okay girls, go on."

Mindy and Allie fell in step beside each other, but Eliza stayed by me.

Before I could say anything, Allie turned, her head cocked. "Aren't you coming?"

"Oh. Well, I, sure if you—"

"Well, duh," Mindy said.

Eliza grinned. "Yeah. Great. I'd love to."

"Mom, that's okay right?"

"Of course, it is," Laura said with the kind of smile I'd seen her use more than once when she was frustrated by a PTA meeting. "You guys go on ahead."

They did, and Laura and I lingered behind as they hurried toward her house.

"Do you need help with this guy? Or the one in your backyard?"

I shook my head. "No. Just tell me where he is."

"Under your garden bench, covered in weed barrier. It was the best I could do."

"It'll be fine. There's nobody who goes in my back yard who doesn't know the score these days."

That was true.

Once upon a time I'd jumped through hoops to hide bodies in the storage shed without Stuart finding out. Now, I could actually enlist his aid to help me move the body if need be. Hopefully I wouldn't need to do that. Although I did need to give Eric another call and let him know that I needed him to take care of two bodies, not one.

I needed to tell him the rest of it too. That there was a new enemy in town with a new agenda I didn't understand, or maybe I just didn't want to understand it. Because the demon who had attacked me said that I wasn't *her*, and the demon who had attacked Eliza had said that she wasn't *her* either.

I had a feeling I knew who they were looking for. Allie was *new*, after all. Newly aware. Newly annointed by battle. New to the world of demon hunting.

She'd returned from Rome with more strength than just training could account for, although I'd kept that assessment to myself. And there was still the question of what—if anything—that golden glow in the chamber beneath Rome had done to her.

Bottom line, my mommy instincts were on overdrive, and I was concerned about my baby girl.

I caught Laura's worried expression, and pulled myself back to the moment. "What's wrong?"

"Nothing—just about Eliza…"

"Do you not want Eliza to stay with them?"

"No, it's not that. It's just… Okay, maybe it is that…"

"What?"

She drew in a breath. "You're sure about Eliza?"

I didn't have to ask what she meant. "I am. Why do you ask?"

"That demon. The one on top of you. He said you weren't new. He was looking for someone who was new. And she's the new one, right?"

"Oh." I nodded slowly, happy that she hadn't made the same leap toward Allie as I had. "You might be right. But if so, it's not because she's bad."

"I get that. But it might make her a target. And is that who we want around our girls?"

"Are you going to stop hanging out with me?" I asked. "Are you going to ask Mindy to stop hanging around Allie?"

I saw her shoulders slump in defeat. "No. Of course not."

"Good," I said. And then, because I couldn't hold it in any longer, I added, "Because it's Allie, Laura. My baby's the one that's new."

CHAPTER 6

"*A*llie?" Laura gaped at me. "What are you talking about?"

"She's the one the demons are all twitchy about," I said. "The one that's new. Or, at least, I think she is. I don't know," I admitted, sagging down to the ground and pulling my knees up to my chest.

After a moment, Laura settled onto the damp grass, too. "I think I need a little more context. How the heck is Allie *new*? And what does that mean, anyway?"

"What it means? Not really sure," I admitted, then gave her the quick and dirty rundown of everything I knew.

She nodded sagely. "So the bottom line is that Father Donnelly and Eric's parents weren't expecting that Eric would be the kick-ass Demon Hunter. His child would."

"Pretty much."

She let that settle for a bit, then her eyes widened. "Is she—I mean, not to worry you, but Eric went a little off the rails."

"I know. But it's different," I said firmly, as much to convince myself as her. "She locked the gate to hell. What's inside her is there for good."

"So she's the happy ending, and Eric was the tumultuous third act."

This time, it was my turn to gape. "Huh?"

"It's Mindy," she said dismissively. "Now that she's in that musical, everything is about plays and movies and story structure. Last Friday, she spent dinner telling me about the story structure in the episode of *The Simpsons* we'd just watched. Then she told me that Paul's affair was the inciting incident in my romance with Cutter. What does that even mean?"

I bit back a laugh. "And I thought I was the one with problems."

"Nah, I'd say we're about even."

"Thanks."

Her brow furrowed. "For what?"

"For surprising me. Or really, for not surprising me. For acting the same way that I knew you would but was afraid you wouldn't."

"There's a lot to unpack in that sentence, but I'm guessing you're trying to say that you worried that I'd freak out, then tell you to get your daughter out of my house?"

I felt the tears prick my eyes, and my throat was thick as I said, "Yeah."

"Oh, Kate. I love Allie, you know that. Like you said, she's the same kid she always was. With more issues than most teens, but nothing we can't handle. But on that same note," she added with a mischievous grin, "I bought one of those tasers Rita used on Eric. If Allie gets out of hand, I'll just give her a jolt."

"And by out of hand, I assume you mean something more nefarious than leaving your best dishes scattered about."

She shrugged. "Hey, whatever works."

And you know what? She had a point.

"The demons are gearing up for something," I said once I was back in the house with Timmy and Eddie. "They want Allie for some reason."

"Harumph. She's the same kid she's always been. Nothing's changed, right? Now you just know what's inside her. But it's always been there."

We were in the living room, and I dropped down onto the couch, pulling a pillow up into my lap and hugging my knees to it. "I know. I know, I do. It's just— well, you weren't there. In Rome, I mean. There was a glow. This golden glow that covered everything after Allie locked the gate."

His brow furrowed, and he squinted as he rubbed his straggly beard. "A glow? Or fire?"

It was a fair question. I didn't know anything about the golden glow that had been in that crypt after Allie slapped her hand onto the dais and stopped the gates of Hell from opening. But I did know a little bit about Cardinal Fire.

Years ago, back when Eric and I were still hunting, we'd been on the trail of one of the most vile High Demons out there—Abaddon. We were the only two surviving members of the team of Hunters that had gone into a series of caverns beneath the streets of Rome. We'd found Abaddon, and we'd been trapped. We'd managed to escape through the use of Cardinal Fire, mystical fire that could cleanse away and destroy demons.

It hadn't destroyed Abaddon that day—he'd managed to escape back into the bowels of the earth, the fire not touching him. But it did touch Eric, and in doing so, it eradicated the mystical bond that kept the demon inside him buried deep. Another round of Cardinal Fire would have probably killed both him and the demon. But there was no more, and we were able to escape, none the wiser at the time.

I only recently learned about the demon that had been hidden in my first husband, then loosed within him that day. The demonic presence affected him, all the way down to a cellular level, and he passed that essence to his daughter.

And because of that heritage, she'd been able to shut the gate in Rome.

That, of course, was a very good thing.

But there's no escaping the fact that the source of her power is demonic, and I don't know what that means. For that matter, I don't even know if she *has* special powers. Sure, she's faster and stronger, but she really has been training. And, yes, she shut the gate. But for all I know that was a one-time thing. Handy in the moment, but not a useful trick most days. (And thank God for that! I have plenty to do without gates to hell popping up all over creation.)

So maybe Eddie was right. Unless the golden glow changed her, she's the same sweet kid she's always been. Even if it did change her, it wouldn't necessarily be for the bad. She kept the demons at bay, after all. All of which made me feel like a horrible mother to even consider the possibility that there was something dark growing inside her.

"Momma, momma, MOMMA!"

Speaking of being a horrible parent...

I pulled myself away from my thoughts to find Timmy bouncing in front of me. "Do you need to go potty?"

"No, Momma. Wanna be the band!"

Across the room, Eddie groaned.

"You want to have a conversation or not?" I asked. "Because if I don't let him, he's just going to whine."

"And if you do let him, we ain't gonna be able to hear ourselves think."

He had a point.

"Band it is," I said, standing and leading the way to the kitchen. "But this is quiet band." I took my voice down to a whisper. "It's for special music. Can you do whisper singing and quiet playing?"

He shook his head. "No, Momma."

At least the kid was honest.

"I bet you can. And if you let me and Gramps finish talking, you can have a packet of Goldfish crackers."

His little face lit up the way it often does when he tells me he loves me and gives me big cuddles. Considering that put me on the same par as cheesy crackers, I wasn't entirely sure what to make of that.

Wisely, I chose to table that question, focusing instead on putting together his music studio. A rubber spatula with a wooden handle. Tupperware instead of metal bowls to serve as drums. A plastic spoon still wrapped from ice cream take-out one day.

And, the pièce de la résistance … an empty paper towel tube.

"You're all set, kiddo," I whispered. "Remember, it's *quiet band*."

"Aye-aye, Momma," he said, putting Boo Bear on the floor beside him, then saluting me with the tube.

I mentally crossed my fingers that I'd just bought seven to ten minutes of quality adult conversation time, then headed back into the living room.

Eddie snorted. "You really think that'll keep the boy occupied?"

"A girl can dream."

"Fair enough." He pointed a bony finger at me. "And a girl should quit worrying about things she don't understand."

It took me a second to shift gears back to my daughter, but I'd caught up with the conversation by the time he added, "You got to look at the basics. Allie's your daughter. You love Allie. Allie's a good kid. Allie's the same kid she's always been. Ergo, unless you know for certain something's different, not a damn thing's changed."

I nodded. He was right. It's not as if this just happened yesterday. We stayed in Rome after saving the world, and part of that was so that Allie could talk with the priests at Forza and train and learn more about what she was. Nobody saw any hint that there was anything evil inside her.

But even without the possibility of evil forces gathering inside her, I was still worried. Because it seemed to me that for *some* reason, the local demon population was looking for my daughter.

"Still might be Eliza," Eddie said when I voiced as much. "For that matter, could be someone else in town."

I scowled at the thought. "All that means is that I have more to figure out. We need to know who the demons are after and why. You remember what it was

75

like before. And I'm not keen on having the oldest and most powerful demon in the world come back again."

He made a snorting noise. "You sent that Lilith bitch and her consort Odayne packing. She's gone. She's dead."

I sighed, then glanced toward the rising noise now coming from the kitchen. I figured we had maybe four minutes left for a real conversation.

"Lilith's not dead, and you know it," I said. In addition to being a High Demon, Lilith is also one of the first and most powerful demons. Getting rid of her is like trying to remove a purple Sharpie stain from a white T-shirt. It just never quite seems to work. Ask me how I know. "And how could a demon ever really be dead, anyway?" I continued, because thinking about demons is almost always better than thinking about laundry.

To be brutally honest, I should have known the answer to that—and I sort of did, even though I never really wrapped my head around it. It's the kind of thing they taught us in the long, boring classes that every Hunter-in-Training had to take. I was always more about kicking ass than learning the details. The book stuff was Eric's love, not mine. Theory, theology, the whole shebang.

From his recliner, Eddie let out a long-suffering sigh. "I stepped in as your *alimentatore*, but that don't mean I do your thinking for you, girlie. You know how it works. Don't pretend like you don't. Because you're right, she's not dead, not what we consider dead, anyway."

"Right," I said, tacitly admitting I did know this, even if I didn't understand the science—or theology—behind it. "When a demon is expelled from a body, they go back to the ether," I recited, feeling like I was nine again and presenting to Father Corletti. "The only way to kill a demon is to kill them in their true form—their true, nasty, monstrous form that manifests in this world. That takes them out completely."

"You cutting corners in your explanation there, girl?"

I made a face. The way it works—simplistically speaking—is that a demon expelled from a human body goes back to the ether. If killed in its true form, however, it's sucked back into a completely different dimension.

The ether is an accessible dimension. Not easily, but it's possible for human souls to get diverted there even though the heavenly dimension is a much better place. That's what happened to Eric's soul after he was killed in San Francisco. He was floating formless out there, surrounded by throngs of equally formless demons.

The thought still made me shiver.

And, of course, there's a hell dimension. That's where demons hang if they just want to live their little demon lives in their own demonic neighborhood. The ether is like a way station. Demons leave hell and go there if they're planning on coming here.

Regular demons tend to hang out in hell or the ether, and when they die, that's where they return.

High Demons have more power, but that also means it's harder for them to manifest in our world, even inside a human body. They just radiate too much demon-ness, and burn through the body quickly.

When they're killed in a human form, they're weakened. Instead of the ether, they return straight to the hell dimension to regain their strength. Which is a good thing, because it keeps them out of commission for a while. Usually years and years in earth time.

But once you kill a demon in its *true* form, it goes someplace else entirely. Call it Uber-Hell, though I'm sure the Church has another name for it. It's another dimension altogether from which there's no escape. At least, not as far as I know. A truly dead demon is the brass ring for a Demon Hunter, because it means that's one beastie that really isn't coming back.

I've taken a few High Demons out in my time— more than the average Hunter, that's for sure. In fact, I'd sent one to Uber-Hell right before the trip to Rome—Lilith's consort, Odayne. He'd burst out of Eric in his true form, and I'd nailed his demony little ass.

Lilith, though … well, I wasn't entirely sure what had happened to her. She'd created Odayne, and that meant they were connected. When Odayne died, she had, too.

But had I sent her back to Uber-Hell, there to be

trapped forever? Or had she merely gone back to the regular hell dimension to regroup?

I didn't know. I *couldn't* know. But if she hadn't followed her lover into that deepest, darkest hell, that meant that Lilith—one of the most ancient and powerful of all demons—was off somewhere licking her wounds and regrouping.

Not the happiest of thoughts, but so long as she's not on earth, I can live with that.

"Exactly" Eddie said, after I told him all of that. "You two kicked her mighty ass to the curb, and more power to you. And if she's injured, it'll take a while to heal in human years. Bitch probably won't make it back until Allie's got grandkids."

"I hope so," I said. "But that doesn't necessarily mean there aren't more demons coming out of the woodwork."

"Eh." His shoulders rose and fell in a Gallic gesture. "There's always demons coming out of the woodwork."

"True. But there were three tonight," I added, getting back to my original point. "*Three.*"

"You think that means they're up to something? Phhhbt. I think it means that there are more demons because you weren't here reading the papers, chasing down the dead bodies that aren't really dead. Not you or your snooky-wookums."

I cocked my head to the side and stared him down. "Eddie…"

"Just calling them like I'm seeing them."

The fact is, he was probably right. Allie said the same thing. I hugged the pillow tighter. "I'm just worried," I said. "She may be fifteen, but she's still my baby."

His shoulders sagged, and for a moment he looked ten years older. Finally, he nodded slowly, lifting his head to meet my eyes. "I never had kids you know."

"I know."

"But I do think of you as a daughter. Or at least a granddaughter. And you know how I feel about Allie."

My smile reached all the way to my toes. "I know. Us, too." And then, because between the two of us, we could only handle so much sappiness, I added, "What about Stuart and Eric?"

He snorted. "Guess I'm more like a father than anyone could have anticipated, because as far as I'm concerned neither one of them is good enough for you."

"Eddie," I said with a hint of warning in my voice. But at the same time, I couldn't hide my grin.

"But…" he continued, holding up a finger, "they're both good men. And they both love you. You figure out a way to keep those two from killing each other, and I think all three of you will end up doing just fine."

"Yeah? Wow, who knew?"

"What?"

"You have a sweet side."

He made a deep grunting, guttural sound. "I'd appreciate it if you didn't tell anybody that."

I laughed. "I never had a dad."

"I know."

"Never had a grandfather, either."

I saw the hint of a smile touch his lips. "You did. A father, too. You just didn't know either of them. Your father's dead, we know that. But as for your grandpa … well he could be alive for all you know."

Considering my age, I doubted it. But technically it was possible. And it really was a nice thought. "Maybe." I shot him a mischievous grin. "For that matter, maybe it's you."

He chuckled. "Stranger things have happened. Between the two of us, we've probably seen most of those stranger things."

"True enough."

"What about Eliza?" he asked.

I shook my head, having lost the thread. "Eliza?"

"She's family ain't she? She must know what your grandparent situation is."

He had a point. "She doesn't have any living relatives, though. But you're right. She might have the information. I'll ask her. But she wouldn't know about my paternal line."

"Well, as far as I'm concerned, you've got a good family. Good tight family. Who cares about blood?" His eyes met mine. "Blood's always causing trouble."

He was right about that. I pushed the pillow away, shaking off my doubts and fears and worries. "It doesn't matter anyway. My family tree is doing just fine."

I pushed off the couch then went over and gave him a quick kiss on the cheek.

He rubbed the spot brusquely. "Ah, now you're going to go and get all sappy."

"It happens."

"Harumph." His eyes narrowed as he stared me down. "Just no crying. Can't stand the crying."

I laughed. "Fair enough. Want to watch something mindless on television before I go put together dinner? Or we could do a short movie. G-rated," I added with a nod toward the kitchen, where the decibel level was rapidly increasing.

"Not a bad idea, but I got me a date." He lifted his wrist and tapped the crystal of the watch we brought him from Italy along with the stiletto. "Time for me to go get ready. You going to be okay alone, girly-girl?"

"Don't worry about me," I said as I heard a clatter and the shrill sound of a toddler's cry. I know how to take care of myself."

"Yeah," Eddie said as I sprinted to the kitchen. "You definitely do."

"No, no, no!" I screeched, my eyes bugged out horror as I stood stock still, completely stymied with absolutely no idea how to deal with this … this … *hell.*

Seriously, I was looking down into the vast pit of hell in all its slimy, writhing grossness. It had touched me—infected me—and the pure horror of it all had festered a murderous rage inside of me. A rage so intense that I whipped out my phone and hit the speed dial for Allie.

"Hey, Mom! We're fine. All quiet. No need to check in."

"Do. You. Have. Any. Idea. What. You. Did?"

The silence hung heavy on the other end of the line for a full count of five. I know, because Timmy was on the floor beside me, counting the writhing little critters as they wriggled on the concrete.

"Um, no?"

"*Maggots*, Allie. The outside pantry is teeming with maggots!"

"*Ew!*"

"Yes," I said. "Yes, that about sums it up. I opened the doors to get one of the cases of green beans and a bazillion of the creatures practically leaped out at me."

A slight exaggeration, as only a few had squirmed off the shelf. But it had seemed like a bazillion at the time. As far as I was concerned, one maggot was one too many.

As a rule, I'm not squeamish. I'll put up with all sorts of things. I've shoved my finger through eyes to expel demons. I've changed the dirtiest of diapers. I've scraped dishes that my teenager forgot about in her bedroom for over three weeks, not to mention half-finished fast food milkshakes that had solidified into some sort of concrete-like substance.

I've even tackled a bathtub ring so intense I actually considered a full bathroom remodel because it would be an easier job.

But I do not—*not*—deal well with bugs. Especially bugs of the slimy, wriggling variety.

"Um," Allie began. "Was it that roast?"

I tilted my head, both annoyed and a little bit proud. Annoyed that she so clearly knew the source of the problem. Proud that she confessed.

"I would say yes, but I'd have to guess since I'm not going to get close enough to be sure. How is it that *you're* so certain?"

"I, um, might have gotten distracted unpacking the groceries you got for Eddie."

We'd gone shopping before leaving for Rome. Stuff for the freezer and dry goods for the pantry. One call from a boy—because I'm certain it was a boy—and her mind turned to mush, and a roast ended up defrosting in the pantry. For almost a *month*.

Seriously, we might just have to sell the house.

"Tomorrow," I said. "You're cleaning tomorrow."

"I know, I know. I will. I'm sorry! But, um, will you help me?"

"Not in a million years."

"But—"

"Maggots, Allie. I really and truly do not do maggots."

"Fine. Can I ask Mindy? Or Daddy?"

"You can hire a cleaning service with your allowance money for all I care. I just want to be able to get the Odyssey out of the garage without the floor squishing under my shoes."

"Ewww. Mom. Gross."

"That, my darling daughter, is my point."

"Can I go now? Aunt Laura made pasta."

Bile rose in my throat at the very thought, but I managed to keep it together. "Sure, go on. But tomorrow, you clean."

"Love you, Mom. And I'm sorry."

I melted at the unprompted affection. "Love you, too, baby. Have fun."

"Will do. Kiss Timmy for me."

And just like that, I melted a little bit more.

CHAPTER 7

*A*fter the maggot encounter, sitting down to fold laundry seemed less onerous than usual, even with Timmy helping.

And by helping, I mean that I folded, and he mangled. But his grin was so wide, and he kept telling me how much he loved me, that I wasn't exactly going to correct him.

We'd just finished a basket, when Stuart called. "I'm still with Bernie," he said. "He found a company that should be able to handle the tile work for a decent price. They're usually booked, and so I'd hate to miss out. And then I really need to run by the office. I've got a pile of paperwork to look over. Do you mind if I'm late?"

"Of course not," I said, even though I did mind. At least a little. It felt like we'd been going on fast-forward since we got back into town, and I'd been hoping for a

little bit of time to sit and chill with my husband. But I understood that he had things to get back to, not the least of which was repairing the investment house that an extremely powerful—and extremely pissed off— demon had pretty much destroyed.

For that matter, I thought, as I glanced out the window at the backyard where a demon carcass still hid beneath the gardening bench, maybe it was best that he wasn't home yet.

I frowned, wondering why I had yet to hear from Eric. It was getting dark, and he was supposed to have swooped in and taken care of the bodies by now. Surely he would have texted me that it was done right? I mean, yes, I could have gone into the backyard and checked for the body, but if it wasn't there, I'd really like affirmation that it was Eric who moved it. And, honestly, how much trouble was it to send a quick text?

"Kate? Did I lose you?"

I straightened. "Sorry, I'm here. I was preoccupied by Timmy." I glanced at my little boy who was being remarkably well behaved, grateful that the kiddo wasn't yet old enough to realize he was Mommy's little scapegoat. "Do you want me to swing by and bring you some dinner?"

As soon as the words were out of my mouth, I cringed again, because I really didn't want to leave the house. Instead, I wanted to waylay Eric when he came for the bodies and ask his opinion on the various demonic goings-on.

"Love the idea," Stuart began, making me tense with frustration, "but I'm good."

I sagged with relief.

"We're going to meet with these guys, then grab dinner out so we can go over some of the numbers and see where we are. Is that okay?"

"Sure. Of course. That's absolutely fine."

Dead air lingered between us. "Kate … is there something going on?" His voice dropped to a whisper as he added, "You know. Something about *demons*?"

"No, no. Nothing like that at all." Honestly, the man knew me too well. And while I *should* have told him, I also knew he had work to do. Plus I didn't want to get into it right now. And, yeah, the truth is I was still a little nervous about his reaction. We'd repaired things in Rome, but I didn't yet know if the repairs were concrete or kiddie paste. Because it was demons in San Diablo that drove him away in the first place.

Maybe it was unfair, but I felt better holding some stuff back. At least until I understood more. And until I could look at his face as I talked to him.

"Kate?"

"It's all good here," I told him, which at that exact moment in time was totally true. "It's only that I was hoping that you and I could have an early night. Maybe chill on the couch. Hang out. But it's fine. Really. I'll take a rain check. Truly."

I sincerely hoped that when I end up at those Pearly Gates the number of demons I've taken out over the years outweighs the number of fibs I've told my husband.

"Definitely a rain check," he said, his voice shifting from business mode into night-with-my-wife mode. "A night in … a glass of wine … imagine the possibilities…."

"Believe me," I assured him. "I am."

With his perfectly honed sense of timing, Timmy started banging on his plastic truck with a wooden stick, which, I realized was the end of my spatula, now missing the flat, rubber piece that gave it those spatula-like qualities.

I ended the call with Stuart, then plucked the stick from Timmy's hand. "It's you and me tonight, kiddo. You hungry?" I started toward the kitchen, tossing the no-longer-a-spatula onto the counter. I'd look for the plastic piece later, but I had a feeling it was buried deep in a toy chest or shoved into the couch cushions. "Want to do dinner on the sofa with a movie?"

"Can we watch puppies?"

The beginnings of a headache trickled up the back of my spine. Not that I have anything against *101 Dalmatians*, but I'm pretty sure I've seen it more times than there are actually Dalmatians in the movie.

"Of course we can, sweetie pie. What do you think about fish sticks and apple slices while we watch?"

His little head bobbed eagerly, and I immediately kicked myself, because I hadn't actually checked to make sure there were any fish sticks in the house.

I said a quick prayer to Saint Monica, the patron saint of mothers, then zipped over to the freezer. I pulled it open, peered inside, and sagged with relief. "Hey, where's my little chef?"

"Here, Mommy!" He scurried into the kitchen easily, as the baby gate that separates the living area from the kitchen wasn't closed. It's usually not these days, though we haven't entirely disassembled the thing since he's mobile enough now that I want the kitchen shut tight during the night.

Now, Timmy stood there holding the chef hat we keep in the toy box behind the couch. "You ready to cook, Chef Connor?"

He nodded eagerly, then opened the bottom cabinet and pulled out a cookie sheet. I dragged over his stool so that he could get to counter height, then opened the box and let him put the fish sticks on the cookie sheet.

He arranged them, then sipped his milk while we waited for the oven to preheat.

"Okay, Timster," I said when the oven was ready. "Tell me how many minutes."

"Three!" he said, holding out three fingers. "Me three!"

"You will be soon, buddy. But let's set the timer for fifteen. Remember? Put it right there at the red mark." The oven has a timer, but I use the dial kind in what may or may not be a misguided belief that letting him fiddle with it will enhance his education.

"Five!" he squealed as he moved the dial to fifteen.

"And who am I to argue with my little Einstein?" I asked, then kissed him on the forehead.

He pointed to his hat. "Chef, Mommy. I'm a chef."

"Right you are. Okay, Mr. Chef. Hop down and let's go get your apple juice out of the fridge."

I pulled open the door, but instead of grabbing a juice box, he snatched a huge Honeycrisp apple.

"Please, Momma?"

Since who was I to argue with a kid who wanted to eat fruit, I took the apple, washed it, then put it on the cutting board as Timmy climbed back up on the stool. "Me cut! Me cut!

"What's the rule?"

"No knives. I know Momma..."

He sounded so much like his sister I almost laughed. "You go find the movie and I'll cut up the apple. Deal?"

"Okay...."

He wandered off, and I quickly sliced the apple. I was putting it on a plate when he shouted that he'd found the video. I checked the timer, then headed over to pop in the disc.

Timmy was two slices into his apple when the timer dinged, and I went to retrieve his fabulous meal, making him promise not to take a bite until I said so because the sticks needed to cool.

Meanwhile, I cut up some cheese for me—enough to share, because I know that's inevitable—and another apple, because it really did look good. Soon enough, the fish sticks were ready to eat, and I was snuggled with my little man on the sofa, juice for him and wine for me.

We finished our food, and I gathered our plates and headed into the kitchen. I'd just dropped them in the sink and trash respectively, when I heard Timmy shouting, "Uncle David, Uncle David!"

I poked my head back in, then glanced at the TV screen. But, honestly, the animated man who was the composer and human lead in the cartoon movie didn't look a thing like David. I told Timmy as much, at the same time silently acknowledging that it was pretty cool of Stuart, despite his dislike of Eric, to let us put the uncle label on him.

The "David" label came because as far as the world was concerned, Eric was David Long, a high school chemistry teacher. In reality, David Long died in the car accident that injured his leg, and Eric had moved into the body. Not the typical family situation, but we've gotten used to it.

Adding the uncle title made it easier on Allie since she and her father had been spending so much time together both at and away from school. I'd been concerned that their time together would be frowned upon by the school staff at best, and deemed creepy and inappropriate at worst. The uncle solution nipped that potential problem in the bud.

"He doesn't look at all like Uncle David," I told Timmy, still looking at the television. When he only bounced more enthusiastically, though, I realized that he'd actually shifted his attention from the show to the French doors that lead to the back yard.

I turned that direction and, sure enough, "Uncle David" was standing right there.

Well, hell.

Not that I don't want to see Eric. As a general rule, I do. But not today. Not after the earlier argument with Stuart. As far as I was concerned, Eric was supposed to have slipped into the back yard, removed the bodies, and slipped right out again.

Knocking on the back door—especially when for all he knew, Stuart might be home—wasn't on the agenda.

Then again, Stuart's the one who got all pissy and then left....

I shook my head, scattering the thoughts. The bottom line was that none of this was about the relationship between Stuart and Eric. Those two were going to have to figure that out on their own. But if Eric was having some sort of demon disposal issue, that wasn't something that I could avoid.

By the time I got to the door, Timmy, thankfully, had turned his attention back to the screen. "Is there a problem?" I asked.

"There's no problem. The bodies are in my trunk." He frowned. "I really need to get a new car. That was a tight squeeze."

"Okay. Well, thanks." I shifted from foot to foot, not sure why we need this conversation if he had the bodies. "And sorry to make you come all the way back from Los Angeles."

He moved his shoulders in the casual shrug. "Yeah, well, about that. I never left San Diablo."

"What?"

"I was still in San Diablo when Allie called."

"Oh. Well, that was convenient. Why?" I realized as I asked the question that I was asking it with a hint of jealously, wondering if he'd decided to stay because he was seeing someone. Which, of course was insane. The last woman he was with was a demon who had pretty much taken control of his mind. Right after that, we'd bopped to Rome. I sincerely doubted he'd started up with the dating thing.

"Why?" he repeated.

"Yeah. Why didn't you head home? You know, down to Los Angeles where you moved when you decided you had to get away from me?" That probably came out with a bit more angry-hurt than I'd intended. "What happened to needing to be away? To having time for yourself? Healing and all that stuff?"

All legitimate questions. What I didn't ask was what I was supposed to tell my husband who'd been very happy to learn that Eric had decided to move to Los Angeles in order to give my family unit a little time to heal. A decision I'd both supported and loathed.

"None of that has changed," he said. "I do need the time. But at the end of the day what I need isn't really what matters, is it?"

"Allie."

He nodded. "She needs me."

"Eric—"

He held up a hand, cutting me off. "I'm sorry if it complicates things for you, but this isn't about you or Stuart. It's about me and my daughter. Maybe before, I could have justified being over an hour away. But not anymore. Not knowing what we know now."

I nodded, because he was right.

"It's about *our* daughter, and I get it," I admitted. "But I need the truth, Eric. Is it only about Allie? Or is it about me, too?" I knew I was being bold, but I didn't care. I needed the truth, because without it, I couldn't navigate these murky relationship waters.

His shoulders dropped with a sigh. And though he reached out a hand for me, I didn't take it. "Yeah, it is," he said, pulling his hand back and shoving it into his pocket. "But it shouldn't be."

CHAPTER 8

"At the risk of pissing off your husband," Eric said, "you and I need to go patrolling tonight."

"Why do I not believe that you care about pissing off Stuart?"

I'd invited him in and now we were sitting at the kitchen table. Timmy, who had given his "uncle" one big hug, was back on the couch with his puppies.

To his credit, Eric chuckled. "Good point. I don't. But I do care about you and about seeing you happy. And I know that it will make you unhappy to go behind Stuart's back."

"It will. Especially since it's our first night home."

"True. But I have two demons in my trunk, remember? And there's another one running around out there who attacked the girls."

"I know." And, honestly, it's not like Stuart was home anyway. I sat back, meeting Eric's eyes. "About these attacks today—Eddie and Allie both think that the demon population probably expanded significantly while we were in Rome. They have a point."

"Makes sense. You and I weren't here keeping the beasties at bay."

"You're right," I agreed, pulling out my phone. "I'll send Stuart an FYI text, and then one to Laura to please come play babysitter until we get back or Eddie comes home."

I concentrated on my phone, grateful for the temporary distraction. Once the messages whooshed away, I looked up at him again. "It really would be easier if you'd just go back to Los Angeles," I said. "But even so, you should know that I'm glad you still have my back."

He tilted his head in acknowledgement. "Always."

I pushed back from the table and stood. "I need to change. You keep Timmy company, okay? And one more thing," I added, pausing as I walked away. "Tonight can't just be about hunting. We need to capture and interrogate."

"Already thought of that," Eric assured me. He pulled a folded sheet of paper from the back pocket of his jeans. "I went through a few old issues of the newspaper before Allie called about dead demon duty. Looking for those miraculous recoveries and survived accidents, you know?"

He knew very well I understood. "You found some likely candidates."

"Oh, yeah. Lot of death and dying going on last month."

"And to think I thought that coming home would be relaxing after Rome."

"Sorry to disappoint." He tapped the paper. "I pulled as many addresses I could find, along with the locations where they died. Well, *didn't* die," he amended with a small shrug. "We'll start there and maybe we can decrease the local demon population by one or two tonight. And you're right," he hurried to continue before I could get a word in. "Interrogation first. As far as I'm concerned, the goal is to end this night with a better understanding of what's going on with our daughter."

Our daughter.

The words seemed to hang in the air between us until, finally, I cleared my throat and mumbled something about changing clothes.

"Just one a sec," I said, then scurried upstairs. Honestly, it was a relief to step away. I needed to get my head straight. As much as I intellectually knew that we needed to do this—and as much as I emotionally wanted Eric nearby—I couldn't get past the reality that the whole situation was beyond awkward.

And my deep, dark secret? I'd been harboring the unlikely fantasy that somewhere down the line, he and Stuart would become friends. That this would all become easier.

But the truth is, even if they became best buds, it

would only be easier for *them*. Because I was really and truly in love with both those men, and that reality had no easy outcome for me.

I changed into jeans, sensible shoes, and a long sleeve tee to combat the nighttime chill from the ocean, even in late summer. I also slipped on my hunter's vest, a *Forza-issued* addition to my wardrobe that looked a bit like something a photographer might wear. I'd stocked it with pointy things and holy water, just like any good Hunter, and headed back downstairs ready to rumble.

By that time, Laura was settled on the couch with Timmy, who was thrilled to see her, especially when she promised him that he could stay up late so that they could build a city out of his Duplo collection. Then—once I'd gotten hugs and kisses and promises to come kiss him good night even if he's already asleep, and once I'd called Allie and told her and Eliza and Mindy to be vigilant—Eric and I set out.

We took separate cars to his old apartment, me following him. He'd moved to Los Angeles before the lease had expired, so coming back to San Diablo wasn't going to be a hassle. The apartment came with an assigned garage, and we stowed his car there.

"I'll deal with the bodies later," he said as he slid into my Odyssey.

"How do you get them upstairs with out anyone noticing?" I asked. He'd been handling demon disposal for a while now, but this was the first time I'd actually thought about the details of that particular workflow. I wrinkled my nose as I pondered the question. "I mean, you don't hack them up and then schlep a demon-filled duffel up the stairs, do you?"

He tilted his head to the side, then said, very simply, "No."

"Good. Glad to hear it. But…?"

"Kate, do you really want to know?"

"No … but kinda?" What can I say? It was like picking a scab. I was certain there'd be something weirdly satisfying about hearing the details of how this business of ours worked on the practical, behind the scenes side of things.

"Let's just say that there are a lot of chemicals stored in the high school basement, and I managed to wrangle a commitment out of *Forza* to send a disposal team every other month. They pretend to be a supply company coming up from LA monthly to pick up the barrels and drop off fresh lab supplies."

"Oh. Right. I get it. Melted demon goo. At the high school. Where our daughter goes." I wrinkled my nose.

"Sorry you asked?"

"Maybe," I admitted. "But melted demons are probably better than cadavers in the Cathedral. And it's not like we can let the bodies pile up. Eventually, someone would notice."

That's a constant worry, actually. When Eric and I were young, we might have been based in Rome, but we were sent all over the world. Leaving a few demon corpses strewn about wasn't that big a deal, even though the poke in the eye made it look like foul play.

For one, the odds of tracing it back to us were slim. For another, most of the time a *Forza* disposal team would take care of the problem before the body was discovered. But a few bodies here and there are different than dozens of kills in a single city. Disposal is necessary if we want to avoid the human world noticing. And we *really* want to avoid that. Not only would it be incredibly inconvenient, but Stuart is still friends with the District Attorney. And how awkward would that be?

We parked at the beach, starting our search at the boardwalk. San Diablo is famous for its riptides, but there's also a very low mortality rate. As far as the public knows, anyway.

That's because most of the people who get sucked out into a riptide and drown come back again with a demon inside them—like the *four* who so miraculously survived while we were off saving the world in Rome.

Since demons tend to return to the place where they became enfleshed, it's a rare patrol when I don't encounter a demon near the boardwalk. For that matter, the largest local nursing home, Coastal Mists, sits on a cliff that rises just past the north end of the boardwalk. And, surprise, surprise, Coastal Mists is also a popular demon spawning location. And quite a few make a home there, too. At least until we discover them.

"Henry Blankenship and Esther Waters," Eric said, pointing up toward Coastal Mists. "Henry had a stroke four days ago, but survived. Esther, a heart attack just yesterday morning. The staff doctor was able to revive her."

"I bet he was," I said, tilting my head to look up at the nursing home that had once been a prison for Eddie, who'd been stashed there by a band of determined demons set on discovering a secret he held.

When I'd first found Eddie there, I'd also discovered that many of the employees were demon "pets"— humans who know the score and are willing to take on tasks for demons in order to gain something. Usually money, but sometimes the demons promised magic, invisibility, immortality, all those shiny goodies.

Most of the time, the promises were lies and the pets just ended up dead.

Humans, I've learned, can be pretty damn gullible.

"Shall we go up and have a chat with Esther and Henry?"

Eric shook his head. "I called Coastal Mists on the way to your place. Both of them have wandered away," he said, adding air quotes around the last because, of course, we both knew that they hadn't wandered at all, but deliberately left.

"That means family and the Coastal Mists staff will be looking for them, too," I said.

"Staff, yes in theory, but we both know that place

doesn't have the manpower. It'll fall to the local cops. And neither of them have family."

"Which means we need to make sure no cop is around when we find them." I shrugged. "That's pretty much par for the course." After all, when your primary weapon is a sharp stick through the eye, and your efforts to save mankind from the scourge of hell leave evidence that most people would think points to murder, avoiding the local cops ranks high on the mission plan.

"If they both skipped out on the nursing home, they're probably holed up in town somewhere." I glanced around, considering our options. "Let's check the caves, then we can do a few passes in Old Town." San Diablo doesn't really have a downtown. A few miles inland, there are office buildings and shopping areas, and the tourist-friendly area near the beach is Old Town, with it's classic-style theater, cute shops, and popular restaurants.

Suburban neighborhoods like mine arc around the town, the more expensive homes located on the coast, and the more affordable neighborhoods inland and abutting the hills. We live close to, but not on the beach, on the north side of town. An easy drive to Old Town, but not close enough to walk.

Inside the perimeter of relatively new construction, the town boasts neighborhoods near Old Town with cute cottages—like where Eric and I used to live—as well as incredibly ritzy areas tucked away in the cliffs.

That's where the Greatwater Mansion is, a rundown historic home from the Hollywood heyday that Stuart and Bernie thought they could fix up and then sell as a boutique hotel through their real estate development company.

Then, of course, a pissed off demon put a damper on those plans.

A fresh wave of guilt washed over me. It wasn't my fault the place got destroyed—it wasn't even Eric's, though he was at the heart of it—but I still felt responsible.

"All right," I said with a sigh. "Let's hunt them down."

Immediately, Eric laughed.

"What?" I demanded. Turning to face him.

"You." He didn't say anything else, and I rolled my eyes. I'd never been a patient Hunter. Show me a demon, and I'll go after it. Tell me I have to search them out, and I wonder why I even signed up for this gig. Of course, technically I *didn't* sign up for it. The first go-round, I was orphaned and raised by *Forza*. The second, the demons pulled me back in by bursting through my window and attacking me in my kitchen. But even so, I could have walked away. I didn't. I made the decision to stay in to protect my family, not to mention the world.

But that doesn't mean I like the drudgery that comes with the job.

I sighed again, then lift a foot, showing off the

comfy sneakers with awesome arch support I bought before we headed to Rome. "At least I have the appropriate footwear for tonight."

Eric grinned. "Remember that summer in Paris? You were wearing the right footwear then, too."

I had to clap my hand over my mouth to stop from barking out a laugh as I recalled that night. We'd taken out a nest of feral vamps and decided to celebrate our victory with an evening of dinner and dancing. I'd worn a pair of fabulous shoes that hurt my feet—but the stiletto heel came in handy when a demon attacked us on the way back to the hotel.

"How many names are on your list?" I asked as we continued north to where the boardwalk ended, giving way to a beach area often used for volleyball and picnics. We continued across the sand, Eric's cane making indentions as we walked along.

There's no additional lighting in this area, so we had the beach mostly to ourselves, as everyone not coming to the dark section to make out or hunt demons was on the beach area closer to the shops and restaurants. We moved as quickly as the rocks and uneven terrain let us, heading toward the narrow strip between the surf and the cliff base where we'd find series of small caves that provided some shelter even at high tide. I'd nailed more than a few demons there, and I make a point to always check it for strays.

As a rule, a demon's going to prefer a comfy house.

But especially when they're newly turned, a demon will hole up anywhere while it's getting its bearings.

"I pulled fifteen names," Eric said, and I paused to look at him, shocked by the number.

"*Fifteen?*"

"Of course, two of them are in my trunk already."

"When we take out Henry and Esther, we'll be below a dozen. But that's still a lot for a town this size." I shook my head, already exhausted from the thought of non-stop demon hunting. "We really need to make a pact to not leave town at the same time again ever."

"*You* left. I was already gone, remember? And trust me when I say there were plenty of demons in Los Angeles to keep me busy before I headed over to Rome."

"Are there?" I've never particularly liked LA, but that didn't mean I wanted the place to be teeming with demons.

His shoulders rose and fell. "Actually, considering the population, no, which is a good thing because I was hardly on my A-game. I'd check the papers and do some patrolling, but not as much as I should have." He paused and looked at me more directly. "Mostly, I blew off work in favor of a few mental health days."

I snorted. Neither one of us had ever worked in corporate America and as far as demon hunting is concerned, we really don't get enough mental health days. "Considering you had a demon inside you fighting to get out, *and* you lost an eye in the process, I figure you earned the downtime."

"And now I'm not only back in action, but back in the hot zone."

I paused outside the first cave. "It really is, isn't it?"

His brow furrowed. "What is?"

"San Diablo. It really is a hot zone. We always believed that it was special because it repelled demons, what with the Cathedral being so chockfull of relics and whatnot. And maybe it did for a while. But something's changed. Now this town is practically a demon magnet."

"Can't argue with that," he said. "Though probably not something the chamber of commerce is going to set up as an advertising slogan."

"Oh, that was really lame," I said, trying not to laugh as I start walking again toward the cliff. "And, seriously, *that's* what we need to get Eddie and Laura researching. Because if we can figure out what's making San Diablo so rumbly all of a sudden, then maybe we can—*hey!*"

I stumbled as Eric grabbed my upper arm and tugged me back. I spun to look at him, then immediately saw what had caught his eye—an old man shuffling toward us through the sand.

More specifically, an old man who looked remarkably like the Henry we were looking for.

"He could just be a lost Coastal Mists resident."

"You don't believe that any more than I do," Eric said.

"No. But we have to consider it before putting a stick through his eye."

"Words to live by," he said. "But we're interrogating, remember? This is a capture mission first. If he's human, he'll be pissed, but he'll be alive."

We walked slowly toward him, and as we did, the possible demon approached us as well. I felt my body tense, going into that familiar, heightened state of awareness. Ready for a fight or flight. Ideally fight. Even more ideally, interrogation. The kind that gets answers. Solid answers. There are questions about my daughter lingering out there, and I don't intend to rest until I know what's going on with her.

Allie filled my mind as the elderly man trudged even closer. He was moving slowly—appearing to be more elderly man than spry demon. The body might be aging, but once a demon enters, even the most broken down body had remarkable strength and agility. Still, most demons are smart and will play old and feeble in order to blend in.

Eric and I stopped in the sand as he came closer, and Eric put a hand on my back. Just a casual couple out enjoying the night. Except I noticed the way he shifted his grip on his cane, ready to use it as a weapon.

Another step toward us, then another. Then one more.

That's when the old man looked up, his eyes going first to me and then to Eric.

I saw a hint of recognition, and I knew without a shadow of a doubt, that this man was a demon.

I took a step forward prepared to grab him around the neck, hold him close, and let Eric bombard him. Not with his fists, but with questions.

But before I had a chance to do that, he went down on one knee. His head dipped, and right then I could have killed him without even breaking a sweat. Honestly, I was too shocked to even try.

Then he looked back up, his glassy eyes staring straight at Eric's face. "Sire," he said.

Sire?

I glanced at Eric, wondering if he had a clue what that was about, but I know his face well, and there was only confusion and misery written there.

"I am not your Sire." His voice was as hard as stone and as sharp as a blade.

"You are the consort. She does not now wish you harm."

Eric took a step back. "She? Who?"

"The glorious one."

Eric shook his head, and my hand went to my stiletto. There was nothing physical going on, but I could see that this was torture for him, a reminder of what he'd gone through before. And the unwelcome certainty that it hadn't ended with the release of Odayne.

"Why?" Eric asked, his voice low and dangerous. "Why are you bowing before me? Odayne is not inside me anymore. I've been unbound."

The demon tilted his head to one side then lifted his nose to the air and sniffed. Slowly, a smile spread across his face. "The scent is still on you. Did you think it was only Odayne? The one she created? Do you think it is he that makes you what you are?"

"No. *No.*" He swallowed, his jaw tense. "Do you think I don't understand what you're doing? Do you think I don't realize the mind games you're playing?"

The demon rose, then took a step closer to Eric until they were only inches away. I stood frozen, unsure what to do, but my knife was still at the ready. If I had to, I'd use it.

But the demon spoke, and the entire world seemed to shift. "It was you, Eric Crowe," the old man said. "You whose blood runs dark. They are in your debt, and you will be rewarded."

CHAPTER 9

"*Consort? Rewarded?*"

I heard the rage in Eric's voice as he took a step toward the old man. "I'm nobody's consort," he snarled, the unfamiliar violence coloring his voice matched only by the fury with which he lunged forward.

In an instant, he'd kicked the rubber cap off the end of his cane, revealing the steel point. Then, in one lightning quick move, he whipped the cane up and sank the tip deep into the demon's eye. "You can keep your damn reward," he added, as the body of Henry Blankenship fell lifeless to the sand.

"Eric!" I grabbed his arm and yanked him toward me, then stepped closer until I was right in his face. "What happened to interrogate? Hello? Things we need to know. Like whose consort you're supposed to be? Lilith? Because if that's the case—"

I shook it off with a shiver. "But no," I continued. "We kicked her ass back to hell, maybe even for good. But even if she's not permanently banished, she can't be back again so soon. Can she?"

He said nothing, and I rattled on. "But if not her, then who? And why? For that matter, when?"

I was spewing out questions, but dammit, I was pissed. Not to mention scared. "Do they want you alive? They seem to, but, again, *why*? We don't know, Eric," I said, finally winding down. "We don't know, because you just killed the demon who could have told us." I gave his chest a shove out of pure frustration. "What the hell were you thinking?"

I expected him to look frustrated. I expected him to run his hands through his hair, to pace back and forth on the sand, to tell me that we needed to hide the body and get someplace safe where we could talk.

Instead, I watched as this man I loved reached up, pressed his hands on either side of his head, then fell to his knees with a guttural howl that seemed to curdle my soul.

When he looked up at me, all I saw was fury in his eyes. "It never ends," he said. "I mean it just never, ever ends."

He released a low, sour string of curses, and when he stood again, his eyes were filled with infinite sadness. "Kate, I—"

I held up a hand. "Not now. We have to get rid of

the body." I bent down to hook one of the old man's arms around my shoulder. "*Now,*" I said.

For a moment he stayed as he was, his expression a reflection of pure misery. Then he drew in a breath, squared his shoulders, and took the man from the other side. Together, we dragged him through the sand, trying to make it look as if we were just two friends helping our drunken third buddy stumble along.

Once we were around the bend, the ocean on our left and the cliffs on our right, we shifted the angle so that we were dragging his feet even more. We were leaving a trail, but we'd take care of that when we left, and what we didn't cover, the tide would take care of.

By unspoken agreement, we maneuvered him into the first cave, far enough back that he would be in the shadows even once the sun came up. "It will look like an accident," Eric said as I turned on my phone for light. And though I knew that both Mr. Blankenship and the demon were gone and we were holding nothing but empty flesh, I still flinched when Eric slammed the face against one of the barnacle-covered rocks in the cave.

We had to do it. Had to make this look like something other than a stake through the eye. An old man, lost and confused, had stumbled into the cave, tripped, and fallen on the rocks, the body left to the ravages of the weather and the tide.

I looked at the body and then Eric. Then crossed

myself. To be honest, I wasn't sure if I was crossing myself for the old man, for Eric, or for all of it.

I sat down on another barnacle-covered rock near the cave entrance that would be under water when the tide came in. "We need to talk."

"Do you think I don't know that?" He drew in breath, then sighed, long and low. "I'm sorry. I lost it out there. I'm so, so sorry. I just—" He lifted his shoulders in a shrug.

"You want answers. So do I."

He took a step toward me, then fell to his knees in front of me, almost as if he was supplicating himself to me. Begging me for forgiveness.

Maybe he was.

"Tell me I didn't screw it up for Allie," he said when he finally lifted his head. "Tell me she'll be—"

"She's going to be fine," I said, because he needed to hear it. "And you didn't screw up anything. It was your parents. It was those renegades in the Church."

He dragged his fingers through his hair, then tilted his head back, so that his neck was stretched as he looked up at the dark rock above. "They thought they were doing good," he said, possibly to me, possibly to his dead parents, possibly to God.

"Maybe. But they were playing God. And that never works out well."

He brought his head down, his eyes locking on mine. I saw the pain, and knew I'd put it there.

I slid off my rock and sank to my knees in the sand before him. "Except maybe once," I said gently, taking his hands. "Despite everything they did to you, you turned out fine, Eric."

He made a guttural noise. "Now you're just being kind. Or blind. I'm not sure which is worse."

"Eric—"

"Don't play games, Kate. And don't try to sugarcoat this. You can't erase what just happened. What I did."

"What you just did? You killed a demon. That's what we do. And, yes we'd planned to interrogate him, but I understand why you lost it. He blindsided us."

I bit back a frown. *Didn't he?* Had Eric understood what the demon meant? Why he revered Eric? Did Eric know who *she* was?

Considering his reaction, I didn't think so, but was he putting on a show for me?

Mentally, I shook my head, telling myself not to let the past poison the present. He'd been possessed by a demon when he'd lied to me before, when he'd hurt both me and Allie. Now though … well, now he was back to being just Eric.

Wasn't he?

"I mean I should have controlled my temper," Eric said. "I got mad, and then I went and killed our best lead as to what's going on. And now I can't even blame the demon living inside me, because he's long gone and now I know it was never just him."

"You've always had a short fuse," I agreed. "But I think anybody would be angry when they're accused of being the consort to a demon. Especially a demon they don't know."

"It must be Lilith. She's back. Somehow, she's come back."

I shook my head. "No. We killed her." I spoke with more certainty than I felt, but it couldn't be true. I wouldn't let it be true.

"Not in her true form. She was in Nadia."

"But she was bound to Odayne," I reminded him. "He died, she died. And even if we got all that wrong, she still has to regroup. That should take generations of our time. Not weeks or months."

"So we were told. But where was the proof? Ancient texts? Runes? Hieroglyphics? No one really knows. They only think they know." He shrugged. "Maybe we're about to get the proof of how it all really works."

"I don't care how it works," I told him. "The bottom line is she's not corporeal. We would know. We would have gotten word somehow. We know she can't move into any old body like lower demons. Her energy would burn right through them. And I have to believe there aren't too many like Nadia willing to timeshare. It's a rare person who both wants to share their body with a demon and is strong enough to house their energy."

Of course, I'd witnessed exactly that twice within

the last two years, so my certainty that it hadn't happened again was a bit misplaced. But, dammit, I didn't want that bitch back in my life.

"We'll do the research," Eric said. "We'll figure out if she's back. But that wasn't what I was talking about."

I frowned. "Oh?" Try as I might, I had completely lost track of the conversation. "What do you mean?"

"I said I couldn't blame the demon for my temper. For losing my shit. It was never just the demon."

Dread prickled my skin. "What are you talking about?"

"That time in the house," he said, his voice cold and harsh. "With you. What I did."

I didn't want to, but I tensed. "I remember."

"It didn't feel like me, but it must have been because I remember it. In the house with you—what I did. And then with Allie at the theater. In the street. Dear God, Kate, I almost hurt my daughter."

"But you didn't," I said gently. "We've been through this before, Eric. Demon. Living inside you. You need to get past it." I reached over and took his hands. "I've told you before. That wasn't you."

"But wasn't it? Wasn't that the point? It was so deep inside of me that it was part of me? An essential, core part." He drew in a deep breath, his face lined with pain. I wanted to pull him close and hold him, but at the same time some part of me was scared to touch him. Scared of what he was thinking, because dammit,

I knew what he was thinking. Hadn't I been thinking it too?

"After the battle," he continued, as if in response to my thoughts, "before Rome, I mean, I thought it was finally, truly out of me. Maybe it is. But that doesn't really matter now does it? Because that infected part was bound in me for long enough. Because it's in Allie now. It's part of her. Of my daughter. So you tell me, Kate. Did I screw it up for our daughter? Is she—"

"She's going to be fine," I said again. "Allie is going to be just fine. She's the same girl she's always been. And that girl is wonderful."

At the same time though, I couldn't argue with him. Because he was right. Somehow the demon was in him deeper than we ever knew, and because of that it was in our daughter now. A geneticist would say it was part of her DNA. I wasn't entirely sure what the Church would say.

I thought about Father Corletti. He knew the situation. Knew that Allie's human-demon blood had the power to lock those gates to Hell. He knew, and he still loved her, still wanted her to be part of *Forza*. For that matter, he thought that she might even be the most important part.

But he was just one man. Father Corletti knew, but the Church as a whole didn't. For that matter, neither did the other priests in *Forza*. Only Father Corletti. Not even Father Donnelly, who was set to take over after Father Corletti passes.

And once Father Donnelly was running Forza. What would that mean? Especially since he had been among the renegades who'd worked with Eric's parents to put a demon inside him in the first place, all with the goal of making the ultimate demon hunter. A noble goal, maybe, but they'd been playing with powers that they had no right to meddle with.

"Kate?"

Eric's voice pulled me away from my thoughts.

"Talk to me," he said. "We're in this together."

"We are," I squeezed his hand. "Always." Because no matter what, we were tied together by Allie.

"I'm sorry," he said. "I'm so, so sorry."

"I'm not. It's inconvenient as hell, but I do love you, Eric. And that makes it good to have you around, and terrible too. And all of that is notwithstanding this whole demon blood thing."

He chuckled and for a second the moment felt lighter. "I appreciate that. But I meant Allie. I'm sorry this is happening to her. I'm sorry about my role in it. I'm sorry even though I know that there wasn't a thing I could do to change it."

I made a show of staring him down. "Except maybe not killing the demon who might have given us answers?"

To his credit, he nodded. "Yeah, except that. We'll find Esther. Hopefully she'll tell us. Maybe Henry didn't even know anything."

"Yeah," I said. "I doubt he knew anything at all."

We both know that wasn't true. And that one single word, *consort*, seemed to linger in the cave between us.

"You should head on back," he said. "I'm going to sit here for a little bit and get my head on straight, then I'll walk home."

"Eric, no. Let me drive you."

"It'll do me good."

I glanced at his cane. "You're going to walk all that way?"

"I'll be fine. The break healed nicely, and I don't even need the cane all the time any more. Fortunately, David was never going to be permanently injured. Except for the part where he died in that wreck. Besides, it's only five miles. The walk will do me good. Really. I want to think anyway."

I considered arguing, but knew I'd get nowhere. Instead, I simply nodded. I got up and gave him a hug.

Then I left him alone in the cave as I slowly walked back to my car.

Since the horrible grinding of our garage door going up and down was loud enough to wake the dead—though not literally, I hoped—I parked on the street and headed up the sidewalk to the front door. It was already well past eleven, and I turned the lock slowly, then pushed open the door with equal care, hoping the hinges wouldn't creak.

Miraculously enough, they didn't. I shut the door behind me, the used stealth tactics to lock the place up again. Then I took off my shoes and padded in socks toward the living room.

The only illumination came from the light in the kitchen. A dim light that I assumed originated from the single bulb above the kitchen sink. I saw no sign of Laura or Eddie, and I hoped that meant that Eddie was in bed and Laura was back at her house with Allie and Eliza and Mindy.

I headed down the short hallway to the living room, and as I did the lamp on the table beside the couch clicked on and I saw my husband sitting there, his eyes on me.

"Patrolling, Kate?"

I shrugged in either acknowledgement or apology.

With a sigh, he pushed himself off the couch and came to me. I was still in the entrance hall, and he stood at the place where the tile met the carpet, essentially blocking my path. "I thought we were over the secrets, Kate."

"I'm sorry. There were demons. I needed to go."

"There are always demons. Like I said, I thought we were done with the secrets."

"It wasn't a secret," I said. "But it also wasn't something I wanted to get into over the phone, and you weren't coming home, remember? Mansion, then office." I pushed past him and went into the living room, then fell exhausted onto the sofa.

"So this is my fault?"

"Fault? Why are we even talking about fault?"

He seemed to mimic me, sagging down onto the sofa as well, then shifting his body so that we we're looking at each other. I expected him to say something, but of course he just sat there. Lawyer tactics. And entirely unfair as far as I was concerned.

I tried to wait him out, but failed. "I assume that everyone's here and asleep?" I asked, when I couldn't take the silence any longer.

"Eddie was here when I got home. He went to bed, I gave Timmy a bath, and put him to bed."

"He'd already had a bath today."

"Trust me," Stuart said. "He needed another one. Apparently he likes jam sandwiches, and Eddie is more than happy to serve them to him."

I bit back a smile but kept my face down so Stuart wouldn't see it. "I'm sorry. I should have told you about tonight. Like I said, I didn't want to get into it."

"Do you think it's a secret that you hunt demons? This isn't exactly a new revelation."

I looked up at him, and he tilted his head to the side, watching me. "Or is there something else you that you didn't want to tell me? Like who you were patrolling with?"

"Stuart, not now...." I knew he was upset. "I know you wanted it to just be family, but you have to understand. Eric's family, too. Whether you like it or not, he's

Allie's father. It's a big messy family, and we have to deal with it. And just because you got all pissy and stormed off doesn't mean that I don't need to go out and do my job."

"Kate, all I wanted—"

"No." I held up a hand, giving him the same look I fire at the kids when they backtalk. "All you wanted was to punish me. To get rid of Eric so I couldn't talk about the situation with Allie." I could hear my voice rising with my pent up frustration, but couldn't seem to dial it back. "And then you played power games and headed off to the mansion so you could work with Bernie and have the little wife at home. You want to play alpha male with Eric, do it without me at the center of it."

"Kate—"

"Dammit Stuart, you left." The force of my words propelled me off the couch, so that I ended up standing in front of him. "Remember? You walked off and left me when Eric moved to Los Angeles. You both left me alone and you took my son with you."

I was breathing hard and tears pricked my eyes.

"Our son," he corrected gently. "And I came back. I came back because I love you." He reached for my hand, but I didn't take it. He drew in a breath, then let it out slowly. "I came back because I want to make this marriage work. This family work."

I turned, looking away from him, trying to organize

my thoughts. It wasn't easy. I knew he meant it. But still…

"We came so far in Rome," I said, my back to him. "We really did." I turned to face him through tears. "I thought we were really back on track, you know? But now we're here and demons are popping up all over San Diablo, I don't know how I'm supposed to deal with this testosterone-laden bullshit. I mean, seriously Stuart, it's too much. Especially when there are things to figure out, and I need Eric around to do that. There are things I have to find out about him, because those things will make a difference to Allie."

I shook my head, then barrelled on. "No," I correct. "It's not just because of Allie. I need to know because of Eric, too. Because I do love him, Stuart. And you're just going to have to find a way to deal with that."

The words seemed to fly out at me out of me, and I feared that they were battering Stuart. Not that I could tell since he was wearing his courtroom expression. In other words, he had no expression. He was taking it all in and not showing a single reaction.

"Is that what you want?"

I blinked, truly surprised by the question. "What?"

"Do you want me to figure out a way to deal with it? Or do you just want me gone?"

"Oh, Stuart." I sank onto the sofa, then took his hands. "Of course that's what I want. You here with me and not at Eric's throat. But you have to understand it hurt when you left, and being home again just brought back all those emotions. But I'm not mad about it anymore. I'm really not."

I watched his face, giving him space to talk, but he said nothing. Just held my hand.

I swallowed, then continued. "You say you want us to be a family, but if that's the case, then you have to understand that Eric is part of it. I love you, Stuart. I do. But Eric is part of our life as well, and he's not going anywhere. He's Allie's father. And," I add, as hot tears snaked down my cheeks, "the brutal truth is that I love him too. I'm sorry, but I do."

"He's moving back, isn't he?"

"Yes."

"I don't like that." The words were flat, as if he was reporting the weather.

"I know you don't. But honestly, Stuart, I do. I need help. I'm afraid things are going to get bad. And I'm afraid that all the badness is going to center around Allie. And I had to go out today because I need answers and we tried—"

I didn't realize I was crying until he put his arms around me and pulled me close, letting me bury my face in his shoulder. I didn't like the way it was now, this strange disconnect between us. Before Eric came back, there'd been no barriers. At least not until that first demon had broken through the window. I wanted to get back to that easy comfort. That total familiarity.

But the truth was, even then it wasn't real. It wasn't real because he never really knew who I was. Who I am. I may not have been active, but I hadn't told him the truth about myself. About what I'd done, what I'd experienced, what I knew about the world. And now I could only hope that knowing all of those things—seeing all of those things—we could work this out.

I pushed back, the certainty that I *did* want to work it out giving me the energy to face him. "We're going to make this work, Stuart," I said. "We may have to fight it out, but we'll figure it out. And I'm not going to give up on us."

For a moment he just studied me, then he nodded. "I believe you." He reached out and cupped my cheek. "I want the same." He paused, then added, "so when you go patrolling, you'll let me know? Even if for no other reason than I want to know that my wife is out fighting demons?"

"I promise. And I'll let you know if I'm with Eric. Not only so you'll know that I have someone watching my back, but so that you'll know who it is."

"I'm not jealous that way," he said.

"What do you mean?"

"I trust you, Kate. Don't you know that? It's not that I think anything will happen between the two of you. I don't believe you'd do anything even if you wanted to. And honestly, I couldn't blame you if you did. I know that you love him, that he was your husband before me and that this is one of those situations that I can't even imagine a marriage counselor would know how to deal with."

"Then what?"

"He can be there in a way for you that I can't."

I took his hand. "Maybe," I said. "But you're getting pretty badass at throwing that knife."

He laughed. "I've gotten lucky a few times."

We shared a grin. "Yeah. You have. But you still need practice. At that, and pretty much everything else."

"Thanks a lot."

I shrugged. "Just calling it like I see it."

"But the bottom line is no more secrets, right?"

"Yes. On my end. And on your end, if you're pissed off or mad, don't just walk away. Don't use the real estate projects as an excuse to get away and not talk about it."

"Fair enough."

"Wow. Look at us being all practical and working things out."

He lifted my hand and gently kissed it. "We've always been able to work things out. You could have told me everything before we even got married, and we would have worked it out."

"I guess I know that now, but at the time, I wanted you to know a different Kate. I didn't understand that there is no different Kate. I'm just me, and I should have realized it would all catch up with us eventually."

I drew in a breath, then held his gaze. "I'm sorry."

The corner of his mouth curved up as he shook his head. "Don't be. All I'm sorry for is the lost time. You could have told me whenever you wanted to, and I would have still loved the real Kate. I *do* love the real Kate."

He pulled me close, and for a moment we just sat like that on the couch, me leaning against him and enjoying the masculine way he smelled, a hint of sweat mixed with his cologne and topped of with a tinge of paint and plaster.

"Kate?"

"Yes?"

"Do you remember what I said about how it's time to stop with the secrets?"

"Of course. That was four minutes ago."

His chest vibrated as he chuckled. "In that case, is there anything else you want to tell me?"

"Um?" I said, trying to think of what other secrets I still had. To be honest, I was surprised to find that I actually couldn't think of any. "I always use the cheaper canned tuna in the casseroles?" I thought a bit longer. "And even sometimes when I tell you that I'm just really good at marinating steaks, it's because I bought the more expensive cuts?"

"What did Eddie mean when he said he couldn't love Allie any more even if he really was her great-grandfather?"

Oh.

I cleared my throat. "Oh, right. There's that."

I pulled away from him, shifting and straightening, afraid that there might be an explosion any moment. But when I looked at his face, he seemed remarkably calm.

"That's a little complicated, but the bottom line is that as far as I know, Eddie's not related to anyone in this family. But also as far as I know, he could be."

"And this all started because you needed to rescue him from that nursing home, and you needed a place for him to live where you could keep an eye on him, and you thought I wouldn't understand unless he was Eric's grandfather?"

"Did Eddie tell you that, or did you figure it all out?"

"I didn't graduate at the top of my law school class for nothing," he said.

"You're not mad? I really would have told you sooner, but the only times I think about it are when it's come up in conversation, and that never seems to be the ideal time. And honestly, for all intents and purposes that is who he is. He's a member of the family. Please, Stuart, don't make a thing about it."

"Just tell me this—do you love him? Does Allie love him?"

"You know that we do."

"Well, I guess that answers it, doesn't it? Of course he can stay."

Love and relief washed over me. "Thank you." I gave his hand a squeeze then stood. "I don't think I ever started the dishwasher, and I'm sure Eddie didn't."

He tugged me back down. "You said that Allie is at Laura's house all night?"

I nodded.

He pulled me closer and brushed my lower lip with his thumb. "Sweetheart," he said, "I think the kitchen can wait."

CHAPTER 10

I lunged upright in bed, not sure what awakened me.

My heart pounded in my chest, and I tossed the sheets aside as I hurried to my feet, glancing sideways at Stuart, who was sleeping soundly.

I grabbed my switchblade style stiletto off the side table where I keep it next to my hand cream. Then I shoved my arms into my robe, and hurried out of the bedroom.

I paused just outside the door, listening. I didn't hear a thing, and I wasn't sure if that was good or bad. Maybe this was all my imagination?

I checked Timmy's room, happy to see that he was completely sacked out on his toddler bed, and since I knew Allie was over at Laura's, I didn't bother sticking my head in there, especially since I'd just heard a scraping noise downstairs. Instead I moved quietly down the stairs, avoiding the few squeaky ones that we've been planning to fix for years, but have never managed to put that plan into practice.

I found Eddie at the base of the stairs, one of my steak knives tight in his grip.

I started to ask what he thought, but he held a finger up to his lips, then pointed toward the living room, only a small section of which was visible from the base of the stairs. I pointed that direction to indicate that I was going first, and he fell in step beside me.

I wasn't scared—I'd been on the hunt too many times for that—but I was pissed. This was my house. My home.

My family.

I'll fight demons all day long if I have to, but a demon coming in my house? That really elevates the stakes.

As for Eddie, not for the first time I realized how nice it was to have another Hunter in the house. My whole life I'd worked in tandem, and in those months before Eric had become David, I'd missed that assistance and camaraderie.

I took a step forward, then another. I paused, having heard a small, whining moan.

I burst into the living room, blade at the ready, then stopped short when Allie's scream pierced my ears.

"Mom!"

In a split-second, I assessed the situation, realizing there was no demonic threat at all. Just my daughter, scrunched in the corner of the sofa, a pillow hugged tight to her chest.

I tossed the stiletto onto the coffee table as I sat beside her. "Baby, what is it? Are you okay?"

She nodded. "I'm fine. I just feel ... I told Aunt Laura I feel bad. I needed to come home."

I glanced over at Eddie. "It's okay. I've got her. Go on back to sleep."

He shuffled forward, his sleep tousled gray hair sticking up in all directions as he focused on my daughter. "You need anything, kiddo?"

She shook her head and hugged the pillow tighter, looking a little queasy as she did. I frowned, wondering how much ice cream and other sweets they'd binged on while watching hours of television. A lot, I knew, since it would take the monster of all stomach aches to get her back home from a sleepover with Mindy.

"I just want to sleep," she said. "Can I go to bed, Mom?"

"Of course you can."

I felt her forehead, but it was cool. "Do you need anything for your stomach? Tums? Chicken soup? Mine's famous you know?" As a rule, I'm a terrible cook, but I have amazing can opening skills, and always keep chicken broth in the pantry.

Usually any reference to my utter lack of cooking skills gets a smile out of her, but this time she only shook her head and pushed herself off the couch.

"Okay," I said starting to get concerned that she was

truly ill and not just suffering the after effects of a junk food binge. "Let's get you upstairs and in bed. Then we'll see how you feel in the morning. This lingers too long, and we'll take you to the doctor."

She nodded, and as Eddie watched, I led my daughter back up the stairs. I glanced at him one more time from the landing, and saw the worry carved into his craggy face. It was the first time that either of the kids has been sick since he came to live with us, and he'd never been a parent himself. "She'll be fine," I said. "Probably by tomorrow morning."

He nodded, but he didn't look convinced, and I wished I had the time to go back downstairs and give him a hug, for no reason other than the fact that he loves my daughter, too.

I got her into bed, tucking her in the way I'd done when she was little, then bent over to kiss her forehead before heading to the door and turning off the light.

"Mom?"

I stopped in the process of pulling the door shut. She pushed herself up in bed, the brown floppy-eared dog that had been her favorite children's toy in her lap.

"You okay, baby?"

One shoulder rose, but she didn't look up at me. A tight knot of worry formed in my chest, and all of the relief that I'd been feeling whooshed out me with the same speed and force as if I'd impaled a demon through the eye.

I hurried to her side, then sat on the bed beside her.

"You're going to rip that ear right off again," I said, referring to the time she was eight and had carried the stuffed dog everywhere by his ear.

She met my eyes, hers glistening with unshed tears. "If I do, you can fix it, right?"

My chest tightened in response to the unspoken question. "You won't," I said.

"But what if I do?"

I moved to the bed and sat on the edge. I took her hand from the fuzzy ear and squeezed tight. Then I abandoned the pretense that this was a conversation about a stuffed lovey. "Father Donnelly said—"

"—that it's only the good stuff in me. Strength. Speed. Blah, blah, blah. I know what he said. But how do I know he's right?"

"You're scared," I said. "Rightfully so." Considering how scared I was I knew she must be terrified. "But Father Donnelly's as close to an expert as we've got. And it's not as if you've ever showed the slightest sign of being evil."

I forced a grin, gave her hand a squeeze. "I mean, there are times when I've thought your room represents the kind of chaos you might find in one of the circles of hell, but—"

"You are *so* not funny," she said in that *my mom is an idiot* tone I knew so well.

"Maybe a little funny?"

Her mouth twitched and I forced myself not to

show relief when she cocked her head and said, "Nope. Not even a little."

"And yet I try so hard."

I waited for her to say more, but she stayed silent. "What happened?"

She licked her lips, then drew a breath. "I had a nightmare."

I wanted to relax. I wanted this to be like all those times when she was in elementary school, and I would have to go get her from slumber parties because she'd had a bad dream. But I knew in my gut that wasn't what was going on this time.

Whatever she'd seen in her sleep, it wasn't just a nightmare. It was something important. Something horrible. Something that was going to spook me as much as it has spooked her.

I forced my expression not to change as I looked back at her, this time taking both of her hands and leaving Floppy Dog between us. "Can you tell me about it?"

She bit her lower lip, but nodded. Then she closed her eyes and started to speak. "It was—it was that night. You know, the night we got the demon out of Daddy. And in the dream, there was this black slimy goo that seeped into the ground and then oozed over to where Nadia was. Only she didn't even look like Nadia anymore. She just looked like Lilith. Or, what I think Lilith looks like."

I nodded, encouraging her to continue.

"I mean, I don't really know what she looks like. I guess nobody does, but I've done all that research and seen all those ancient books with the pictures of demons and stuff. She was supposed to be beautiful and horrible all at the same time, and that's how she was in my dream."

She drew in a stuttering breath, then swallowed like she was holding back tears. "But Mom, it wasn't anything like I'd seen in those books. I think—I think I was seeing what she really looks like."

I winced, but not from her words. She'd been squeezing my hand, almost cracking my bones. "It's okay, baby. Go on and tell me the rest."

"That's really it. I just— I just think she's coming back. I think she may already be here. And I'm afraid that she's going to go after Daddy again."

I forced my expression not to change as I nodded, trying to pretend like her words didn't terrify me. Before the beach, I probably would have written this off as a bad dream. Now, though…

Well, now I'm scared.

Consort.

The one who's blood runs dark.

The demon's words rattle in my head, haunting me. Terrifying me.

I wanted to hug her close. To reassure her that even if it was a premonition, it didn't matter. That we would fix it.

But those would be hollow words. Because with

every gain, we have losses. And how am I to know what we might lose this time?

So I did the only thing I could do. I hugged her tight, then whispered, "Whatever happens, baby, we'll face it together." And then, because she was still my little girl, I added, "I'm not going to let anything happen to you or your father."

At that, she actually laughed. "A nice thought, Mom, but I'm old enough to know that you can't make that promise."

"Yes, I can," I said fiercely. "I can make it, and I will do everything in my power to make it come true. But you're right. I can't do better than that. All I can promise is that I'll try." I hugged her tighter, then pulled back to face her. "Is that enough?"

She nodded. "I love you, Mom."

"Love you, too, Al. More than you'll probably ever know."

She swallowed, then wiped her eyes before looking straight at me again. "Eliza was right, you know."

"Eliza?"

"That knife that I threw—the one that hit the demon right in the eye. I'm not that good. Or, at least, I wasn't. I wasn't before we went to Rome. I wasn't until we were in the crypt. But there was something about that chamber…"

"What?" I asked, though I already knew. I'd seen the way she'd run and leaped and battled her way to the dais.

"I don't know how, but even before I got to the dais and closed the gate there was something about that room. We went in there, and I felt something inside me change. I thought it would be the same for you and Daddy."

"Not me," I said. And as for Eric … well, I really didn't know.

"Here's the thing," she continued. "What if that was the whole point? What if the demons always knew that we'd be able to close that gate? What if it was like some really long con to get me down there? To make all this stuff happen inside me so that some demon buried deep inside me comes out? What if I was never the result of a plan by good people wanting to fight demons, but of bad people wanting to make me be some sort of weapon for their side?"

With ever word, my mouth went dry and my heart beat faster. I forced myself not to let my fear show as I shook my head hard, her hands gripped tight in mine. "No," I said firmly. "No."

"But—"

I shook my head again. "No. You are you. You're good, Allie. You always have been. Nothing in you has changed. Whatever you are now, you always have been."

"But what if I've always been dark?"

"Do you want to be dark?"

She shook her head so forcefully the bed moved. "Well, then. That's your answer. If we have to fight something in you, we will. But we'll deal. I promise. Because you're Allie. You're sweet and you're smart and you're snarky and you're badass, and you're a pain in my butt sometimes, but you're a good kid and I love you."

A single tear streaked down her cheek as she nodded then ran the back of her hand underneath her nose. "It almost got Daddy. We almost lost him."

"But we didn't."

"Because of you," she said.

I thought of that horrible moment when I'd watched a blade slide deep into the eye of a man I loved. I'd expected him to die that day. But he hadn't, and that had been one of the biggest miracles of my life. But I can't guarantee that will ever happen again. Could I ever do the same with Allie? Let someone do it to her?

I didn't know, but the truth was, I didn't think so. And surely, whatever demons lived in the ether around us, knew that too.

Time moved differently in those in other dimensions. I'd been told that, but never had proof. Now, though, I did, because Eric had told me. He'd been in one of those dimensions, after all, and to him returning to me had seemed almost instantaneous.

Which means that a long con for a demon, would not be very long at all.

But none of that was the kind of thing I was willing to tell Allie. Not yet. Instead, I'd carry her worries as my own burden for a while. And somehow, I would try to fix this.

"We all have your back, sweetheart," I finally said.

"I know you do. But..."

"What?" I pressed when she trailed off with a shrug.

"I guess I'm afraid that it won't even matter. Because someday, I'm going to have to do what you do all on my own."

I saw the fear in her eyes when she looked directly at me. "And Mom, I'm really scared that in the end, we're all going to lose."

CHAPTER 11

"*A*h, Katherine," Father Corletti said. "Of course, you are worried." I'd called him from Stuart's office after leaving Allie's bedroom. It was morning in Rome, and I'd been lucky to catch him. The moment the line had connected, my tears had spilled out with as much force as my worries.

I laid it all out, giving him the details of the demonic encounters since we'd returned to San Diablo. He'd listened as he always did, and it had been a relief to share my worries with him, to let him carry some of that horrible weight for me.

I couldn't remember a moment when Father Corletti wasn't there for me. When I was a little girl, I would sit on the edge of my bunk and he would come in and speak with me at night. I would tell him about the adventures of the day, the excitement and the terror. Most of the time he would sit quietly and simply listen, and even without a conversation, it made me feel better to know I had both his ear and his heart.

Now, I wished I was still there. In Rome. In those dorms. Back before I truly understood how what truly fragile creatures we are. I wished I could look into his eyes, and see that reassuring gaze look back at me.

Tonight, his voice would have to do.

"Don't discount your fear," he said. "But also do not forget that sometimes a dream is just a dream."

"But what does it mean?"

He chuckled. "You always were a terrible listener, my child."

I rolled my eyes. That was true enough. "You're saying I shouldn't be worried?"

"As her mother, part of your job is to worry. But we know that God has a plan, and I do not think that Allie closed the gates of hell for nothing. I believe in her, Katherine. What do you believe in?"

I closed my eyes. I believed in the power of good. I believed in my faith. How could I not? Hadn't I been raised, literally, in the bowels of the Church. I believed in my family, as crazy and as mixed-up as it was, and I believed that this kind, brilliant, gentle-hearted priest loved me like a daughter.

But I also knew that bad things happen. That evil fights hard. And if it was now fighting for my daughter, then as much as I wanted to believe that we would win, I couldn't know that for sure.

"Then you must arm yourself with what you have left," Father Corletti said when I told him as much.

"My faith."

"*Si*. Believe in the power of good. Believe that Alison is the sweet, wonderful child you have always known her to be. Believe that she has a higher purpose to serve. Most of all, have faith that somehow you and Allie and your family will get through this together."

I nodded. No matter what, Allie was my daughter. I loved her. And at the end of the day, that had to be good enough.

Didn't it?

By the time I was ready for Mass the next morning, Allie was already up and waiting impatiently downstairs.

"Is Stuart still getting dressed?" she asked. "We're going to be late!"

I stared at this kid. On any other day, I'd be wondering what was up to make her so eager to get to the Cathedral. Today, my heart broke a little because I already knew—Lilith. The demons who'd attacked me. And that demonic essence hiding deep inside her.

I went over and gave her a hug, and was actually relieved when she shrugged out of it with a typical teenage, "*Mom*."

"We have plenty of time," I told her. "And Stuart's

got Timmy duty this morning. He's getting him dressed, and he'll be down. Did you eat already?"

She nodded, then pointed at the table where a half-empty bowl of Kashi sat, along with a box of Frosted Flakes and Timmy's cartoon emblazoned bowl. "Do you want me to make something for you or Stuart?"

"No thanks. But go bring in the paper while I make myself a bagel." I glanced at the clock, relieved to see that we still had plenty of time, then shouted up the stairs to urge Stuart and Timmy to move faster.

Since things never go as planned with a toddler in the house, that *plenty of time* fantasy went poof quickly. My plan to arrive at the Cathedral with plenty of time to drop Timmy in the children's center before heading to Mass, ended up all shot to, well, hell.

Instead, we arrived with only five minutes to spare, and I was feeling sweaty and rumpled by the time we crossed the threshold and took our places on one of the pews. I fell into mine with a sigh, happy to be back in the sanctuary for this Sunday instead of the Bishop's Hall.

San Diablo is a charming small town tucked in among the hills and the California coastline. Its origins date back to well-before California was a state —or the US was a country, for that matter. Pagan rituals took place here for centuries before the town became part of the mission trail. One of those missions, in fact, stood right where the Cathedral stands now, like a shining star atop one of the highest hills, a focal point for our artsy and seemingly sleepy town.

I, of course, am one of the few who understand that while the town may seem sleepy, there are monsters lying dormant.

Not that long ago, I'd believed the opposite. The Cathedral is special in that the very mortar is infused with holy relics. For years, Eric and I had believed that was the reason the town had such a low demon population, making it the perfect place for us to retire.

Now, despite those relics, it seems that the Cathedral—or at least the town itself—is a demon magnet. And damned if I know why.

Renovations to the Cathedral had been going on for what seemed like forever, and that meant the beautiful sanctuary often went unused and services were regularly held in the Bishop's Hall. Today, I'd been thrilled to see that the sanctuary was open, though much of the stained glass was covered and many of the pews were roped off.

The rumor is that the project would be complete by Christmas, and I fervently hoped that was the case. The Bishop's Hall is designed more for potlucks than reverence, and I miss being in this awe-inspiring sanctuary.

Beside me, Stuart turned so that he was looking my direction. "What?" I whispered.

He shook his head and shifted so that he was looking forward again. My stomach twisted as he did, because in that moment, I understood what he was doing—looking at Allie as if to make sure she hadn't grown horns.

"Seriously?" I whispered, though there was a definite edge to my voice. I'd noticed the way his body had tensed as Allie and Eliza had crossed the threshold to enter the Cathedral ahead of us. Then again, when we'd paused at the basin of holy water, each of us touching it and then crossing ourselves. He'd relaxed only after Allie had done as much without bursting into flames.

Now, he looked back at me, guilt written on his face, then shrugged.

I let it go. The truth is, I really can't blame him. I had, after all, been wondering the very same thing, and my relief that she is able to walk through the Church without any signs of discomfort is a huge relief. To her, too, I imagined.

At the same time, I reminded myself that David had been able to do so as well in those first months after Eric had come back in the chemistry teacher's body. Over time though, as the demon inside him grew more powerful, it had become more and more difficult.

That, however, wasn't something I was going to think about. Instead, I was going to do what Father Corletti had said. I was going to have some faith.

The service began, and a new priest—Father Joseph —stood at the altar. Since the horrible death of Father Ben, my previous *alimentatore* before Eddie took over, we've had no priest in residence, and the Bishop or a steady stream of visiting priests have filled in. Now I wondered if this young priest who looked fresh out of the seminary would be a permanent addition, or just another one passing through.

That wasn't something I pondered long, though. Instead, I quickly lost myself in the familiarity of the ritual, Father Joseph's words reminding me of the many reasons to come to the service. For some, it's a reminder that there is a world beyond ours. That's not why I come though; I'm reminded of that every day of my life. Instead, for me, church is a weekly reminder of the power of good. Of friends and family and hope.

It's a reminder of what I'm fighting for, and even though protecting my family is truly at the heart of it, it's so much bigger than that. There's a world full of people who haven't seen the big picture that I have. And those of us who've seen beyond the curtain have a responsibility to hold that curtain shut. To keep the rest of the population safe. Not because we owe them, but because it's the right thing to do.

The service passed quickly, and even though I felt guilty about it, I breathed a sigh of relief when Allie took communion with hellfire raining down on us. After Mass, I asked her to go get Timmy, as I'd been waylaid by Delores, the Cathedral's volunteer coordinator, in the courtyard.

A retired teacher in her late sixties, Delores Sykes showed absolutely no signs of slowing down. She'd created the position of volunteer coordinator at the Church, and managed her domain like a well-oiled ship. I liked her a lot even though she intimidated the hell out of me.

"Kate! I was hoping I would see you this morning. I was wondering if you were up for a little bit more volunteer work."

"I'd love to," I lied, remembering the bug-filled boxes I'd been tasked with sorting through the last time I'd volunteered. "But I've been so overwhelmed lately with family stuff." I dropped my voice and shot a glance toward Stuart. Considering my marriage was back on track, I should probably feel guilty about referencing our recent separation that, I knew, had been the topic of much gossip. But that's the length I was willing to go to avoid spiders and other slithery critters.

Her expression shifted into one of prurient compassion. "You poor dear. I do hope things are improving?"

"Absolutely," I said. "But the family needs my attention. Tend your garden, and all that."

"Of course, of course," she said. I expected her to walk away and waylay some other innocent parishioner. Instead, she added, "It's just that the Bishop pointed out that since you already have a sense of what's in the archives, you could head a new committee for organizing and enhancing the collection. It would only be a one day a week thing. We're hoping to look at the collection, see what might be missing, and find out if we can acquire any related material. As you know, some of the donors split their collections. But the Bishop believes it would be better for a donor's collection to be held in one place. And as you know, San Diablo has the best collection of arti-facts and relics relating to the Church of any Catholic institution."

I did know that. I'd gotten sucked into doing research in the archives when I'd been duped by a High Demon. A long and messy story, but with a happy ending since I'd brought him down.

But even with that happy ending, I had never been happy about the bugs.

Still, it wouldn't be a bad idea to have access to the archives, especially while I'm trying to learn more about Allie's situation. As far as I knew, Allie was one of a kind. But I couldn't help but wonder if this was a sign. If I was being guided to take this volunteer position.

Even if this gig wasn't divinely ordained, at the very least, I could use the position as a good excuse to get books from the Vatican. Much easier to go through the Church system than by the regular mail. And I knew that Father Corletti would approve. Especially since it had become more difficult to get access to records at the Cathedral after Father Ben's death since the Bishop knows nothing about who I am.

It also provided a terrific opportunity to help with Allie's training and Eddie's research. "You know what? I'd love to. I can't dive in for at least a week—I'm deep in planning Timmy's birthday party—but you can count on me to coordinate. And," I added with a bright smile, "I'll even recruit Allie and Eddie Lohmann to be my first committee members."

"Oh, sweetie, I am thrilled to hear that." She reached out and squeezed my hands. "And I was going to ask you..."

"Yes?" I tried to keep the trepidation from my voice. Had she heard rumors about me of the demon hunting variety? Worse, did she want me to sign on for yet another volunteer job?

"Well," she said, dropping into a whisper. "I heard you were teaching a self-defense class for women."

"Oh! I am, yes. Although the lessons have been less than regular. I'm hoping to start that back up next week, too. I'm still recovering from our trip to Rome."

She drew herself up. "Well, when you do, you let me know." She nodded firmly. "After all, every woman needs to know how to kick a little ass."

I barely managed to refrain from slapping my hand over my mouth to hold back the laughter. Because those were definitely *not* words I'd expected from Delores's mouth. "Yes," I said, my voice tight with fighting back laughter. "She absolutely does." That was the absolute truth. I'd just never pictured Delores as the type to do anything more proactive than carry a can of mace deep inside her purse. "I'll send you an email as soon as I know when the next session is."

She smiled. "I look forward to it."

She turned away, and I turned the opposite direction, shaking my head in wonder at the surprises that life sent you. I was about to pull my date book from my purse to look and see when I could schedule the next training session, when I noticed Allie and Eliza hanging out on the playscape, near the swing set. Timmy, however, wasn't on any of the swings. They were just standing by the vertical support posts. Allie had her eye on her little brother, who was playing quietly in the sandbox.

As for Allie and Eliza, they weren't alone. There was a boy with them. A dark-haired boy, who stood tall, his shoulders thrown back with the confident bearing of a full-grown man. Not the usual slouch I was familiar with when confronted with teenage boys. Especially teenage boys who were chatting up teenage girls.

I realized I'd crossed my arms, my jaw tight as I watched him watching Allie … and Allie watching him right back. My focus was so intense, in fact, that I almost jumped a mile when Eliza said from beside me, "Not a bad service. I like the priest."

I hadn't even realized she'd left the playscape.

"Who's that?" I asked, not interested at all in Father Joseph right then.

To her credit, Eliza didn't pretend to misunderstand. "That's Jared," she said casually. "He's the guy from the before. The one who chased away the demon."

CHAPTER 12

"She likes him," I said to Eliza.

Beside me, Eliza shrugged. "What's not to like? He's cute, and he scared off a demon. Which means he already knows the world we live in. Makes him better boyfriend material than most of the guys at her school, I bet."

"Boyfriend?" I heard my voice rising into squeaky tones.

She shrugged again. "Well, duh."

"Hmm."

I turned my attention back to Allie, who was completely oblivious to the fact that Eliza had left, much less the fact that I was watching her. Instead, she was deep in conversation with the boy—*Jared*, I reminded myself.

I was about to turn back to Eliza and demand every tiny detail about the boy— because I assumed that the three of them had rehashed him in detail last night before Allie came home—but Stuart joined us.

"Eric wasn't here," he said without preamble.

Eliza and I exchanged confused glances. "So?" Eliza asked, before I could say that very thing.

Stuart's attention was on me as he answered. "He *can* come into the sanctuary, can't he?"

"Really, Stuart?" I heard the irritation in my voice and tried to dial it back, but I wasn't entirely successful. "You were there, remember? The demon's out of him."

"But are we sure about that?" It was quick, but I saw his eyes shift towards Allie and then back to me.

I crossed my arms over my chest, my temper rising. "Yes." My voice was icy. "Of course I'm sure. You saw him walk through the Vatican, remember? If he can walk there, I think he can manage St. Mary's."

He exhaled, his shoulders sagging a bit in the process. Then he ran his fingers through his hair, something I knew he did out of habit when he was frustrated. "I'm sorry. Honestly, I'm sorry. It's just that I'm—"

"Worried about Allie? Do you think I didn't notice the way you were looking at her?"

"So you're not worried at all?"

I started to say that I absolutely was not worried, but I caught myself. No more secrets, right? "A little," I admitted. "But what mother wouldn't be?"

"She's fine," Eliza said loyally. "She walked all over

the Vatican. She took communion there. What more do you want?"

"Exactly," I said, both to myself and to Stuart. "No writhing. No head spinning. No vomiting bile. She's Allie, Stuart. She's our daughter."

"Right," he said as he shoved his hands into the pockets of his slacks. "Right. Of course, she is. I'm sorry."

The words were perfect. But he didn't look at me as he said them. I wanted to blame him for being worried. To lash out in anger, but how could I? I was worried too. For that matter, so was Allie herself.

"You guys," Eliza said, drawing out the word. "Come on, already. Allie's fine. For that matter, Allie's probably more than fine. I mean, she's got to have serious bonus points for closing the gate to hell, right?"

She looked between me and Stuart. "So if anything happened to her down there, it was on the good side. That was the whole point, wasn't it? Behind what she is, I mean. Those Church dudes messed with Eric because they were trying to breed someone who could win over the demons, right? And she *did* win. So yay for the crazy breeding folks. Or am I wrong?"

"I hope you're right," I said. "And I believe in my heart that you are." But how was I supposed to know if my faith was justified?

Eliza rolled her eyes. "Does she know you guys are being so weird about all this?"

"We're not being weird," I said. "We're just aware. And so is Allie. She's worried. Didn't you know that?"

"Yeah. I did," Eliza said. "We talked a little bit about it yesterday when Mindy wasn't around. And I told her what I'm telling you. Don't worry about it. She's a cool kid. She's going to be fine."

My smile felt watery as I put my arms around Eliza and gave her a quick hug. "If I haven't said it recently, I want you to know that I'm glad you're in my life. And I'm glad I didn't kill you when I met you in Rome."

"Yeah, well, same goes."

For a moment we all stood in silence, remembering those early days when she'd both longed to get to know me, but also was secretly betraying me in the hopes of saving her mother, the aunt I'd never known.

It hadn't worked out for my aunt, but at least I now had a cousin. An actual family member who shared my blood. It was a new feeling, but a nice one.

Beside me, Eliza cleared her throat. "Um, listen, I should probably get back down to San Diego today."

Cold shock crashed through my body. "What?" I realized then that I'd assumed she was going to move to San Diablo permanently. It was probably a foolish assumption, since she'd grown up in San Diego. Her family might be gone now, but surely she had friends she wanted to get back to.

Even so, I didn't want her to go, for her sake as well as for mine and Allie's. "Do you think you should be alone right now?"

"Oh, no. I'm okay. Really. And I'm not moving back there. I mean, if it's okay with you, I was, you know, thinking about moving to San Diablo."

I exhaled, surprised by the intensity of my relief.

"Of course, that's okay. I was hoping you would. So why do you need to go today?"

Her cheeks flushed a bit, and I wondered if there was a boy. I was about to ask, but then she said, "It's just that I have stuff. I might have some stuff in my mom's boxes that you would want. Sentimental stuff and maybe demon-hunting stuff. She was tracking your mom after all."

"I'll happily look through anything you have." I'd grown up an orphan, and now I was eagerly clinging to any piece of my history that crossed my path.

"I've got to get some of my stuff, too. I've been wearing the same clothes since I left for Rome. I thought I'd check the bus schedule and head down today."

"Are you sure? I don't like the idea of you out there on your own. Why don't we go shopping today for new clothes? For that matter, you could probably put together a whole wardrobe between me and Allie."

"Yeah, but I really want my own things. And this isn't about me, right? I mean *the one who is new*? Does anyone really believe they mean new to town? It's Allie, right? It has to be."

"All the more reason to have you here."

She nodded. "I get that you're worried. But it's not

like there's ever a good time. There will always be demons, right? And it's not like you're going to let her go wandering around on her own. I mean, she usually has Mindy with her, and now it looks like she may have someone else watching her back…."

She said the last with a glance toward the playscape, and I grimaced. I had no idea what this guy's story was, although I couldn't deny that he had come to her rescue once. That alone makes me want to trust him. But then again, maybe that was all part of his game.

"I'm not staying away forever. A week, if that. I need to get my stuff and contact my mom's friends. And I need to see about selling the house. All that stuff. Father Corletti's getting me a death certificate, and we're saying she had a heart attack. I can't tell them the truth."

She sniffed, then looked at me with tear-filled eyes. "I'm going to arrange some sort of memorial service for sometime next week. Can you guys come down? And then maybe I can follow you back in my car?"

"Of course," I said gently. "Of course, we'll be there for you."

"I might miss Timmy's birthday party," she said. "I don't want to, but—"

"I get it. You have things to take care of." Now I was kicking myself for not having already helped her to deal with that, but having met her in Rome, already seeming so independent, I'd let myself forget how she'd come to be alone in the first place. "And as for Timmy, he won't have a clue. Give him a hug and a candy bar when you come back, and you two will be more than squared away."

She laughed at that. "Right. Okay. Well, I'll tell Allie I'm heading out and then get on my way."

"Not by bus, you aren't," Stuart said. "I'll drive you." He looked at me. "I'll take Eliza to San Diego, then stay overnight in Los Angeles. The firm's got an office there, and I've been meaning to go take care of a few things anyway. A few meetings, then I'll head back home."

"Really?" I asked. As a rule, Stuart hates road trips.

"Totally not a problem," he said.

"That will work great," Eliza said, then turned to look at me. "I can send Stuart back with a few boxes of my mom's, too. Family stuff that you and Allie can look through if you want. Or you can wait until I get back. Whatever."

"Okay," I said, still uncomfortable about her not being here. But she was right. She had a life to go back to. One to wrap up so that she could move here, and the sooner the better. Now that I had found my cousin, I wanted her where I could watch out for her. "When are you two leaving?"

Eliza shrugged.

"Might as well go as soon as we can," Stuart said. "It's a five hour drive."

"Okay by me," Eliza agreed. "I just need to say bye to Allie and tell her I'll be back."

"And you have a car down there, right? One you left the airport?"

She nodded. She'd flown to Rome from San Diego, but had changed her return to come back with us into the coastal airport that services the area around San Diablo and Santa Barbara, transferring through LAX.

Stuart turned to face me. "This means I'll need you at the mansion on Monday for a delivery. Is that okay? Bernie will be out of town, too."

"Sure," I said. "I can do that." The truth is, I wanted to go back. I'd been right there when Lilith had wreaked havoc on the place. Now, I wanted a reminder of just how dangerous that bitch of a demon truly was.

"So it's all settled?" Stuart asked.

"Sure," I said, but I couldn't shake the feeling that Stuart had another agenda. That maybe, just maybe, he was avoiding Allie. A fear that seemed more likely when Allie came over with Jared beside her, and instead of smiling in greeting, my husband glanced down as if examining his shoes.

Thankfully, Allie didn't seem to notice. Instead, she was all lit up with what I'd recently come to learn was her *I've met a cute boy* glow.

"Mom, we're going to go to the beach, okay?"

"Who is we?"

"Me and Jared and Mindy and, hopefully, Eliza?"

Eliza looked between Allie and me. "Sorry, Al. I'm popping down to San Diego to deal with packing and my mom's funeral and stuff."

"Oh. Right. I'm sorry."

Eliza shrugged. "Yeah, well, the good news is I'm moving here permanently."

"Yeah? That's awesome." She turned her attention back to me. "So just me and Jared and Mindy. I texted her and she's totally into it, so you can't say no. We'd disappoint her."

"Allie…" I gave her the Mom Stare coupled with the Mom Tone.

"I know, I know. I should have asked first, but we were planning and it's a gorgeous day, and—"

"Don't you think there's something you've forgotten?" I asked.

She stared at me blankly, and I cast my eyes sideways in the direction of Jared.

"Oh! Right. Duh." She cleared her throat. "Mom, this is Jared. Jared, this is my mom."

"Nice to meet you, Mrs. Connor," he said, sounding like a perfectly polite teen. So far, so good.

"You, too. How did you—"

I was about to ask how he came to be around Allie and Mindy and Eliza yesterday, but Allie barreled on.

"Jared goes to Coronado High, too. He's the guy I told you about. The one we met on the boardwalk last night," she added, glancing toward Eliza.

Considering Jared knows exactly what he did on the boardwalk last night, I would have expected her to be less cryptic, but I appreciated that she realized we might be overheard. So kudos to my kid for thinking responsibly.

"Jared, I appreciate what you did for the girls. Do you drive?"

"Yes, ma'am. I'm seventeen, but I've had my license for two years. I had a special permit when I was fifteen because my parents don't drive and I had to get around. I'm happy to drive us all to the beach and then home again."

"I appreciate the offer," I told him. "But why don't you meet us at the house in fifteen minutes? I'd like the chance to get to know you better."

My daughter dropped her head, looking absolutely mortified.

"Mom, is that really—"

"Yes." I understood her frustration. Other high school friends had been driving her around for the last year without me running a background check. But those friends weren't living with one foot in the demon world. Jared might have helped the girls out, but before I trusted him to drive them, I needed a lot more information.

I dug in my purse for a piece of paper and a pen, then scribbled our address on the back of a grocery receipt. "Meet us there?"

"Sure thing Mrs. Connor," he said.

"For crying out loud, Mom!" she said, after he waved and headed off towards his car. "Do you have any idea how embarrassing that was?"

"Allie, sweetheart, this isn't a boy thing. It's a demon thing," I added, lowering my voice to an almost inaudible whisper.

"But that doesn't mean he can't like me."

"I'm sure he does like you, but I need to—"

"*Mom.*" She winced a little, as if she didn't mean to get so loud. "Mom, I just want—Oh, never mind. It's fine."

She shot a frustrated glance toward Stuart and Eliza, then turned and headed back to the playscape where she plunked herself down beside her brother.

I exhaled, guilt welling inside me. Because in that moment I realized why she was so frustrated.

It wasn't a demon thing.

It wasn't a boy thing.

It was a teen thing, and right then, all my daughter wanted was to feel like an average teen, even if for just one last, lingering moment.

Since I once again got waylaid by Delores on the way to the parking lot, Stuart and Eliza easily beat us home. I found a note from Stuart on the kitchen table telling me he would text with an ETA tomorrow. I texted back that I would fill him in on all things demonic when he arrived back in San Diablo, and though he returned a smiley face, I was quite certain that he was mostly smiling about being away.

The truth is that I'd never wanted to get Stuart involved in this part of my life. Of course, I'd never anticipated that this part of my life would come knocking on my suburban doorstep. But now that I was back in the demon hunting game, I couldn't help but want him to be all-in. I wanted him fighting the good fight, telling me that we were going to figure this out. Telling me that we were going to be able to protect Allie and help her get through whatever was coming.

I didn't want him running scared from her, but I couldn't help but fear that was exactly what he was doing.

I shoved the thoughts aside as Allie called my name, the shrill sound of her voice sending terror shooting through me. "Allie?" I turned, grabbing a knife leftover from breakfast off the kitchen table as I practically leaped into the living area, only to find that there was no demonic crisis. *This* crisis had little brother written all over it.

The guilty party howled on the floor, clearly upset by this sister's reaction to the chocolate milk he'd spilled all over her favorite white T-shirt, not to mention my beige sofa.

"Mother! I just changed!"

"Not a crisis," I said calmly, picking Timmy up and soothing him. "Go change again. I'll wash your shirt, and I'll see what I can do about the couch. And you, Mister," I said, tapping Timmy, nose, "you get to go play quietly in the corner."

"Play band?" Timmy asked as Allie huffed in frustration before pounding up the stairs.

"That, kiddo, is not quiet." I plopped him on the floor. "Coloring books."

"*No, no, no, no, no, no, no, no, no.*" He'd behaved so well earlier that this meltdown was probably inevitable.

"*Yes, yes, yes, yes, yes, yes, yes, yes, yes.*" I got down on my haunches as I said the word over and over again, matching his loudness. This wasn't a trick I tried often, and it must have been absurd enough to distract him into submission, because his eyes went wide and he burst out laughing.

"Coloring books?"

"Okay, Mommy."

Score one for the adult team.

I gave him a kiss on the forehead, then dragged over the basket where we keep the coloring books and crayons, not to mention the blanket that goes under them in a somewhat futile effort to protect the carpet. Meanwhile, I walked back into the kitchen to get the Shout and a rag, fervently hoping that the people who'd Scotchgarded the couch had done their job properly.

"You could've helped, you know," I said to Eddie, who had watched the drama play out from his front row seat, better known as the recliner.

"I could have, but I didn't."

I rolled my eyes. There was really no point arguing. I glanced toward the stairs to see if Allie was on her way back, but saw and heard nothing. "What do you think about the boy?"

Although Eddie had skipped Mass this morning —"What's the point of going if Rita ain't gonna be there?"—I'd brought him up to speed in the first few minutes of our return home.

Before we'd gone to Rome, Eddie and Rita had been pretty much inseparable. She'd even gone so far as to give Allie a taser for her fifteenth birthday, a gift I'd thought entirely inappropriate until it proved its worth in a demon-related crisis.

"I think I'm glad Rita stood me up today," Eddie replied to my question about Jared. "I wanna meet this kid who helped Allie out the other night."

On that, we were agreed. "So why did she stand you up?" I scowled at the stain on the cushion. From what I could tell it was expanding, not shrinking.

"Eh," he said. "She's got a cousin in town or some such. Niece, I think. Maybe a nephew. Don't know, don't care."

"Really? You two are so tight. You don't want to meet her family?"

I gave up and flipped the cushion over, relieved to see the other side was clean and I hadn't used that trick on this particular cushion before.

Eddie grunted and shrugged his shoulders. I wisely decided not to press the point, because it occurred to me that maybe it was Rita who didn't want her family to meet Eddie. And if that was the case, I could see why he was grumpy. Although to be honest, curmudgeonly defined Eddie's usual state.

The doorbell chimed, and I headed that direction as Allie's footsteps pounded on the stairs. She managed to skid into the entryway ahead of me, now in a pink tee and shorts over her bathing suit. "You're still going to say okay to the beach, right?" She looked at me with pleading eyes. "A boy hasn't liked me in forever. I asked Mindy to go with us, but she's got rehearsal for the musical. But I'm the one he asked out, so please let me go by myself. Please, Mommy, please."

It was the Mommy that got me. It had been a long time since she'd called me that. "Sweetheart, the last time you went out, you were attacked by a demon." Although to be fair, *attacked* wasn't really the right word.

"Mom! Think about where we live and who we are. One, I go out all the time without getting attacked. Two, it's not like there was an APB put out announcing that I've got some weird funky powers, was there? And, three," she added before I could answer that there might very well have been, "Jared'll be with me, and he already proved that he knows how to handle himself where demons are concerned. So it would be the two of us together."

"Allie..."

"Mom..." she said in exactly the same tone.

"Just let the boy in," Eddie said. "We're leaving the poor kid out there in the elements."

Considering it was a gorgeous California day I wasn't too concerned about his health and well-being, but Eddie had called it right with regard to politeness. I nodded to Allie, who hurried forward, gathered herself, then opened the door. "Hey," she said. "Come on in."

"Hi." His smile was equally wide and equally shy, and I gave him points for that. Then he looked at me and extended a hand, which I took. "It's a pleasure to see you again, Mrs. Conner."

"Thanks for coming by. I heard about what happened on the boardwalk. So I just want to get to know you a little better before you two head to the beach. It, um, sounds like we may have a few things in common."

"Yeah. I guess so."

I gestured toward the living room. "Have a seat."

"Thanks." He headed toward the sofa, and I was glad I'd flipped the cushion. "It smells great in here," he added, making Allie beam.

"Cinnamon rolls," she said, sounding as proud as if she'd kneaded the dough herself and hadn't just popped them out of a cardboard canister. "I thought you might want a snack before we go."

She said the last boldly, as if my consent were a given.

"Sounds delish," Jared said.

Allie joined him on the sofa, Eddie stayed in his recliner, and I tried to look casual on the pouf we use as a footstool. Timmy ignored us all, wildly coloring one of his Animal Kingdom coloring books.

"So how do you know about demons?" I said, jumping straight onto the back of the elephant in the room.

"Um...."

"It's okay, boy," Eddie said. "We're all friends here."

"So you know too?" Jared asked Eddie.

"Yup," Eddie said. "And while you're at it. Why don't you tell us what you were doing following the girl in the first place?"

"Gramps!" Pure mortification colored Allie's voice.

"No, no," Jared said. "It's okay. I mean, I get why your family would be nervous. It does look a little weird, I guess."

"So?" Eddie pressed, and I hid a smile. He hadn't had many times in his life to play the parent, or the grandparent, for that matter, and I was enjoying watching his style.

Jared shrugged again, one of those full-body boy shrugs, and then sort of disappeared into the sweat jacket he was wearing over his tee. "Yeah, it's just, you know, my peeps like to keep it on the down-low."

"Your peeps?" I said. "What are you in a gang?"

"Mother!"

I held up my hands "Sorry."

"No," Jared said, "It's me. I'm sorry. I'm just a little nervous. I mean, I liked Allie even before."

"You did?" she asked, her voice rising into a squeak.

"Yeah. Sure. What's not to like?"

They shared a smile, and I bit back my own.

Eddie cleared his throat.

"Yeah," Jared said. "Right. So, I'm a grade above Allie, and I noticed her before she quit cheerleading. Just because she's cute, is all. But then we started hearing things. About a demon hunter in town, I mean, and I started paying more attention."

"Why would you be hearing about a demon hunter in town?"

"My parents are kind of in the trade."

"Kind of? You mean they're rogue?"

"Huh?"

"Who do they work for?"

He shook his head slowly. "Work for?"

So he wasn't involved with *Forza.* Either that, or the kid could keep a secret.

"Oh," he continued. "Right. Well, my great-grandfather was killed by a demon. Turns out he'd been hunting them. Nobody else knew, but they took out the whole family. So my parents don't work for anybody. Well, except themselves."

"The whole family?" Eddie asked.

Jared managed a combination eye roll and scowl, which was about as teenager-y as you could get. "You know what I mean. Not *everybody* obviously. But it became like the family vocation, you know?"

I looked at Eddie and Allie, my thoughts going to

Eric and Eliza. As much as I hated to admit it, I did know.

"Why didn't you say anything?" Allie asked.

"Dunno. I guess 'cause it's this huge secret. And then recently, like right at the beginning of the summer, we heard about a demon hunter who was being targeted. We figured it was you," he said looking at me. "But I wanted to keep an eye on Allie, too, because, well, you know," he said looking down at his shoes.

Except I *didn't* know. Did he mean he liked her? Or that he knew about what made her unique?

Which meant I had to ask. "Why? Why did you feel like you had to keep an eye on Allie?"

His shoulders rose, then fell. "'Cause she's your daughter. And if you're hunting … well, like I said. A demon took out almost my whole family even though most of them didn't know the score. And, well, you know." His eyes darted to Allie, then to the ground. "I like her."

Allie's cheeks turned as pink as her shirt.

"I get it," I said gently. To be honest, I liked this kid. He seemed genuine, and he seemed to genuinely like my daughter. Plus, if she was going to date anybody it was good to date someone she wasn't going to have to keep secrets from. Not that I was ready for them to start doing the dating thing. Not at all.

The oven timer dinged, and I pushed up off the pouf. "I need coffee," I said. "And one of the cinnamon rolls. You guys want to continue this in the kitchen?

Allie, why don't you go get the rolls out of the oven and put them on the table? Is that good for everybody or does anyone want anything else?"

"I'd love coffee and a cinnamon roll," Jared said. "To be honest, I don't usually get up early enough for Mass. But I wanted to talk to Allie."

"I didn't see you in Mass," Allie said. "But I noticed you when I came out," she added with a shy smile.

"No? I saw you in there. I was sitting pretty far in the back though."

"Allie, rolls. Eddie, you coming?"

Eddie pushed himself out of the chair. "I made a promise to myself years ago to never turn down a cinnamon roll. And I'm a man who keeps his promises."

Allie laughed. "Come on, Gramps. I'll get you a new mug for coffee."

He started shuffling that way, and I went along with him. Jared walked with us, making idle chatter about how nice it was that we were letting him and Allie go out, and how good the cinnamon rolls smelled.

Our living area is right next to the kitchen area, so it wasn't a long walk. But the areas are divided by three things—the currently open baby gate, the line the separates the carpet from the kitchen tile, and a sideboard with an ornate mirror where we keep the good china.

As we passed, I glanced at the mirror out of habit. And that's when I saw it.

At the same time, I heard Eddie's strangled little gasp, and knew that he'd seen the same. I clutched his arm, ostensibly to steady him, but really to prevent him from doing or saying anything.

As soon as we reached the table, Jared hesitated, as if uncertain where to sit. I took advantage of his hesitancy to reach onto the nearby counter top and grab the wooden spatula handle I'd tossed there yesterday.

And then—in one lightning-fast move—I spun around and pushed the kid back hard so that he fell into the chair. I stepped on his feet so he couldn't stand, pressed him against the chair's back with a firm hand on his shoulder, and jabbed the wooden stake right toward his treacherous little heart.

CHAPTER 13

"*M*other!"

Allie's shrill voice stopped me just in time from pounding the spatula stem straight through Jared's unbeating heart. (Okay, that's not entirely true. Demon-Hunting Kate knows better than to immediately stake enigmatic vampires who protect her daughter from boardwalk-trolling demons. Mom-Kate isn't quite so rational about a vampire flirting with her baby girl.)

"Do you think I missed that shimmer in the mirror? Talk," I demanded, pulling the stake back a few millimeters, but otherwise not moving. He wanted to get out of that chair and come at me? He'd encounter the dull-but-still-functional end of my spatula.

"I'm here to help," he said, his hands lifting in surrender. "Swear to God."

"Excuse me?"

He shrugged. "Figure of speech."

I put the end of the stick into his ear. "Another smart aleck remark and you'll be as mindless as a zombie, and immortality will feel pretty damn long."

"Mo-*ther*. Will you please just chill?"

"I promise," Jared said, keeping his eyes on me. "I only want to help."

"The hell you do."

"*Mother!*"

That time, I glanced at her. She was wearing oven mitts and holding the pan of rolls.

"He saved me, remember?"

"Allie, baby, get with the program. He's a vampire."

She froze, her eyes going wide before she backed away, tossing the pan on the kitchen table. Without, I noticed, putting a trivet under it. "Wait. What? *Seriously?*" She looked from me to Jared.

He shrugged, looking more than a little abashed.

"But—" Her brow furrowed as she met my eyes. "But, it's daytime. And the sun is out."

Clearly, my kid still has a lot to learn.

"Back off, girly," Eddie said. He'd crossed to the table, and now he used a fork leftover from the morning to dig out a cinnamon roll. He took a napkin from the holder, opened it on the table, then dropped the gooey roll right on it. Then he took a seat and looked up at me. "If the kid wanted to harm her, he's had plenty of chances."

Since that was true, I backed off. But only a little.

"Don't get too comfortable, though," I added to Jared, brandishing the spatula stick and making a mental note to keep something wooden and sharp in the house. I mean, seriously? Demons *and* vampires? This town was on a definite downward spiral.

"Why didn't you say something?" Allie asked, taking a step forward, then another step back, clearly unsure how close she could safely get to this creature.

Jared shrugged. "What? I'm just supposed to say, 'Hi, I'm a vampire. Demons want to kill you, but you should trust me?'"

Allie looked between me and Eddie, then back to Jared. "Um, maybe?"

"How old are you?" I demanded of the boy-vamp.

"I told you. Seventeen."

"Yeah?" Allie asked, her head tilting as she looked him up and down.

"Let's try that again," I said. "How old are you?"

Jared squinted, studying me. Then he said, "One hundred and twenty-seven."

I glanced at Eddie, whose brows rose as he said, "Huh. Young then."

"Young?" Allie said.

"That explains the sun," I said to Eddie.

"Hello?" Allie said. "Are you guys going to clue me in, or do I have to fly back to Rome for a class on vampires?"

"Yeah, the whole vampire thing is a little bit different than what you're used to," Jared said to Allie.

He looked between me and Eddie. "You want me to explain, or you guys want to take the stage?"

I forced myself not to laugh. I still didn't trust the guy, but I did like him. "You're doing fine so far. Just give her the real deal and we'll be cool."

"Yeah, so the thing is vampires aren't exactly demons."

I started to lift a finger, but he raised a hand to cut me off.

"I'm getting there. The way it works is that way way way back, the first vampire was created when a man killed another man by slicing his neck and sucking his blood. Not the usual thing to do when you kill someone, and no one knows why he did it, yada yada yada, blah blah blah, it's all supposedly written out in some mystical magical books that have long since disappeared. But apparently the guy he killed was a demon, and by sucking the blood he sucked in the demon, too."

Allie shook her head, clearly baffled by this rambling explanation, but to her credit, she said nothing.

"Anyway, according to legend which nobody can completely verify, but's probably true, this original vampire got lonely. I mean there were demons wandering around like the kind you hunt," he added with a nod to me, "but that wasn't exactly the same deal. They were different, right?"

"Different how?" Allie asked.

"This new guy was still the guy he was before the

177

demon went into his body. He didn't die and then get reanimated by a demon. And it wasn't like possession because the demon was there, but wasn't controlling him. Wasn't doing anything, actually. He was just part of him. And after a while, this first vampire realized he was immortal. And immortality can get pretty freaking lonely."

"Go on... " She sounded a little leery, but interested.

"I don't know details, obviously, because I wasn't around back then, but the bottom line is that he did the whole bite and suck routine, which Hollywood got pretty much right, and created other vampires. The thing is, it's all the same original demon, just—I don't know— diluted, I guess. It's not like a new demon who comes in from the ether and invades each time. So it's the original person plus demony bits." He looked at Allie. "With me so far?"

I saw the haunted look in her eye, and knew that she was. She had a demony bit inside her, too, after all.

"Go on," I told him.

"Yeah, well, that's pretty much it. I mean the immortality gig is pretty cool, except I imagine it gets old after a while." He grinned up at me. "I'm not there yet. I mean the last hundred years have been pretty freaking interesting."

"And the blood?" Allie asked. "You survive by drinking blood?"

He shook his head. "Yes and no. Mostly, that's how the change happens. After that, human blood isn't just food, it's like a drug. Hollywood didn't really get that one right."

"Human blood?"

"Yeah. We don't need a lot of sustenance, but we need some. I mean, technically I'm dead, but I still need energy, right? Otherwise I'd just watch television all day."

"Okaaaaay…."

"I can drink pretty much anything—alcohol doesn't do shit for me. And the only way to really get a blood buzz is to drink human blood. That's where you get the horror stories. Think of it like PCP or something. It can really make a vampire lose its shit, you know?"

Allie looked at me, her brow furrowed.

"Do you drink human blood?" I asked.

"Not hardly ever—what?" he added off my look. "If I said never, would you believe me?"

He had a point. "Go on."

"Anyway, let's say you hear about a nest of vampires who are running around ripping necks open and killing the humans? Those are the addicts. And it's bad. When I need to eat—which really isn't that often—it's animal blood all the way. Gets you a little buzzed, but it doesn't have the same effect."

"So you're just good like all the time?" Allie asked. "You're like this shiny nice immortal who walks around forever?"

"Yeah. That's pretty much it." But as he spoke, I

noticed that he was looking down at his Converse tennis shoes.

"They're all addicts," I said gently, letting Jared know I understood even while explaining the truth to Allie. "There's always going to be that urge. There's always going to be that risk. And some vamps fight it better than others."

He looked up at me, his eyes hard and fierce, and in that moment, I could see the demon inside him. "I fight," he said. "I fight hard. And I'm not in line with those demons. I don't want this place to be a hell on Earth. I'm still having a good time here. Whoever wants to hurt Allie, I'm not on their side. I want to protect her."

I didn't challenge him. I wanted to believe him. So help me, I wanted someone on our side, and if this boy really was willing to look out for Allie and watch her back, the fact that he had the strength of a vampire wasn't a bad thing at all. But I was only letting him near my kid if he truly convinced me that I could trust him.

"You still haven't told me about the sun thing," Allie said. "So that's just a whole bunch of bullshit they made up for movies?"

"Allie…"

She rolled her eyes. "Seriously, Mom? I got a demon inside me, remember? I don't think saying bullshit is a big deal."

"I assure you, it is."

She rolled her eyes again, and when I saw Jared laugh, I warmed up to the guy even more.

"Yeah, the sun thing," he said. "So when you're young like me, you can walk in the sun, no problems. But when you get older, a couple of things happen. For one, it's harder to fight the urge for the blood. For another, you burn in the sun. The older you get, the more you burn, until finally you're a crispy critter if you even step out into the light. The more blood you drink, the longer you can postpone that. So it's a vicious cycle."

"Oh. Well that sucks. How far away are you from that?"

He shook his head. "Don't know." He looked between me and Allie and Eddie. "Couple of centuries I guess? But I've known some vamps who it happened to around the hundred and fifty mark. Some around the thousand-year mark. I guess it's different for everybody."

"And killing you?" Allie said, her voice hard and practical. "Stake through the heart?" She nodded to my hand that still held the spatula. "I figure my mom knows what she's doing, right? Or did Hollywood get that wrong too?"

"Yeah, stake to the heart." He spread his arms wide, exposing his chest. "I don't want you to, but if you feel like you have to, I won't fight back."

"No. You keep talking." I held up the spatula stick.

"But until I'm one hundred percent sure, I'm holding onto this."

Relief flooded his face, and he nodded. "Okay. Good. I'm liking that."

"Hello?" Allie said "Sunlight? Can we stay on topic? So you can walk in the sun, no problem?"

"You've seen me in the sun. On the boardwalk. At school. And yeah, so far I don't feel anything. Don't get a tan, which sucks, but I guess that's good. I figure that means the sun is doing something to you, and right now I don't want it to do anything. Like I said, I like being in the world. Heck, I even like high school."

"And the killing thing?" Allie asked. "We know that stakes work. What about holy water? What about sticking something through your eye like for demons?"

"Yeah, staking works. Although I have to admit, I think you'd have a hard time getting that spatula in through my skin and between my ribs to get my heart."

I tilt my head and stare him down. "Want me to test that theory?"

"Really don't."

Allie does a hand roll, as if urging the conversation along. "And? Stiletto through the eye?"

"Nope. Like I said, we're not like the demons you're familiar with. There's no singular demon living inside me, just a piece of that original one. I guess that's why that telepathy thing works."

"Telepathy? You can communicate with other vampires?"

"The old ones can. Not me. I guess it gets stronger as you get older. Like the demon inside you is maturing or something. I just get senses of when other vampires are around."

I tapped the spatula on my palm. "Well, that's interesting," I said. "So how many vampires are around in San Diablo right now?"

"As far as I know, it's just me." He looks at Allie and shrugs. "Lone wolf."

"You mentioned your parents before," Allie said.

"They're long dead," Jared said. "I have to create fake parents for school and stuff. It's not that hard. They exist entirely on paper."

"Wow," she said, with the same awe as if he were a movie star.

"So tell us all the ways to kill a bloodsucker," Eddie said. He'd been watching Jared, his caterpillar brows pulled together as he studied the boy, man, vampire, whatever. "Trust me," he added, "I know them all. Make sure you're giving us full disclosure here, boy."

Jared started s to count off on his fingers. "Staking, like I said, through the heart, not through the eye, and it's got to be wood. Don't know why, don't ask. Burning works, and from what I've seen, it's pretty damn unpleasant. Other than that, I don't think there's much of anything."

"Drowning?" Allie asked.

"Don't think so. Would rather not test it."

"Holy water?"

I fought a grin. Clearly she was getting into this interrogation.

Jared shook his head. "Holy water bothers the older vampires. The older they are, the worse it is. Me, I could stick my hand in holy water and not feel much but more than a warm tingle. But it's not going to burn away my flesh."

"That totally sucks," Allie says, to which Jared's brows rise, not surprisingly.

"Excuse me?"

"No, no, not in ways to kill you. I get that it's probably a good thing from your point of view. I'm just amazed at how badly Hollywood got it. I mean, honestly, they could really use a technical advisor."

"I think the way they do it makes for better movies."

"I don't know," she said. "I saw this one movie about a week ago, that had this horde of vampires that—"

"*Kids*," I said. "Can we stay on topic?"

"What is the topic?" Allie asked, which raised a very good point. I'd lost the thread of the conversation myself.

"Him," I said, going back to the only thing I was sure of. "We're trying to get to know our new friend, Jared."

Jared held his hands up, as if in surrender. "I've told you everything you've asked, and I'll tell you anything else you think of, but do you mind losing the stake? I'd just feel more comfortable chatting with you if I didn't think I was going to be impaled any second."

I nodded, since that seemed more than reasonable, and we ended up around the kitchen table, just like we had originally planned.

"So you don't eat? Or you can't eat? Because these cinnamon rolls are really good," Allie said, pointing at the rolls that only Eddie had been enjoying.

"I can eat. I just don't eat much. It slows me down. Makes me sluggish." He looked between me and Allie. "So there you go. A tip for catching a vampire. Feed him a heavy meal."

I bent my head, and smiled. Yeah, this kid was growing on me. *Kid.* Wasn't that something? The guy had close to a century on me, and I still thought of him as a teenager.

"Tell us how you were turned," I said, as Allie used a spatula to get the cinnamon rolls out of the pan and put one on each of our four plates.

"What I said before about my family was true. They were all killed by demons. But I got away. I thought I was safe, but it turns out I was dying. One of the demons had attacked me, and I'd caught my leg on a nail. Sliced me straight down the calf, and ripped open an artery, I guess. All I know is there was blood everywhere." He bends over and tugs up his jeans, revealing a long jagged scar on his calf.

"So a vampire turned you?" Allie asked. "A vampire saved your life. What do they call that? A sire?"

He shook his head. "No. I don't have a sire. I'm a free agent."

"Free agent?"

"In the vampire world, you're beholden to the one who turns you, even if you don't want to be. You go against a vampire who turns you, even if they're doing shit you don't agree with, and it gets bad. It's a clique-ish world. A little bit like high school, I guess."

"But you don't have a sire? How's that work?"

I picked at my cinnamon roll, proud of the way that Allie was pushing him, asking all the right questions.

"A demon staked him. I ended up killing the demon. I didn't even know how then. It was just dumb luck. I didn't know what I was either. I just thought I was sick from the loss of blood or something. But I passed out, and I woke up craving blood."

"You drank blood? I thought you said—"

"I told you, I didn't know anything. The craving is still there. It's there all the freaking time. So yeah, I drank. There was somebody in my town. A guy who'd come around to steal things. I caught him. I drank from him. I drank more than I should have, and I killed him. And I didn't like it. I don't like—"

"What?" I asked.

"Being out of control," he said. "That's what the blood does to you. It steals control."

"Did you turn that guy? The one who stole things? Did just drinking from him turn him or has Hollywood got that part right about the whole sharing and sucking and back and forth thing?"

"No, they mostly got that right. The demon lives in

the blood, so taking their blood doesn't do it, making them drink from you, that makes it happen."

"Can you walk on holy ground? You were at Mass this morning."

"Yeah, sure. Right now, anyway. Like I said, things change as you get older. I met one vampire who was over a thousand years old. He's not insane. He's limited how much blood he drinks, but he can't go out in the sun and he can't go into a church, and holy water burns the shit out of him. But he mostly feeds on animals, and he's not a whack job."

He looked between me and Allie. "There's a lot of whack jobs out there."

He looked down for a moment and I held up my hand before Allie could ask another question, because I was certain that he was debating whether or not to tell us something.

After a moment, he proved me right. "The vamp who turned me," he said softly, "he was dressed like a priest. Had the clerical collar and everything, you know? I still don't get that. I don't get how he could have been a priest."

"Well he must have been faking it," Allie said.

"Yeah, maybe." Jared shrugged. "Yeah, he must have been."

But there's something in his voice that made me think that he doesn't believe that.

I met Eddie's eyes. I knew that he'd heard the same stories that I had. Stories of vampire priests. Those

who fought the demon by becoming the demon, ultimately sacrificing themselves for the greater good, but
taking out their vampiric brethren in the course.
Surely some of those, if that was true and not just a
rumor, would have succumbed to the powers of the
vampire, sacrificing their duty to eradicate the creatures in order to become one themselves.

The thought made me shiver. I hadn't dealt with
many vampires in my career. As Jared said, compared
to the demons who infiltrate society, they're a rare
breed.

"—your strength?"

I'd lost the thread of the conversation, but caught
on quickly when Jared said, "Yeah. Like I said, I don't
do the human blood thing, so I'm not as strong. But I'm
also not a whack job. I consider it a win-win."

"Why are you in high school anyway?"

"What else am I going to do? I have to grow up, at
least as far as I can. I mean I can pass for twenty-two or
twenty-three, but after that I have to move and start all
over again."

"Move?" Allie asked. "Where did you move from?"

"Yeah. I buy fake documents. I have a parent on
paper who's just never around. That way I can deal
with all of the banking stuff. Most of the time I'm
twenty-one. It's just easier that way. I'm only seventeen
on paper now because I wanted to go to Coronado
High. And I moved here from Vegas. A lot of vampires
in Vegas. And not all of them are whack jobs."

"You moved last year?"

"Yeah, a few months before the end of the last school year. I came in as a sophomore."

"Why?" That time, I asked the question.

"I got word that I might be needed. That there was work to be done. Lots of demons."

"Got word from whom?" I asked.

He looked me dead in the eye. "I got word."

I considered pushing the point, but decided not to. Trust takes time after all, and I understood why he might not trust me yet, just as I didn't completely trust him. "You didn't bother reducing the demon population while we were all in Rome."

"Nope."

"Why not?"

"I didn't want to risk getting staked. I needed to be able to keep an eye on Allie," he added, his eyes going straight to hers.

Her brows rose. "So you're just here to babysit me?"

He shrugged. "I want to fight demons. I want to help. You can call and ask, but I'm not one of the bad guys."

"Call and ask? Who?" Allie looked baffled, but I already knew. Somehow, some way, he had a connection with *Forza*. And I'd lay odds that it wasn't Father Corletti who was his contact, but Father Donnelly.

"Why didn't you say something before?" Allie asked after Jared confirmed my suspicion. "Like last school year?"

He poked at his cinnamon roll, still not having taken a bite. "I don't know. All of this maybe? I mean, your mom's a demon hunter. You're what? A demon hunter in training?"

"I—" Allie began.

"Her job is to kill me," he interrupted, pointing to me. "There's a demon inside me, after all."

Allie looked at me, her eyes full of pain and fear. "That's your job? That's what it boils down to?"

"Oh, baby, no," I said, knowing the question wasn't about Jared at all. "That's not what my job means at all."

CHAPTER 14

"So what do you think, Mrs. Connor?" Jared asked. "Can Allie and I go to the beach?"

"Excuse me?" Allie's voice rose with indignation. "You're just going to ask for me?"

Jared's brow furrowed as he looked from Allie to me and then back to Allie again. "I thought you wanted to."

"Yeah," she said in the sarcastic tone that I was well familiar with. "At least, I did before you turned out to be Dracula with an agenda."

"Agenda?"

"It might not be so bad, girlie." Eddie said. "I worked with a vamp once. Nice gal. Tiger between the shee—"

"Eddie!" I nailed him with a hard glare.

"Yeah, well, just saying that vamps can make good partners. All depends on how much they're on the sauce, just like the kid said."

"He's not a kid," I pointed out. "Not by a long shot." To the extent Allie was interested in Jared as a boyfriend, I needed to nip that one in the bud.

"No, I'm not," he said. "That's why I can protect you," he looked hard at Allie. "You don't have to worry if I'm around."

"I don't need your protection." I could hear the indignation shifting into fury.

"Okay…" He dragged the word out just like your typical teenager who was less than a century old. "You're probably right. But you can ask me questions. I probably have a lot I could teach you."

"There's not a thing I want from you right now." She pushed back from the table and stood. "I'll see you in school in September. Mom, I've got some things I need to do in my room." And with that, she stormed out of the kitchen in a huff.

Across the table from me, Jared looked with wide eyes from me to Eddie. "What? What did I do?"

I fought the urge to shake my head. This poor, clueless boy. How could he have walked this earth for over a century, and still not understood the female population?

"You've been seventeen for most of your life, and you really don't know?" Eddie apparently had no qualms about calling the boy out.

"What? She needs more training. She needs to be in the field. I can work with her. I can help her. I can go

out there with her and let her get some honest to goodness experience hunting demons."

"There are so many things wrong with that statement," I said. "For one—no, actually let's just forget the
first one." I would never hear the end of it if I told this
boy that Allie thought he was truly boyfriend material.
"The bottom line is that I don't know you well enough
to let you take her out on a demon-hunting excursion
with just the two of you."

"But it's the perfect scenario. It'll look like she's out
with a guy from her school. Do you want to bring
along her friend? What was her name? Eliza? The one
at the Church?"

"She's my cousin."

"So, does she know the sitch?"

"She does. And she could take you out if necessary."

He winced at that. "It wouldn't be necessary. But
bring her along."

"She's not available for the next few days."

He sagged in defeat. "Look, I just want to make sure
that Allie's safe. If she is what rumor says she is, she's
going to be important."

I stifled a shiver. "What exactly do you think she is?"

He offered a twisted smile, looking boyish again.
"Honestly? I don't really know. Some new breed, I
guess. But she sure got the demon population buzzing.
They're out for her, you know that right? Because if
you don't, you should. She needs someone watching

her back, all the time. And what better than a
boyfriend?"

I exhaled. For better or for worse, I believed what
he was saying. "Look, it wasn't a stupid plan, at least
assuming I trust you, which I'm still not sure about. But
you may have shot yourself in the foot if the end game
is taking Allie out to protect and train."

"What do you mean?"

Men. Some things never change.

"Jared ... Don't you get it? She likes you. *That* way.
And she thought you liked her that way too."

"Oh." He sat there for a moment. "Oh. Yeah. Well. I
guess that's awkward."

I exhaled. Beside me, Eddie looked like he was
about to burst into laughter. I shot him a hard glare,
and he immediately sobered. With a sigh I turned my
attention back to Jared. "Look, just ... just give us some
time, okay? Do you have a phone number?"

"Um, yeah, of course."

Now, Eddie did snort. "He's a vampire, not a
Luddite."

The sharp blare of a horn interrupted the conversation before I could tell Eddie that I wasn't actually
questioning whether or not the boy was attuned to
technology.

"That's my ride," Eddie said. "You fill me in later.
Normally, I wouldn't want to miss a bit of this drama,
except tonight I've got plans for some drama of my
own." He waggled his brows as he stood.

As he patted himself down, checking for his wallet and keys, I turned my attention back to Jared. "You should go too," I said. "I'll be in touch. I need to talk to Allie. And I need to talk to my husband. And then I need to talk to her father. You get that, right?"

He nodded.

"And after all that, I need to talk to the Vatican." I flashed him the kind of smile that could either be an invitation or a threat. "I guess I'm just one of those overprotective moms."

"Yeah," he said. "But I think most moms don't vet teenage boys through the Vatican..."

"I have not worked directly with this vampire," Father Corletti told me. "But I am aware of him. Over the years, Father Donnelly has cultivated a network of spies. This boy—this vampire—is among them. Apparently he even helped your Mr. Duvall—the demon version—smuggle the key from California to Rome."

"Really?" We'd encountered the Thomas Duvall demon in Rome, only learning that he'd been aligned with the good side after he'd been impaled through the eye by one of the bad guys. His mission, though, had been to hide the key that could open the gate to hell from the demonic minions who were trying to do exactly that. "He really worked with Duvall and that contingent?"

"So Father Donnelly has told me."

"Father Donnelly?" I repeated, feeling a hard rock form in my gut.

I didn't trust Father Donnelly. Father Donnelly was the man who worked with Eric's parents with the crazy goal of breeding the ultimate Demon Hunter. Frankly, I would have thought a priest would know better than to play God, and the fact that he played that role with my husband and daughter just pissed me off all the more.

"I know you do not trust him, *mia cara,* but we must all be forgiven our missteps. His heart was in the right place, and his goal, as is all of ours, is to hold back the evil that wants to invade this world."

"Maybe," I said. "Honestly, where that man is concerned, sometimes I'm not so sure."

"I am."

I said nothing.

"Katherine?"

"I trust you, Father. You know that. But I think you're wrong on this."

"Then we will have to agree to disagree. But if you trust me, I hope that you will at least give him the benefit of the doubt."

I closed my eyes, not liking the direction of this conversation. Because I did trust Father Corletti. The gentle priest was the closest thing in the world I had to a parent, and I loved him with all my heart.

If he said I could trust Father Donnelly, then I

would do my very best to find a way to do that. But that didn't mean it was going to be easy.

"But what about this vampire?" I pressed. "You don't know him at all? He's just one of Father Donnelly's spies? How can I trust *him*? For all I know, he has Father Donnelly duped."

Father Corletti's low chuckle washed over me. "I know that you do not think highly of Father Donnelly. I wish that were different, *mia cara*. But again, I must tell you that you can trust the boy because Father Donnelly trusts him."

I didn't mean to, but I actually snorted in disbelief. "I don't know, Father. I don't think I can."

"That is one of your best qualities, Katherine. You have faith, and yet you do not take the world on faith. But, my child, at some point, we must make the choice to not only believe that good exists, but to see it when we look at the world. Everyone has the capacity for good, no matter what is in them."

"You really believe that?"

"If God created the universe, then He must have created the demons, too. Thus, the possibility exists. You should know that more than anyone."

I closed my eyes, thinking about Eric and Allie. "I do. But this is my baby we're talking about. What if he's —what if we're wrong. What if Jared is only trying to get her alone? Trying to capture her? Trying to hurt her?"

"She's been training," Father Corletti said. "I have

seen her skill, and Marcus has told me many times how much she impressed him. Her skills, her strength. She surpassed his expectations. There's more to learn, of course, but your daughter is not weak. In fact, I think—"

"What? What do you think?" I know what *I* was thinking, I was thinking about what he just said about exceeding Marcus's expectations.

Allie had trained with Marcus in the weeks after she'd sealed shut the gate to hell and before we returned home. I'd told him what we'd been doing training-wise in San Diablo, which frankly wasn't much.

If she had surpassed that—if she'd been as strong and agile as she'd been in that chamber deep beneath the streets of Rome— then I think it's fair to say that something about that day had brought to the surface skills that had been dormant in my daughter.

But whether that was for good or for ill, I couldn't know. Like Father Corletti said, I could only believe. I could only have faith.

And I chose to believe that her skills were for the good.

I realized that Father hadn't answered my question. "Father? What do you think?"

"I think she's more powerful than either of us realize."

"Yeah. Me too." I sighed. "So why doesn't that make me feel better?

"You're her mother, Katherine. You wish to protect her. That will never change. But you can't always do that. In fact, you never really could. You could only do your best."

I closed my eyes and whispered, "You're saying that I'm all out of excuses."

"Perhaps."

"Perhaps? You see something else here? This vampire teen is more than a hundred years older than Allie, but people are going to think that they're dating. And to top it off, she's got a massive crush on him."

Father Corletti chuckled. "I don't know how to guide you on this except to say that he is both seventeen and older. Allie is fifteen, but she's older too."

"So you don't have a problem with this?" I actually pulled the phone away from my ear and gaped at it.

"She's a teenage girl. She has a crush on an older boy. Isn't this often the way of high school students?"

He wasn't wrong. But at the same time this was hardly the same as Allie having a crush on a teacher.

As if answering my unspoken question, Father Corletti continued. "He's a centuries-old vampire who wants to protect a young woman with incredible abilities. Do not create problems that do not exist."

"Maybe..." The truth was, I'd gotten definite crush vibes from Allie at the kitchen table, but Jared had seemed truly clueless when she'd stormed away.

On the whole, I didn't know what to think. The

only thing I knew for certain was that Father Corletti was right—I can't protect Allie forever.

I needed help doing my job, and so did she.

At the end of the day, I was simply going to have to trust her.

And that's never as easy as it sounds.

"I tapped lightly on Allie's door, then slowly pushed it open. "Hey, sweetie. Can I come in?"

I got no response, so I decided to enter anyway. I needed to check on my baby, after all.

I took a step in, then another. The room was dark, the blackout blinds closed against the Sunday afternoon sun. Then I heard the softest shuffle of clothes against the sheets, and I stepped lightly to the bedside. I settled on the edge, my eyes finally adjusting to the darkness, and saw her curled up on the bed holding her favorite stuffed dog. "I thought he liked me..."

"Well, I think he does."

She shifted, the mattress moving as she sat up, then clicked on the dim bedside light. Even in the relative darkness, I could tell that she'd been crying. "He just thinks I have to be protected. But I can take care of myself. And why would he want to protect me anyway? He's a freaking vampire."

I put a steadying hand on her knee. "Like he said, he

likes this world. So do a lot of demons, actually. That tells us something, though, right?"

She scowled. "Dunno."

"Yes, Allie, you do. I know this hurts. I know you like this boy, and now you're not even sure if you can trust him. For what it's worth, I think you can. But whatever your emotions are, you have to turn them off. You have to think like a Hunter, baby. That's what Father Corletti told you, and Marcus, too, right?"

At the mention of the priest and the *Forza* trainer, she nodded. "Yeah. You're right."

"So?" I pressed.

She exhaled loudly, the way she does when I ask her to empty the dishwasher even though she'd rather watch TV. "It tells us that whatever bad thing is brewing, it's end of the world kind of stuff. Like what opening the gate would have done."

"Exactly," I said, as proud as I could be of my daughter. "How'd you get there?"

My eyes had adjusted to the dark, and I could easily see when she rolled her eyes, obviously frustrated with my shift into both mom and teacher mode. But she didn't complain aloud. Instead, she said, "Because it's like you said. He's a vampire. But he likes this world. Which means that he's going to fight the other demons who want to end it all and turn this place into some nasty hell dimension."

"Exactly."

"And you trust him?" she asked me.

"He worked with Duvall," I said. "The Duvall demon, I mean."

"Really?" That perked her up. "Well, that puts him on the good side. Are you sure?"

"That's what Father Corletti said."

"Wow. I guess that means we really can trust him," Allie said.

"Looks like it."

"So I guess we'll let him babysit me, then, since that's all he wants to do." She sniffled. "I thought he liked me."

I reached for her hand. "I know you did, sweetie. But isn't he a little old for you?"

She flopped back against her headboard. "Whatever. Doesn't matter. He just sees me as someone he has to protect. It's not like he likes me."

"Hey, I like you. And I know you can take care of yourself, and I still think you need to be protected."

"That's not exactly the point, Mom."

"Isn't it?"

She huffed again, and said nothing, just waited her out.

It didn't take long.

"Do you mean it?" she asked.

"Mean what?"

"Do you really think I can take care of myself?"

I reached forward and took her hands. "Yes, I do. But that doesn't mean you don't have a lot to learn. About fighting, sure, but also about this," I added, taking her hand and pressing it to her heart. "But you're a remarkable kid. I'm really proud of you."

She smiled, and her whole face seemed to light up. "Thanks, Mom." We shared a quick smile, before hers turned into a frown.

"Oh, no," I said. "What did I say?"

"*Kid.*"

I fought the urge to laugh. "Well in my book, fifteen still qualifies as a kid. Or do you prefer young lady?"

"He's like only one grade above me, but he totally thinks I'm a kid."

"One grade and about a hundred and ten years."

She rolled her eyes, as if those numbers meant absolutely nothing. "There's nothing wrong with liking a boy who's a little more mature."

"Allie..."

She stayed silent and prickles of warning danced over my skin. "He really is too old for you," I pointed out. "Not to mention the fact that he's a vampire."

She stared at me, her expression showing no reaction at all.

I sighed, and tried to call out the big guns. "If nothing else, you'll get old and he won't. You saw *Highlander*, right?"

"Huh?"

"*Highlander,*" I repeated, shocked by her blank stare. "You've really never seen it?"

"Is it one of those really old movies you like?"

"Really old? No. But it wasn't made in the last five years if that's what you mean."

"Does it suck?"

"Allie!"

"Well?"

"I get that you're not in the best of moods, but do not dis one of my favorite movies."

Her mouth twitched. "Is it one of those movies that's only on VHS that you keep in the box in the attic?"

"Now you're just being disagreeable," I said, making her burst out laughing. Which, considering I'd come up here to cheer her up, was a good thing. "It has lots of good fight scenes. We could break them down. Plus, Sean Connery, and that's never a bad thing."

"Yeah?"

"Would I lie?"

"You might," she said.

"Actually, why don't we see if we can find it? I'm sure I have it around here somewhere, if not we can rent it."

"A movie afternoon? Can we make popcorn?"

"Why not? We'll have a lazy Sunday. But we need to get Timmy down for a nap or see if Laura will babysit. In this family, he'll learn all about fighting and pointy things soon enough, but the longer we can hold him off the better."

"I'll call Aunt Laura and take him over while you find the movie. Can Mindy come watch, too?"

"Why not?"

"Awesome. And Mom," she added, pushing off the bed, "I love you."

And that, I thought, was the core of what really mattered.

CHAPTER 15

*S*an Diablo's Greatwater mansion is a once-stately mansion that had fallen into serious disrepair through neglect before my husband and his partner in real estate, Bernie Dorsey, had bought it as an investment property. Now, it's fallen into serious disrepair through the antics of that bitch Lilith who'd been hell-bent on not only walking the earth herself, but on planting her boyfriend in my first husband.

Built during the Hollywood heyday by a legendary film producer who'd spared no expense. The place was massive, with a huge entrance hall illuminated by floor to ceiling windows that commanded a stunning view. The house itself was settled at the top of one of San Diablo's many hills, and the view was epic, encompassing both St. Mary's Cathedral and the San Diablo cemetery, not to mention the ocean beyond.

There was even a spiral staircase that led from the

main balcony down to that cemetery. Because who doesn't want direct access to where the dead sleeps? Theophilus Monroe definitely did, as he was the later resident who had the set of stairs installed. A relative of the town's founder, Theophilus was a bit of a bad apple, as he dabbled in the black arts and made all sorts of revisions to the place.

I hadn't been back here since we returned from Rome, and now I walked through the place assessing the damage. The battered staircase, the crumbling balcony, the gouged wooden floors and popped up tiles. Scorch marks scarred the walls and ceiling, and windows were cracked and covered with plastic sheeting.

I took it all in, and though the condition was horrible, I was even more glad that I decided to come today. Waiting for a delivery was the least I could do, especially since I felt somewhat obligated. All of this damage was the result of demons, after all.

Allie and Mindy were with me, and Mindy hadn't been here since that horrible day when we'd foolishly believed the safe room that had been constructed to guard against demons would be strong enough to protect us from the likes of Lilith. We'd been wrong, as the condition of the house clearly attested.

"Whoa," Mindy said as she looked around the entrance hall. "I guess the safe room looks even worse, huh?"

"You were there," Allie said.

Mindy nodded, hugging herself. "I think I blocked most of it."

"Are you okay being here?" I asked gently. "It's all safe now."

The moment the words were out of my mouth, I wanted to call them back. Lilith was behind all the trouble that had damaged so much of this beautiful mansion. And now Lilith was back in action again. Could I really say that any place was safe?

"I'm okay, Aunt Kate. It's all good." She looked toward Allie. "Is the upstairs a mess?"

"Is it?" Allie asked, her eyes on me.

The truth was, I didn't know. "Why don't we go find out?" I glanced at my watch. "I've got at least half an hour before the delivery's supposed to come. Let's go check out the damage in the rest of the place."

I crossed the entryway to the massive staircase that led up to the second floor, Allie and Mindy following behind me and whispering among themselves. I could hear them as we climbed the stairs.

It's kind of creepy, but it's also kind of cool!

I know, right? Can you imagine all the Hollywood parties?

And that freaky black arts guy? He probably had séances!

I smiled to myself. I wasn't sure if I should be pleased or disturbed that these two girls thought the creepy mansion that had been almost destroyed by a powerful demon was cool, but I decided to go with pleased. It proved they were resilient, and that was a much better assessment than that they were crazy.

"Are you coming on Thursday?" I heard Mindy ask Allie.

I resisted the urge to turn and look at them. Instead I continued my eavesdropping as we walked along the landing toward the ballroom that opened off a set of double doors in the middle of the hallway.

"Are you kidding?" Allie said. "Of course I am. You're starring in the freaking musical."

Thursday was the preview for friends and family, Friday was their day off, and Saturday evening was the grand opening of the community musical in which Mindy had the starring role of The Baker's Wife in *Into the Woods*.

I listened as they continued talking, Allie telling Mindy how excited she was for her, and Mindy telling Allie that she couldn't wait for her best friend and family to be there for the preview and opening night. "My dad's even coming on Saturday. Can you believe it?"

Despite the fact that Paul was coming to town— something that Laura was not going to be happy about —I couldn't help but smile. There'd been a period when there'd been a rift between these girls. Allie had made the cheerleading squad, and Mindy had not. For a while, I'd feared that the easement between our houses would never get used again. Then, fortunately, we realized that Mindy was a miniature Celine Dion. She excelled in the choir, got parts in the school musicals, and generally found her way again. Mindy had been a little jealous of Allie and cheerleading, and Allie was a little jealous of Mindy and singing. It all evened out in the wash.

Now, though, I had to wonder. Would the fact that Allie was anointed with some sort of special Demon-Hunting skills change the dynamic again? As far as I knew, Allie had yet to tell her bestie the situation. Which meant that right now, they were pretty much on an even keel as far as Mindy was concerned—both ordinary teenage girls learning how to fight. But I couldn't help but wonder how that revelation would change their friendship. I hoped it didn't, but I knew better than to believe the road would be easy.

I paused in front of the double doors and waited until the girls were paying attention. "Have either of you been in here yet?"

They looked at each other and shook their heads. "It's a great room," I said, then pushed the doors open with bold ceremony. "*Ta-da!*"

"Wow," Allie said, with just the amount of enthusiasm that I've been hoping for. "It's huge." She glanced around the empty room, which, I was glad to see, had sustained no damage during Lilith's temper tantrum.

In truth, the room wasn't completely empty. There were tables with knocked-over chairs surrounding them. There were even a couple of mattresses on the floor, though they were out of place in a ballroom.

Most likely this place had been a refuge for vagrants over the years.

The room was cavernous, and in the back it opened on to a small staging area for food preparation. A set of stairs connected that service area to a basement tunnel that provided access to the kitchen on the far side of the house.

I explored that back area as the girls stayed in the main room practicing their forms and kicks. When I returned, Allie had executed a perfect spinning back-kick, and Mindy had dodged it like a pro.

"Bravo," I cheered, impressed with how far they'd come in their training. I made a mental note to ask Laura when Cutter would be back. Not only did I want him to start working with the girls again, but I needed to schedule a time for the self-defense class I'd started for the neighborhood women.

"Allie!" I called, realizing that she'd switched from practicing kicks and was about to send the knife she now habitually carried toward the far wall.

She looked at me, her eyes wide. "What? The wall's a mess."

I walked over to the wall and pressed my hand against it. "The plaster's in perfect condition. All it needs is a new coat of paint, and you are *not* leaving dents and holes in it. Stuart would ground us both."

"Fine." She exhaled in a huff. "Whatever."

I forced myself not to smile, but I couldn't help but

wonder how many other mothers had this conversation with their teenage daughters.

"What about one of those mattresses?" Mindy
asked.

"Yeah," Allie said. "We could line them up on the
wall, and make a whole area for practice."

We hadn't brought Mindy a stiletto back from
Italy, but Laura had bought one for her daughter
while we were over there. She'd ordered it off the
internet. Laura was all about ordering things off the
internet.

"Fine." Honestly, I was happy to keep them occupied
while I went down to deal with the delivery. I glanced
at my watch. "Hurry and I'll help you set up. And don't
miss the mattresses when you throw."

"God, Mom. We're not lame. We've been practicing,
remember?"

I remembered Eliza being blown away by Allie
recently landing a knife throw right in a demon's eye.
So, yeah. I supposed she could hit a mattress. I hoped
Mindy's skills were at least half as good.

I started to help, but my phone chimed with a text
as the girls rushed to the mattresses. I paused to pull
out my phone as they each grabbed an end of the top
mattress and pulled it aside.

The moment I glanced at the screen, an ear-
piercing scream shook the room. Immediately I looked
up, only to see that the scream had come from Mindy,
who was backing away from the stick-thin, bearded

man who had risen from the middle of the pile of mattresses.

"I've got him," Allie said, hauling back and readying her knife to throw.

"Stop!" I called. "Are you sure he's a demon?"

"Mom!" But her shoulders dropped, and I knew that she wasn't yet certain. "What do I do? What do I do?"

"Who are you?" the possible demon asked.

"You're trespassing," I said. "We need you to leave this property. This isn't a homeless center. I'm sorry."

The possible demon frowned at me, then shrugged a shoulder. He looked to be in his mid-thirties with filthy hair and yellow fingernails.

"Not fair. Finally find a place to stay out of the weather, and I get kicked out."

"It's summer," I said. "The weather's fine. And there are shelters on the south side of town."

"Whatever." He reached into his back pocket, unwrapped a mint, and popped it in his mouth. Then he shot me a scowl, then another one towards Allie, who was still holding her knife at the ready while she mouthed *mint* at me.

That, however, wasn't enough to go on.

"Don't got to get angry about it," the possible demon said. "I'm going."

As he walked by, Allie slipped the hand not holding the knife into her back pocket. I smiled, realizing I couldn't be prouder when she pulled out a spray bottle and got him right in the face.

My kid came prepared.

The demon—because he was definitely a demon—let out plaintive howl as welts appeared on his face. He lunged to the side, then dove toward Mindy, yanking her in front of him like a shield.

"Do you not understand?" he asked, his eyes on Allie. "I would never hurt you. But this little bitch? I'll break her neck and not even blink." He pointed a finger at me as I started to take a step toward him. "You too, Hunter. Don't move or this one dies. Then you."

"But you won't hurt me?" Allie said, taking a step toward him. "Why?"

I froze, trying to communicate with her telepathically to be careful and stay still. The wrong move, and Mindy died.

Apparently my telepathic skills needed work, because she took another step. "Tell me why."

"You know." The demon said. Allie took another step. "No, I don't. What's going on?"

"Come. No. Closer."

"But I don't get it," Allie said. "Why aren't you coming after me?"

And then, before I realized what was happening, Mindy opened her mouth and let loose with a high note so intense and powerful it's a wonder the windows didn't shatter. What it *did* do was cause the demon to loosen his grip, so Mindy was able to break away at the same time that Allie burst forward, leaped on the demon, and knocked him flat on his back.

A blink of an eye later, her stiletto hit home, and the demon had been released.

And me, the Level Five Demon Hunter in the room had stood there useless, watching it all.

"They what" Eric asked, when I relayed the entire story to him less than ten minutes later.

I'd texted him to come get the body and couldn't help but give him the blow by blow the moment I saw him. "Apparently they were thinking about ways to combine their skills and using Mindy's voice as a distraction was their favorite plan."

"Sounds like it worked."

"Like a charm." I was glowing with pride. "They'll want to tell you all about it, I'm sure."

"I look forward to it. The body's upstairs?"

"Yeah. The girls, too. They're still practicing in the ballroom." He took a step that direction. "You might want to wait. I nodded to the tile deliverymen who had texted right before the demon episode. They were currently bringing huge bundles of tile and hardwood into the mansion. "I don't know how we could explain you hauling out a body."

"A good point."

"How did you get here so fast, anyway?" His apartment is on the far side of town. I'd expected at least a half hour wait.

"I was on my way over anyway. To be honest, I expected to see Stuart."

I lifted a brow. *"Mano y mano?"*

"Just the opposite. I want to make a truce."

"Really?"

He frowned at me. "Is that a problem?"

I shook my head, then pointed to a far corner as one of the delivery men caught my eye about where to unload his bundle. "No," I said to Eric. "That's definitely not a problem for me."

"Are you saying it might be a problem for Stuart?"

There were so many ways I could answer that question, and I wasn't sure what would be the best. I started with the most obvious. "I think Stuart's a little concerned about why you weren't at Mass yesterday."

Eric chuckled. "What? Is your husband afraid I can't walk into the Cathedral?"

"A little. But I think he's more concerned about our daughter."

"That son of a bitch..."

I could hear the anger in his voice, and I grabbed hold of the wrist above the hand that had just curled into a fist. "Hold on there. Truce, remember? He doesn't understand it. Honestly, I don't get it either. It hurt you to walk into the Cathedral near the end of that whole thing with Odayne, remember? And, yes, I know there was a demon inside you," I say lowering my voice in case Allie was listening, or the delivery guys

216

for that matter. "But there's something in her, too. We just don't understand what it is."

"*Did* she have any problem walking into the Cathedral?"

"Of course not," I snapped. "None whatsoever."

Eric rolled his eyes.

"What?" I demanded.

"You make a big production to explain exactly why it makes sense that Stuart is concerned, then you get snippy with me when I suggest that you might be concerned?"

"Our daughter is not a demon. I'm just trying to think logically."

Eric's mouth twitched at the corner. "Don't do that, Katie-kins. It doesn't suit you."

I rolled my eyes. "Back to my original question— why weren't you at Mass?"

"Something came up," he said.

"Something demonic?" I asked, right as the front door opened again, and a burly man pushing a dolly stacked with boxes entered.

The burly man stopped short. "Demonic?"

"You must've misunderstood. I said demo. As in, we've been demo'ing this place." Who knew that lying so easily would be one of my most valuable tools as a Demon Hunter?

He glanced around. "Yeah. Can see that."

I signed his clip-board without reading, hoping I hadn't just sold him the house, then pointed to a free corner, hoping this was the last company scheduled to come by.

"Attacked," Eric said, not even missing a beat once the guy was out of earshot.

"Wait, you're telling me the demons attacked you? On the beach they were calling you Sire."

"I know. Demons are tricky little devils."

I snorted. "I think they just have bad leadership. Somebody's not telling the right hand what the left hand is doing."

"I don't know," he said, his tone turning more serious, "but I wasn't thrilled to be jumped as I walked from my garage to my apartment. I don't have room for another body in my trunk, Kate. Not until I can make a run to the school."

"Not even one? What am I supposed to do with it? Put it in the back of the van and take it where?"

His entire body seemed to slump as he exhaled. "Is it a big guy?"

"Skinny."

"All right. I suppose I can cram him in." He didn't sound thrilled, but I wasn't about to argue.

As we started up the stairs, he gave me the rest of the story. "I had a dream," he said. "A dream about Lilith."

"What about Lilith?" We'd reached the double doors, and I nodded indicating that the girls were inside.

"I'll tell you later."

Since it didn't seem urgent, I pushed the doors open, and we both watched as the girls practice sparring. They were doing well, and I was proud of Mindy who'd been making steady progress. But Allie's skills had increased exponentially.

She moved with speed and form that she hadn't had before we went to Rome, but I knew that her new expertise wasn't the result of training with Marcus in the bowels of the Vatican.

Like it or not, I had to admit that something had happened to my daughter. Something that changed her. But whether that change was for good or for ill, I couldn't know for certain. All I could do was go with my gut and, like Father Corletti had said, have faith that my daughter was fundamentally good. That any skills or powers she now possessed had been given to her so that she could battle the demonic forces that wanted to wreak havoc in our world.

Not—*please, God, not*—so that she could rally those demons herself.

"They really are doing great," Eric said next to me.

"I know." He and I shared a smile as we watched them dodge and parry, kick and spin, their kicks and jabs and grunts echoing in the cavernous room.

As I looked around, I realized how huge this room was. They were moving all over it, but not even making a dent in the square footage.

"I hope Mindy and Eliza and Allie can get some more use out of this place before Stuart and Bernie sell it. It's almost poetic that we've got demon hunters in training practicing in the mansion, when the whole reason we're remodeling again is that demons practically destroyed it."

"Yeah, sorry about that," Eric said.

"Wasn't your fault, no matter how much it might feel to you like it was."

He took my hand and squeezed it. "Thanks for that."

I nodded, thinking of Lilith. Wishing she was out of our lives completely. But considering what Jared had said, I feared we'd soon be facing off again with that determined and ancient bitch of a demon.

I wanted to crack a joke. To tell Eric that if I could get out alive from seventy percent off after Christmas sale, I could survive whatever Lilith had to throw at us.

But I couldn't say it. This was important stuff, and our daughter was at the middle of it.

Sure, I can joke about how I honed my fading skills by practicing sword fighting with Swiffer handles, but that wasn't what I needed now. I needed enchanted swords and lost information. I needed almost inhuman strength. I needed every ounce of the training I'd ever had.

I needed research. I needed help.

I realized then that I'd reached for Eric's hand, and that help was right there.

He squeezed mine tight, and I was certain he understood what I was thinking. Our baby girl was in the middle of this. So was he, for that matter. And none of us understood what was going on.

I knew Stuart was worried about Eric. Worried about Allie, too. But I was certain that they were just as clueless as I was.

Unfortunately, I wasn't sure if that simple fact made this whole thing better or worse.

It wasn't a question I could examine too deeply, though, because the girls noticed us and raced over, Allie crying out for her father, and Mindy doing fist pumps and congratulating herself and Allie on what a great job they were doing kicking butt.

"This place is so cool, Aunt Kate. Can you imagine if it had equipment in it and mats and stuff? It could be like one of those places where gymnasts go to live while they train for the Olympics. I've seen documentaries, you know. Those girls move down there, and they train and they train and they train and then they go and they win the gold."

The words rattled out of her, and I suddenly imagined a Demon Hunting Olympics. If there was such a thing, it felt like we were in the thick of it.

"It really does suck that Stuart and Bernie's company is going to sell this place instead of Stuart buying it," Allie said. "It would've been really cool to live here. Everybody I know could have moved in for week-long parties, and I mean how much fun would that be?" She looked between me and her dad. "Can you imagine? We'd be like movie stars or something."

"Stuart was going to buy it?" Eric asked.

"A passing whim," I said. "I'm certain it wouldn't have happened. The place is prime real estate. And now with all the repairs, it would be too much of an investment. Now I think they're planning on selling it for someone to convert into a hotel."

"Sucks," Allie said, and Mindy seconded it.

Honestly, now that I was standing here, I had to agree.

"Hey lady!"

The delivery guy's voice filtered up the stairs, "Boxes are all in, and someone's down here waiting to talk to you."

Allie and Mindy went back to sparring, while Eric and I went down to find Jared standing right in the middle of the maze of boxes and stacked wood.

"Jared," I said. "How did you find this place?"

He shrugged. His eyes darting to Eric. "It wasn't hard."

That wasn't exactly an answer, but I realized that he used his vampiric senses to pick up on our trail. Obviously, he wasn't sure if Eric knew the situation. Which, of course, Eric didn't. Not yet.

Eric took a step closer, his eyes narrowing, his body stiff in a fighting stance that surprised me considering he didn't tend to get surly around teenagers. Especially since this teenager was a student at the school where David Long taught.

"I know you," he said. "You go to Coronado High."

"Yeah." Jared glanced at me, wary. I shrugged.

"Um, hi, Mr. Long. I was in one of your chemistry classes last year."

"You were," Eric said. "What are you doing here?"

With each word, he was getting closer until finally Eric grabbed Jared's upper arm and pulled him forcibly toward him.

"What the—"

"You're a vampire," he said, his voice low and dangerous. "What the hell are you doing here?"

I saw his free hand go to his back pocket, and though I didn't know what was in there, I feared it might be something sharp and wooden.

"No!" I bolted forward and yanked Eric off. "He's okay. Been there. Almost staked that."

Eric looked between me and Jared. "You're sure?"

"Positive. He's been vetted."

"Vetted?"

"I talked to Father Corletti. He's cool. He was working with the Thomas Duvall demon." I didn't mention Father Donnelly, since that priest was not high on Eric's favorite person list. "You know, the Pepperdine student demon who was trying to get us the key to keep the gates from hell from opening again."

"Huh." Eric didn't sound convinced.

"How the hell did you know he was a vampire anyway?" I asked.

Eric's brow furrowed. "Does it matter?"

"You're Eric Crowe," Jared said, his eyes going wide. "I've heard of you."

Eric stood perfectly stiff, his posture making clear that despite what I'd relayed from Father Corelli, he didn't trust Jared. Not yet. "I go by David Long now, as you damn well know. What do you want, Jared?"

"I want to help Allie," he said, his eyes darting to me. I stayed quiet. If he wanted to win Eric's approval, he was going to have to do it himself.

Jared shrugged, as if he'd read my mind. Considering he was a vampire, I suppose it was possible that he had. Some could, after all. "I want to help train her," he said. "I want to help protect her."

"I'm listening," Eric said.

"Okay, here's the sitch. Lilith wants her dead. She knows that Allie is special and could hurt her."

"Why didn't you tell me that before?" I asked.

"I don't know. I'm navigating this the same way you are. You didn't trust me. I guess I figured it would be too much to dump on you at the beginning. And I knew you were going to call and check on me. But now that I've got the *Forza* seal of approval, I can tell you the hardcore stuff, and you'll know I'm telling the truth."

"We'll *assume* you're telling the truth," Eric said. "Certainty will come later. Certainty is earned."

"Right," Jared said. "I promise I'll earn your trust."

"We'll see," Eric said. He looked at me. "I need to talk to you."

I nodded, and he pointed to Jared. "Don't move a muscle."

Jared lifted his hands in surrender.

"He can't even follow the simplest of directions," Eric said to me.

"Just let it go," I said, pulling him aside. As soon as we were out of earshot—except Jared was a vampire and had extraordinary hearing, so who knew?—I said, "What's going on?"

"I told you I had a dream about Lilith," he said.

"Yeah?"

"I dreamt that Allie was dead, and that Lilith was looming over her."

My heart stuttered in my chest. "So you believe him? About Allie being the one who can stop Lilith."

"Well, he did just say that Lilith wanted her dead, so it lines up with my dream."

"He worked with Father Donnelly," I said, because how could I keep that to myself now?

Eric scowled. "I suppose the kid could still be okay despite that black mark."

I said nothing. With regard to Father Donnelly and whether not he was a help or a hindrance, I really didn't have an answer. I knew what Eddie would say— he didn't trust that priest as far as he could throw him —but I hadn't made up my mind yet.

"The truth is, Jared's been at Coronado High for almost a year. "He could've killed Allie already if he wanted to," I said.

"Unless it didn't matter until after Rome," Eric pointed out. "She changed that day."

"I know. But he also could've killed her that day on the boardwalk. Instead, he sent that other demon running."

"Also true," Eric said. "If he'd wanted Allie dead, it would have been easy enough."

"So you're saying you trust him?" I asked.

"I'm saying let's give him some rope and see if he hangs himself."

CHAPTER 16

*a*s soon as Jared arrived in the ballroom, the girls begged to go outside and practice knife throwing and fighting.

Eric and I agreed, and after giving her "Uncle David" a huge hug of greeting and thanks, Allie led Mindy and Jared down the staircase that led from the ballroom's balcony to the larger balcony one level below.

That main balcony had been damaged during Lilith's temper tantrum, but Stuart and Bernie had already implemented the structural repairs to both it and the spiral staircase leading down to the cemetery.

That's where the kids went now.

As far as cemeteries go, this one was unusual. Not only did its location offer a stunning view of the Pacific, but it had also been mystically enchanted decades ago. As far as I knew, though, there was no active enchantment at the moment.

I considered that a good thing.

As the kids got settled in the cemetery and began practicing with their knives, Eric and I stood in companionable silence watching.

"How bad do you think it's going to get?" I asked.

"With Lilith involved, it could get beyond bad." His voice was steady and conversational, but I knew him well. I also knew what he'd been through. And I knew that he was scared. I couldn't blame him. I was scared, too.

"We beat her before," I said. "We'll beat her again."

He turned to face me, and as he did, his eye-patch came into view. "I believe you," he said. "But at what cost?" He turned his head again so that he could look down into the cemetery with his good left eye.

"I only lost an eye in the last battle. Do you think either of us could stand it if we lost our daughter?"

I shivered and shook my head. "Don't."

"We have to think about it."

"No," I said firmly. "We don't."

"Kate—"

"No." I drew a breath. "I get that you want me to face reality. But I can't face that. As far as I'm concerned that will *never* be reality. If that's a problem for you, you can leave right now. I need you on your A-game, Eric. I need you to know we can win. If you don't know it, how can it happen?"

I could hear the fear and frustration in my voice, but I didn't care. I *was* frustrated. And I *was* scared. But I was determined, too. We would win this. Failing—losing Allie—was not something I would let into my head.

"We'll win," he said. "We'll win even if I have to sacrifice myself to do it."

I closed my eyes. I wanted to tell him that would never be a possibility. I wanted to tell him that he couldn't do that.

But the truth was, of course he could. For Allie or for me, I knew I couldn't stop him. He would sacrifice himself if that's what it took. I might not want to lose him, but he wouldn't care. He would do whatever it took to protect Allie. To protect me. Even to save the world.

And that was just one of the reasons that I still loved him … and always would.

"You won't have to," I whispered as I took his hand, knowing he understood.

For a moment, he said nothing. Then he nodded toward the cemetery. "They're good."

"They are. I'm especially impressed with how well Mindy's doing."

"Not that Allie's noticing. Her eyes are on that boy." I hear both humor and worry in his voice

I sighed. "She's fifteen. I expect there to be crushes. But I'd really prefer the crush wasn't a vampire."

"Yeah, that's what all the moms say," he said, making me laugh.

I was about to say something else, when I saw a burst of something fast and white leap from behind a tall grave marker. It tackled Mindy, and I saw a flash of metal as the creature—I assumed it was a demon in some sort of white jogging suit—started to drive the knife home.

In an instant, Jared flew forward with such speed I almost wondered if he really had flown. He knocked the demon aside, and the two went tumbling as Allie rushed forward to grab Mindy by the arms and help her to her feet.

A second later, Jared had stabbed the demon's own knife into its eye. I saw the familiar shimmer as the demonic essence left the body, leaving the corpse behind, and empty shell.

I realized my hand was numb because Eric was squeezing it so tight.

Jared went over to where Mindy and Allie stood and spoke to Mindy. I couldn't hear, but she nodded, looking more than a little shaken even from this distance.

Allie threw herself at him and hugged him, and he hugged her back, a reaction that made me tense, but under the circumstances made perfect sense.

A moment later, they all three looked our direction, apparently only now realizing we'd been watching.

"Hey, Daddy! Did you see our knife work?" As soon

as the words were out of her mouth, she winced. "Um, I mean Uncle David. Sorry."

Eric rubbed his temples. "I guess Jared knows the truth now," he muttered to me.

"He knew your name, remember? He knows a lot. I want to know why."

"Can we go patrolling?" Mindy called. "We'll be safe. You saw. Jared will make sure of it."

I looked at Eric. "What do you think?"

"Yeah," he said slowly. "I think it's okay."

"Really? Are you sure? I'm going back-and-forth."

He glanced back to the cemetery before returning his gaze to me. "Does Mindy know? About Allie, I mean?"

I shook my head. "I told Laura, but we both think that it's Allie's decision as to whether or not Mindy knows. As far as I know, she hasn't told her yet."

"She needs too. Allie's not just a Demon Hunter right now, she's a target for demons. More so than usual. That puts Mindy in the crossfire."

"Agreed. I'll talk to Laura and Allie. Tell soon, or I will."

Eric nodded approval. "And vampire boy?"

"He must know something. He's the one who said that Allie was the one who could take out Lilith. I assure you that's not because of her Algebra grade last year. Which means there must be rumors floating around about some prophesied savior or something.

The truth is, I have no idea. But he knows that much at least. Assuming it's true."

"Assuming?"

"Well, I hope it's true. If Allie can take out Lilith, that's a very good thing. And like we've said, something happened in that crypt. That light. It was like it—"

"Anointed her," Eric finished for me.

"Yeah."

For a moment, Eric just watched the kids. Then he said, "I'm going to go patrolling with them. If this vampire wants to watch out for our daughter, I need to see if I want him on the job."

"Good. I like that."

I went with him down the stairs and across the patio, following the path that the kids had taken. We passed Mindy coming up. "Are you not coming?" Eric said.

She rolled her eyes. "Allie said she thought I should probably go." She made a face. "I don't know why I should. I don't suck at this, and I've been training really hard."

"She's probably thinking about the musical," I said, proud of myself for coming up with such a reasonable lie. Even if you twist an ankle, they'll use your under-study. You have to dance, right?"

"Oh. Yeah. But she should have just said so."

I shrugged. "You know Allie." Which was really no answer at all.

In fact, right then I thought that maybe Mindy

didn't know Allie, after all. Because it was perfectly clear to me that this was a boy issue, not a hunting issue. But I supposed Mindy would figure that out soon enough.

"Have fun," I said to Eric, wondering if the excitement of patrolling with her dad would outweigh the humiliation of having a chaperone. "Keep them safe."

"Always. And tell Stuart I came by. Reassure him that I bathe in holy water and eat Communion wafers for breakfast. So he has nothing to worry about."

"And your dream?" I asked once Mindy was back upstairs and out of earshot. "Do I tell him about that?"

He reached out, then tucked a lock of hair behind my ear. "Yeah, Kate, I think you have to. You told him no more secrets, right?"

I had, yes. But I hadn't realized what a hard habit that was going to be to break.

I spent a few hours alone in the house, walking up and down the seemingly endless maze of hallways. I found the wing in which the staff used to reside. I found secret doorways that led between the levels. And I found a charming little garden in the backyard, tucked away on the only patch of land that was on the same level as the house. Everything else was down below, the only thing passing for a yard being the cemetery itself.

I stood there for a moment surrounded by flowers

in a garden that had become much too overgrown. I looked out at the ocean amazed at what a gorgeous day it was, because how could it be so beautiful when there was so much danger brewing around us?

My phone buzzed with a text, and I looked down to see that it was Stuart. *Where are you?*

I answered quickly. *The mansion. Back garden.*

Just parked. Meet me inside.

I hurried in, and arrived a few moments after he'd stepped over the threshold. He was looking at the various deliveries, inspecting them for damage. "Thanks for doing this," he said. "I know it took a chunk out of your day."

"It wasn't a problem. I enjoyed having the chance to look around the place. And the girls did some training up in the ballroom. They even killed a demon."

"Well, that's what all the cool kids are doing these days," he said. "Everyone okay?"

"Just another day at the office."

That earned me a grin as Stuart slid his hands into the pockets of his suit. "Bernie thinks a gang came up from Los Angeles, had a wild party, and wrecked the place."

"I always knew Bernie was naive."

"I think he just can't imagine what else it could have been. So he's going with what works."

"You couldn't think of anything better?"

"Honestly, I didn't even try."

He looked around shaking his head. "I told you

once that I wanted to buy this place for us, but now..."
He trailed off with a shrug.

"Is it the expense? Or because you're going to leave
again?" The minute the words were out of my mouth I
regretted them. We'd been down this road so many
times. But I couldn't deny that the hurt was still there.

"Kate... I'm not going anywhere. Not again. There's
still a lot to process, I know that. But I know the score.
And now I know how bad it can get."

It can always get worse...

That, however, wasn't something I said aloud.

"As much as I think it would be incredible to live in
a place like this," he continued, "with two kids to put
through college, it's probably not the best idea."

That was true, of course. But I couldn't deny that
there was something appealing about it. This place may
have been invaded by a demon and owned by a crazy
occultist, but in its bones, it also understood what we
were dealing with.

"— some investors."

"I'm sorry, what?"

"I was saying that I met with some investors in LA
this morning. They're considering turning it into a spa-
style hotel retreat."

"Oh." I was more disappointed in the news than I
should have been. "Well, it's roomy enough. I went all
over the place today. You could house a small army
here. Allie loves it," I added, which wasn't relevant to
anything.

"Where is she?"

She and Jared went patrolling with Eric."

"Jared? The vampire?"

"Um, yeah." I'd brought him up to speed when we'd talked on the phone this morning.

"You think that's a good idea?"

"No. I think it's a terrible idea, that's why I let her do it. Of course I think it's a good idea," I snapped. "And so does Eric."

He held up his hands. "Just asking the question. I worry about her. She's my daughter, too."

"Is she?" A slow fury was bubbling up inside me, and I was tired enough and worried enough not to try to tamp it down. "You haven't hugged her since Rome."

"Of course, I have."

"No. You haven't."

"Are you sure?"

I nodded, and he leaned against one of the stacks of boxes looking a little broken. "I really haven't, have I?" His words were a whisper, and when he met my eyes, he looked bewildered.

"She's scared," I said, taking his hands. "So am I. So are you. But she saved the world, Stuart. Don't you think that has to count for something?"

CHAPTER 17

S tuart was filling his travel mug with coffee when Eric came by on Tuesday morning.

I let him in, and he followed me to the kitchen where the two men greeted each other without fisticuffs or sarcasm. As far as I was concerned, that was a portent of good for the entire rest of the day.

"I called you," I said as Eric took a seat at the table. "I wanted to hear how yesterday's patrol went."

I'd tried to get the scoop from Allie, but all she told me was that it was "awesome," that Jared was "badass," and that hunting with her dad was "really cool." As an aside, she said that they'd killed five demons between the three of them. Then she told me that she was too tired to go into the details, and crashed in her room.

Since I'd thought she might be avoiding talking about it, I peeked in on her when she didn't answer my knock a few hours later. And, yeah, she'd been sound asleep. And not even eight o'clock yet.

Because she's a teenager, despite that early bedtime, she was still sound asleep this morning.

"All she told us was that it went well," Stuart said, "but what's your assessment?"

"Same. She was great. And I like Jared. No signs that he's evil, no sense that this is all a ploy. He seems like a good kid who genuinely wants to protect her."

"Kid," I repeated.

"You know what I mean."

"Great. Allie's finally on the verge of getting a boyfriend, and he's a vampire." With a sigh, I poured him some coffee, then topped mine off as Stuart added cream to his mug.

Eric's face went tight. "I don't think she's ready for boyfriends yet. And I didn't say that I thought he was interested in her like that. Besides, Jared seems like a genuine asset to us, but if he lays a hand on her, I'll stake him myself."

"Not if I get there first," Stuart said, and the two men shared a knowing grin.

I rolled my eyes . "I'll join in with you on the concern about his vampire status, but you two are going to have to get used to the idea that she's fifteen. Boys will be in the big picture. Probably a string of them. Deal with it."

Eric looked at Stuart. "You okay if I just cut to the chase and put a stiletto through their eyes?"

"I know the District Attorney. I'm sure we could pull strings so you avoid the murder charges."

"Guys…" I tried to sound terse, but inside I was doing cartwheels. The two men in my life were actually, finally getting along. As far as I was concerned, this was Christmas.

"She really did okay?" Stuart asked.

"She did amazing," Eric said, his voice full of paternal pride. "It's not her fighting skills that worry me, it's what's going on in this town."

"The demons are getting persnickety," I said, taking a seat at the table as Stuart leaned against the countertop, his brows raised.

Do demons get persnickety?" he asked.

"Apparently they do," Eric said. "Over the last few days, I've had demons calling me Sire and swearing to protect me. Then five minutes later I'm jumped by a demon with a sharp blade. Allie's the same."

"Right," Stuart said. "That day she met Jared…" He trailed off as he shifted his attention to me. "Didn't that demon say he wasn't going to hurt her, and her mother would approve of him?"

"Something like that," I said. "So what do we think is going on?"

"I have no idea," Eric admitted. "To be honest, I don't even trust the ones who say they're not going to hurt us. But it does seem as if we're dealing with two warring factions of demons."

"But why are you and Allie in the middle of it?" Stuart asked.

"It has something to do with the Lilith," I said. "I'm certain of that."

"I can't say you're wrong," Eric said, "mostly because I know you're right. But I really wanted to be done with that bitch."

"I don't blame you," Stuart said, then frowned, obviously considering something.

"What?" I asked.

He turned to me. "Have demons been protecting you, or only hurting you?"

It was a good question. "Just attacks."

Stuart tapped his fingers on the counter the way he does when he's thinking. "Father, daughter," he said. "Same blood."

Eric shook his head. "Not anymore." He gestured to his body. "I've gotten used to it, but it's not me."

"But the demon lineage," Stuart pressed. "That's why Allie is … the way she is."

"We got the demon out of him," I say to Stuart. "You can't possibly have forgotten that." Stuart had been right in the thick of it.

"Yeah, well, I'm all out of ideas. And I'm late," he added, glancing at the clock. He pushed away from the counter, then kissed me goodbye. This time, it was a regular kiss, not the claiming kind that he'd given me in Eric's presence before out of an overabundance of jealousy.

I'll admit I like those kinds of kisses, but today I was happy for a typical goodbye-to-my-wife kiss. If nothing else, it was a good first step—maybe even a second step—toward the two men in my life finally finding their way through this forest of craziness.

Not long after Stuart left, Eddie shuffled into the living room, his hair sticking up in all directions and his chin prickly with whiskers. "So the kid did good?"

Eric confirmed that she had, and Eddie nodded as he joined us in the kitchen. "Always knew she would. So, you going to let her go hunting with vampire boy without a chaperone?"

"Don't call him that," I said with a sigh. "If we're letting him into our lives, we should at least call him by his name."

"Eh," Eddie said as he pulled Eggos out of the freezer, then popped two into the toaster. "I fixed that necklace for her," he said. "You make her wear it when she's with that boy."

"You don't trust him?"

He peered into the toaster as if that would make the waffles cook faster, then looked up at me with a shrug. "As far as that girl's concerned, I don't trust anybody."

His concern for her made me feel warm and fuzzy, but I also didn't want to leave her unprotected. If she had a powerful vampire to guard her back, that was a good thing. And when I told Eddie as much, he shrugged and grunted ascent.

"I can't say I disagree, just saying she should wear the necklace."

I'd purchased the necklace he was referring to for Allie's last birthday from Eyes Only, a shop that sold spy equipment in Old Town. Mostly novelty and cheap stuff, but there was real equipment available to those who asked. Eddie had suggested having her wear a tracker, and his suggestion had proved essential in saving her life. Unfortunately, it had also been ripped from her neck, the chain broken and the setting smashed.

"Thanks for fixing it," I told him. "I'll tell her it's important to you that she wears it."

"To me?" Eddie asked.

"She loves you, old man. Go figure."

At that, he turned positively pink and even offered Eric one of his waffles, a clear sign of a good mood.

Eric declined, saying he needed to get to the school for a faculty meeting now that we were getting close to the beginning of the school year. "Plus, there are a few bodies I need to disintegrate in the basement."

I grimaced, and pushed the yogurt I'd pulled from the fridge away. I'd eat it later.

After that flurry of morning activity, things slowed down. Eddie had gone to go meet Rita before going to work a few hours at Eyes Only. Allie was reading in bed. My friend Fran had picked up Timmy for a play-date with Elena, leaving me alone with a Swiffer, a vacuum, a can of Pledge, and a dust rag.

Not my favorite way to spend the day, but it had become inevitable. The dust bunnies were forming a union, and Timmy had started writing his letters on the surface of the coffee table. Normally this wouldn't bother me too much, but we had people coming to the house on Saturday. Considering my terrible skills at housecleaning, I figured Tuesday was a good day to start with the whole process.

With luck, the place would be shiny and presentable by Saturday, when a horde of toddlers would destroy it all over again.

An hour or so later, Mindy had bounced through the back door and trotted upstairs with barely a wave in my direction. Other than that, nothing much changed. Except that I'd shifted my focus to the kitchen and was in the middle of scrubbing the stove top to within an inch of its life. How it became so dirty when I used the microwave for almost everything is one of the mysteries of the universe.

I was desperate for an excuse not to work, but the loud, high-pitched voices of the two girls coming down the stairs would not have been my first choice at a distraction.

"You're seriously blowing off our shopping day tomorrow to go patrolling with him? And I can't even come along?"

"I told you. You don't want to get hurt before you go onstage." I'd told her the excuse I made up. Apparently, she thought it was a good one.

"You're shoving me away because of a boy, Al. We were supposed to be learning to fight together." Mindy's voice carried all the way to the kitchen. "I mean I get that you're better than me, but I don't suck."

"Come on Mindy. It's not like that."

"It is. Ditching your best friend for a boy. Totally lame."

"You just don't get it. I—"

"What? What don't I get? You've been acting different ever since you got back from Rome. You're not talking to me, Allie. What happened to best friends forever?"

"I am *not* being different." Her voice was hard and harsh, and I knew that Mindy had inadvertently cut deep. I took a step toward the stairs, then forced myself to stop. This was something the girls had to work out between themselves.

"Whatever," Mindy said. "You know where to find me if you want to hang out. And as for hunting tomorrow, good luck. I hope you don't die."

The words were nice, but the tone was bitchy. Then, from my perspective near the sink, I saw her open the back door, and disappear into the backyard. At the same time, Allie came into the kitchen with a huff, then pulled herself up short when she saw me. "You heard all of that?"

"I heard."

She flopped down at the table. "She's being totally unreasonable."

"Is she?"

"Mom. Don't even start with me."

"Why haven't you told her? She's your best friend. You haven't even told her that Jared's a vampire, have you?" I realized that I hadn't told Laura, either. But that was an oversight, not intent. I was so used to her knowing everything, I'd forgotten to bring her up to speed, something I'd do as soon as I saw her.

At the table, Allie let out a teenage-quality sigh of frustration. "She knows I like him. What if Daddy had decided he was evil and killed him? I really didn't think I wanted to have that conversation with anybody."

I went and took the chair beside her. "Allie, you need your friends. You and Mindy have been through a lot, and she loves you."

If it was possible, she seemed to sag even further. "I know. But..." She trailed off, not meeting my eyes.

"But?"

She leaned back in her chair and huffed again, her attitude switching from dejected to teenage frustration. "Mom. You know what I am. Or you don't know what I am. And that's the problem. What if she looks at me different? What if she's scared of me?"

My heart broke a little. "Why would she be?"

"Duh. I mean I'm scared of me."

I reached over and took her hand. "Oh baby. I know it's hard, but you are you."

"Yeah. I am me. But what is that? A freak?"

"No. Definitely not."

She scowled as she pulled her hand away so she could hug herself. "I don't know. Maybe I am."

I fought back tears, hating the realization that I could do nothing to help but be there for her. There was no Band-Aid I could put on this boo-boo, and kisses wouldn't fix it anymore than a Popsicle before dinner.

All I could do was trust that we'd raised her right and be there for her as she worked through it all.

I didn't like the feeling. I wanted to do, to fix.

But I knew I couldn't. And like Allie, somehow, I was going to have to find a way to live with this new reality.

"So have you looked at Eliza's papers yet?" Laura asked that afternoon as we walked through Old Town toward Eyes Only. I'd filled her in on everything—from girl drama to vampires to demons who couldn't seem to decide it they wanted to kill my family or worship it. I'd also told her about the boxes of family information that Eliza had mentioned, one box of which Stuart had brought back with him from San Diego.

"Mostly random papers and stuff," Eliza had said when I called to thank her. "A few pictures of our moms, that kind of stuff."

My throat had tightened as I'd thanked her again, but I still hadn't opened the box. I didn't have any photos of my parent, and I didn't want to open that box until I was ready to deal with whatever emotions were packed in there with the photos.

I didn't tell Laura that. Instead, I just told her I hadn't had time, what with being so busy cleaning.

Laura stopped on the street, her hand going to her heart as she reaches out. "Steady me. I think my heart skipped a beat from the shock."

"You're so very funny."

"Just lightening the moment. You okay?" Her words were gentle, and I realized she knew exactly why I hadn't opened the box.

"I'm good. Thanks."

"Okay, then." She cleared her throat, her tone lightening as she said, "And the cleaning? How's that going?"

I groaned.

"That good? Why didn't you call me? I would totally help you get ready for the party."

"I considered it, but to be honest, I wanted something mindless. Something where I wasn't worrying about demons or my marriage, or the rivalry between Eric and Stuart."

"Or Allie?"

"Most of all, Allie," I admitted. "She still hasn't told Mindy. Not about Rome. Not that Jared's a vampire."

"I know. Mindy thinks Allie's all in a twist because she has a crush on Jared."

"That's probably part of it, although she won't

JULIE KENNER

admit it to me. But the bigger part is that she thinks
that Mindy will freak. About Allie, I mean. The whole
being bred to fight demons thing. Especially since that
means there's something demonic in her. She's afraid
of how Mindy will react. So she's damaging the friendship by trying to protect it."

Laura paused on the sidewalk, then shook her head
slowly. "I get it, but I think it will be fine. She might
stumble a little bit at first, but I did too."

"Yeah, but I'm just me. I don't have any supernatural
essence running through my blood. Apparently, Allie
does. Would that have changed things for you?"

"I don't think so. I mean, you're still you. You can't
clean a house to save your life, and before everyone
comes, I really want to check your baseboards."

"Why am I not surprised?"

"Seriously, do you want me to get involved? I could
tell Mindy so that she has some time to process before
Allie finally gets around to the big reveal."

I considered that. "No. It's Allie's story to tell. But I
do think Mindy deserves to know. I've been meaning
to give Allie an ultimatum. Tell or I will. I just haven't
done it yet."

"It's hard," Laura agreed. "Did you mean it about
Mindy being a target?"

"Directly, probably not. But since this whole thing
seems to have shifted the demonic focus in this town
off me and onto my daughter, that puts you in the clear
and Mindy in the target zone."

"Well, that sucks."

I drew a breath. "Maybe it would be for the best if they have a rift. Keep Mindy safer."

For a moment, I feared Laura would agree, but ultimately she shook her head. "No. They're besties. Once Mindy understands, she'll be right there at Allie's side. Trust me. I know how that feels."

I swallowed the tears that had gathered in my throat. "Thanks."

"As for the drama that might happen if Allie has a boyfriend—vampire or not—I really can't say."

"Mentor," I said. "Not boyfriend. I wouldn't even let her go out with a nineteen year old, much less someone who's crossed the century mark."

"Crush then."

We walked in silence for a while, then Laura sighed. "Teenagers. You don't even have to throw demons in the mix to have drama. How lucky are we to have this extra layer of angst?"

I laughed at that. She wasn't wrong.

By the time we reached the shop, we'd decided to give the girls a few more days to work it out. Hopefully, Allie just needed a little more time to work up the nerve to tell Mindy, and I'd give her that leeway. But if Mindy didn't know by Timmy's party on Saturday, I was going to insist that Allie either tell her or Laura will. Especially since keeping the information from her could be dangerous.

The little bell jangled as we pulled the door open, an

anachronistic sound considering the shop was full of cutting-edge technology.

"Don't tell me our girl lost that necklace again?"

"She didn't," I said. "For that matter, she didn't lose it the first time. She loves it. The demons ripped it off."

Eddie snorted "That just means she'll lose it again. When aren't the demons going to be after her?"

"*Eddie.*"

"What? Like you didn't already know that? That's this life. Always was, always will be."

I knew that, of course. Before Eric and I retired, demons had been a daily part of my existence. Practically an hourly part.

But I'd always wanted something different for Allie. Hadn't I?

Is my problem the fact that she's suddenly neck deep in the family business?

Or am I more concerned about the fact that I don't understand what her larger role is in this hazy world that we were moving through? A world that most people don't see, but that my family sees all too clearly?

"You two just coming to say hi?" Eddie asked, pulling me from my thoughts. "I don't see a bag of bakery goods in your hand, so you're not bringing me lunch."

"We're here to enlist your aid," Laura said. "We're on a mission."

"Are you now?" His eyes twinkled beneath his bushy brows. "So how am I helping?"

"We need something that lets us listen to Allie and Jared," I said.

Eddie's face turned nine shades of red as he barked out laughter. "Hoo boy. Our girl is going to be pretty ticked off if she finds out you're doing that."

"But she's not going to find out because you're not going to tell her, and your equipment is so awesome that we will be far enough away that she won't notice us. Right?"

He snorted. "That so?"

"You do have something like that, right? I see it in movies all the time. Special amplifying headphones or telescope-like microphones that bad guys aim at windows so they can hear the conversations inside. Or, I don't know, something?"

I realized that perhaps I'd been watching too many movies, and I was about to be utterly defeated in my plan to listen to what my daughter and her vampiric protector were talking about. But then Eddie gave a low snort and said, "Yeah. I got you covered."

As Laura and I shared a smile of victory, Eddie dipped below the counter. I heard him rummaging in the cabinetry before popping up a moment later with a shiny cardboard box, the kind where the top lifts off to reveal the contents inside.

I peered in and saw something about twelve inches long, very slim, and silver gray in color. "How does it work?"

He took Laura and I through the instructions,

which were actually pretty simple. All we had to do was turn it on, put on some headphones, then aim the receiving end toward the kids. (Although *kid* really is the wrong word for Jared, and I needed to remember that.).

Once again, Eddie disappeared behind the counter, then came back up with a small packet. "Auxiliary headphones," he said. "So Laura here can listen in, too."

"Terrific," I said. "I'll take it. How much?"

Eddie waved the question away. "You're looking out for our girl. Let's just say this one's on the house."

"Should I remind you that you don't actually own this place? You work here part-time, Eddie. Do you really think your boss is going to be okay with that?"

He snorted. "You let me worry about that."

Since I was more than happy not to have to explain to Stuart why a charge for spy equipment had appeared our credit card, I didn't protest any longer. I put the box in one of the plain brown shopping bags the store offered, told Eddie, goodbye, then headed out to go spy on my daughter, my best friend at my side.

We paused just outside the store. "Where are they?" Laura asked.

I rummaged in my purse for my phone, then turned on the app. I'd recently learned I could also track her phone, but considering my daughter was out in the world kicking ass, I knew it was likely she'd fall on it, too. And that phone she loved might easily get lost or crunched if she kept it in her back pocket.

Besides, the necklace had been a gift from me. A reminder to her that I loved her. And that I would always be looking out for her.

I expected to see that they were at the beach, and I was surprised when I found them at the park, just a few blocks away at the east end of Old Town.

"Oh, that's an easy walk," Laura said. She glanced up the street, then pointed to a small art gallery. "There's an alley between the gallery and that little cafe, and if we use it to cut through to the next street over, we can grab some ice cream at that cute little shop. We'll just have time to finish before we get to the park."

The alley isn't actually intended as a throughway, and it was clogged with Dumpsters and plastic milk crates. It was cooler there, too, the buildings on either side keeping it shaded and gloomy. "Well this is charming."

"Trust me," Laura said. "Shortcut to ice cream. It's worth it."

We walked a few more steps, and then I stopped to adjust the shopping bag, the handle of which was cutting into my arm. As I did, I heard another step behind us.

I whipped around—at the same time mentally kicking myself, because I really should have been paying more attention—and found myself staring at a familiar-looking woman with a sullen expression standing behind me. I tried to remember where I'd seen her before, but before I could place her, she leaped on me.

That's when I remembered.

And, dammit, I *knew* I should have impaled Sour-Bitch that day at the checkout stand.

CHAPTER 18

"*T*here must be no obstacles," SourBitch said, looming over me as I thrust up with my index finger.

"*Kate?*"

I froze, my fingertip a millimeter from SourBitch's eye . *That wasn't Laura.*

"Oh my God, Kate!"

I glanced over SourBitch's shoulder to see my friend Fran gaping at me as Laura raced to her side. Her shout had startled SourBitch, who clearly hadn't anticipated someone behind her, and it gave me a split second in which I could change my course of action.

So instead of impaling the demon with my non-acrylic fingernail, I smashed my palm hard against her face, forcing her off me. Then I shifted my weight as I rolled to the right. I thrust up and out with my left leg, my hands on the concrete giving me extra leverage.

Blam—I got her right in the chest, and she stumbled backward as Laura moved protectively in front of Fran.

"Go," I said, now on my feet with my knife in my hand. "If you don't," I added for Fran's benefit, "I'm calling the cops."

The demon showed yellow teeth, then turned and sprinted out of the alley.

"Kate! Why did you let her go?"

"She'd been drinking," I lied. "Got upset when I accidentally bumped her with my shopping bag." I winced, hoping the listening device hadn't broken when I dropped it. "I think she just needs to sleep it off. And, honestly, I don't want to deal with the paperwork and fallout."

And wasn't that the understatement of the year?

"Well, I still can't believe it. But my gosh, Kate! That was even more impressive than what you and Cutter have shown us in class."

"Thanks," I said. "I guess we can call it an in-the-field demonstration." Fran's one of the mom's in the women's self-defense class I started. She's also a good friend, though nowhere near Laura's place on the hierarchy. Since her daughter Elena and Timmy are the same age, we've bonded over play dates and birthday parties. And now that her mother, Rita, is dating Eddie, I imagine I'll be seeing even more of Fran.

I frowned, wondering how much of the truth Rita knew. She'd seen Eric lose it once at Allie's birthday party, but as far as I knew, she thought it was temper or drugs—not a demon. Honestly, I'm not sure that's a plus.

I made a mental note to ask Eddie the status. In the meantime, I was operating on the assumption that Fran was clueless about the demon situation.

"Wow," she said again. "Sorry, but my heart is still pounding."

"It's all fine now," I said, although it wasn't. Sour-Bitch was still out there, and I hoped I'd made the right call in letting her go. After all, I could have killed her and then told Fran the truth...

"Kate's going to start more classes up soon," Laura said. "I'm setting up an email list. You're on it."

"Great. I can't wait. And speaking of anticipation, Elena is so excited about Saturday."

"Timmy is too. I think the kids will have fun." Yesterday, we'd looked at all his party decorations and he'd practically vibrated with energy.

"That's why I came here, actually. The alley, I mean," Fran told me. "I was in the toy store and saw you through the window. I wanted to ask about Timmy's present. I saw the cutest little box with stuffed monsters and monster coloring books. I thought it was adorable, but wanted to make sure that was okay. Some kids don't even like the cute monsters. Too scary."

"No," I said. "That sounds great."

After all, as far as I was concerned, the more he knew about monsters, the better.

~

"What did she mean by no obstacles?" Laura asked, once Fran had returned to the toy store and we were hurrying to the park, foregoing the ice cream so I could make certain that SourBitch didn't show up to give Jared and Allie a hard time.

"I have no idea," I admitted. "Something to do with Allie?" That was where my mind went, of course, but only because as far as I was concerned, everything in the demon world these days had to do with my daughter.

Still, I had to acknowledge that my thinking was probably a little bit narrow. I was worried about her, yes. I didn't understand what had happened to her, true. But that did not mean that everything happening in the supernatural realm revolved around my daughter.

"I guess we need to do research."

Laura actually smiled.

"What?"

She shrugged. "I'm a complete klutz where fighting is concerned, but with research, I'm a whiz."

"You are," I agreed. "Not a lot to start with, though, is there?"

She shrugged. "Well, I'll poke around. Who knows, maybe we'll get lucky."

As far as luck went, we managed to find Allie and Jared without needing to look at the tracking app again. They were exactly where they'd been before, near the little duck pond in the center of the park. An excellent location for two reasons. First, there were hardly any people there today. Just a few random joggers on the path that ran by the pond, but most people were over on the soccer field or at the playscape. And second, because the pond stood near a cluster of trees and flowering plants that made for excellent camouflage.

I felt a little bit like a parent out of a comedy movie as Laura and I tried to hide behind those tree trunks. But Jared and Allie seemed so intent on talking to each other, that neither even looked in our direction.

I made a mental note to talk to Allie about that. She needed to be more aware of her surroundings. Right now though, her lackadaisical attitude towards her safety worked in my favor.

Laura and I each put in our headphones, and then I aimed the device, feeling a bit like James Bond. Moments later, I had it set properly and Laura and I could hear their conversation.

"—so embarrassed. I know, it's stupid, but I thought that you were really in high school and you liked me. I can't believe I'm telling you that," Allie said. "Except I guess you should know why I was so bitchy before."

"I get it. And I'm flattered. And, honestly..."

"What?"

He shook his head. "Nothing."

259

"Is it weird? Looking seventeen but being, like, *so* much older?"

"Yeah. Some. I don't know." Jared shrugged. "I'm just me. I've lived a long time—well, not *lived*—and seen a hell of a lot, but at the end of the day I am who I am. Do people really change that much over the years?"

"I don't know," Allie said. "I only have fifteen to judge by. You're the only one who's been around long enough to ask."

Even from this distance, I could see their shared smile. I could also see that the age difference hadn't dimmed Allie's crush at all. Which meant that I needed to add Talk With Daughter About Older Men to my very long To Do list.

"Listen," he said. "I'm flattered that you think of me that way. If I didn't think your mom would stake me—"

He was cut off by the sharp sound of Allie's squeal as a passing jogger veered off the path and leaped toward Allie. I started to race that way, but Laura pulled me back, and I watched as Allie expertly dodged the jogger even as Jared caught the demon by the shoulder and spun her around.

Two more joined the fray, and I held my breath, mesmerized, as Jared and Allie worked in tandem in a violent ballet of fighting skills that made me proud.

They took out the jogger first, then the second assailant, both demons going back to the ether without Allie or Jared breaking a sweat. Though, honestly, I was pretty sure that vampires didn't sweat.

Jared was poised to take out the final demon when it spoke. "He cannot walk again. He cannot have his mate."

"Just go back to hell you bastard." And Jared slammed the stick through the demon's eye. I saw the demon rise into the ether, and once again, I wanted to run forward.

Once again, Laura stopped me. "Don't," she said. "They've got it under control. Allie needs to know she can do this on her own. And that she can trust Jared."

I nodded. She was right.

It wasn't just me and Eric who had Allie's back anymore. This boy—this man—was watching out for her too.

I didn't understand why, but right then it didn't matter. He'd saved her, and for that he would always have my gratitude.

"Are you okay?" Laura asked, once Jared and Allie had walked away from the pond.

I nodded. I'd been catching my breath, thinking about my past and my family. Remembering that rhythm I'd had with Eric and the other fighters on my team. The way we'd all practice in the *Forza* training rooms below the Vatican. It had been intense, but the training had saved my life more than once.

For that matter, it had saved the world.

I turned to Laura as something else occurred to me. A thought, just taking form. "Is Cutter back in town?" I asked.

"Yeah. Later tonight. Why?"

"Do you think he could meet us at the mansion tomorrow?"

"Sure. What for?"

"I'll tell you tomorrow," I promised. "But I think I have a really interesting idea."

Because Cutter had classes all day, he was only available first thing in the morning. Which explained why I was awake and at the mansion far earlier than should be allowed during the summer when the kids didn't have to get up early. It was especially unfair since Timmy was finally sleeping in these days, and most days I could stay gloriously asleep until at least eight o'clock.

Not so today. It was seven-thirty in the morning, and I was wandering bleary-eyed through the entrance hall, giving the side eye to the contractors who were awake and perky and working hard.

Laura was with me, also awake and perky, and Cutter was beside her, equally bright-eyed.

I clutched my coffee closer and tried not to show how much I would prefer to be back in my bed.

"Stuart's not coming?" Cutter asked.

I shook my head. "I wanted to get your thoughts on this before I talked it over with him. But we do need to wait for—" I cut myself off as Eric stepped in through the open doors. "Never mind. He's here."

"He is," Eric said. "But why is he here at this hour? It must be important since you're up and dressed."

After all these years, he still knows me so well…

"Come with me, and I'll tell you all what I'm thinking." I led the way, heading up the stairs and straight to the ballroom the girls had worked out in yesterday. "You've all seen this before, of course. And I think most of you have seen the former servant's quarters, right?"

"I haven't," Cutter said, so I took them to the nearby wing and showed them the row of rooms with plenty of space of two twin size beds plus dressers, a table, and even a few other personal items.

A few of the rooms still had musty old beds inside, and we took a moment to sit, Eric and me on one as we looked across at Cutter and Laura.

"It's like a dorm room," I said. "Don't you think?"

Eric gave me a sidelong look. "Kate, what's this all about?"

"Just humor me. Dorm room. Right?" I looked at each of them in turn, and they all shrugged, as if not certain what I wanted the answer to be.

"There are six rooms on this floor. That would house twelve people. And there's a slew of guest bedrooms in this place, too, so that could bring in a few more."

"Are you thinking about a hotel?" Laura asked.

"High-end but with these rooms for kids doing the hostel thing?"

"No. Mindy actually gave me this idea."

"Mindy?"

"Well, the kernel of it." I looked at Cutter. "Do you think that ballroom could be transformed into a training center? With mats and punching bags and the whole shebang? And could the salons be set up for archery practice, knife throwing and stuff like that?"

His brow furrowed. "Are you asking me to set up a training center here?"

"No, not really. I mean, if you were interested in doing some of the training and participating, that would be amazing. Right now, I just want your opinion."

I looked between the three of them, feeling the excitement rise in me. "I told you all how Father Corletti thinks that I should start training Demon Hunters. Apparently they've discovered a lot of potential hunters in the Southwest and California. What if *Forza* diverts them here and we train them?"

I watched their faces, but only Eric said, "Go on."

"Right. Well, I'm thinking that Forza should buy this place. I'm thinking that I should turn this into a training center. A full-blown, live-in training center." I shrugged. "Anyway, that's the idea. What do you think?"

The three of them exchanged glances, but nobody said anything.

"You hate the idea? Really? I thought it was kind of great."

"No," Eric said, with a crack in his voice. "Honestly, I think it's brilliant. And you can totally count me in to train."

"Really?"

He took my hand, and I knew he'd been thinking about our past. About our own time in the dorms. "Absolutely."

We headed back to the ballroom so that Cutter could take another look now that I'd told him how I wanted to repurpose it. "Honestly Kate, I think this place is about as perfect as it gets. The ballroom will convert easily. You have the kids in the dorms. They're living together, so there will be that camaraderie."

"It would almost be like *Forza West*," Eric said, making me laugh.

"Forza, the sequel," Laura said in a low movie trailer voice. "This time, it's personal."

"I'm really glad you guys think it's a good idea," I said when I'd stopped laughing and could breathe again. "I was afraid you'd say I was thinking too big, taking on more than I could chew."

"Well, you might be," Eric said. "But I have your back. And we can move my book collection here too," he added. Eric had been the Rare Books Librarian at the San Diablo Public Library before he died. Because of who he was and what he was trying to learn about himself, he had built quite a collection of rare books,

particularly on the topics of demons and demonology.
I'd assumed that he'd used the library fund, but it
turned out he'd bought the books himself or through a
research account with *Forza*.

Having those manuscripts here if we were trying to
train hunters would be a huge boon, but I didn't see
how it would happen. They belonged to the library
now.

"No," he said when I pointed that out. "My will
authorized the library to hold them in trust for you,
but ultimately it's your decision where the books go."

"Your decision," I said.

"No. Eric's dead. David Long has no claim on those
books."

I said nothing. He knew perfectly well I'd do whatever he wanted with those rare manuscripts.

"I'm getting excited," I admitted, as the four of us
continued to chatter about the possibilities.

"We can hold your women's self-defense class here
too," Cutter said, "It's not that convenient for me to
come, but if I'm going to be consulting here anyway..."

I shook my head. "No. I want to keep this separate.
And we'll have to arrange for some sort of private
school accreditation. I figure with his law background,
Stuart will be able to navigate those channels.
Assuming he signs off on this whole idea. And Father
Corletti, of course."

"I'm sure they will," Eric said.

Below, the contractors were still hard at work. We

walked through them, trying to avoid their bits of equipment and stacks of tile as we headed toward the exit. We'd almost reached reached the door when one of them launched himself at Eric, a pry-bar tight in his hand.

Cutter, in the kind of move that he doesn't show off in class, whipped his leg around high and fast and sent the guy sprawling with a solid kick to the chin .

From the floor, the guy snarled. "Fool. Your trust is misplaced."

Eric grabbed him by the collar and hauled him up off the ground. Cutter held his hands behind his back as Eric got right in the demon's face. "What happened to you creatures bowing before me? Calling me Sire?"

"I would never bow before you. But if you kill me, another will come. He won't rise. He cannot rise. We will not let him rise."

Laura looked at me. "What does that mean?"

I shook my head. I didn't know. Around us, the other contractors were staring. I could see the blood lust in Eric's eyes, I knew he wanted to shove something sharp and pointy through the demon's eye, but this wasn't the time or the place. And I desperately hoped Eric realized that, too.

After a full five beats, Eric tossed the demon back on the ground. "Get the hell out of here before you lose an eye."

The demon looked as if he was going to attack again, but then he turned and raced for the door, crying out as he went, "He cannot rise, he will not rise..."

Cutter looked at me, breathing hard as he reached for Laura's hand. "Cryptic little guy, isn't he?"

"Yeah," I said. "They almost always are."

CHAPTER 19

"So you really like the idea?" I asked Stuart as we sipped coffee at the breakfast table the next morning. "I mean, you really think it makes sense?"

"You're sure this is something that you want to take on?" he asked. "I mean, my part is the easy part. Paperwork and signing checks and documents. You're taking on quite a load, Kate."

"Not alone, though. You'll help with the office administration, right? And Eric will be training and helping with overall operations, and Cutter will help, too. Plus, Father Corletti will send others to help train as well."

"I think it's a great idea," he said. "What are we doing about high school, though? Is Allie going to go all in at your new academy? Or will she stay at Coronado High?"

"*Forza West*, for Allie," I said. "But we'll be bringing in academic teachers, too. I have a feeling those will be the classes she tries to skip."

He nodded slowly. "That makes sense. What about Mindy?"

I grimaced. To be honest I hadn't thought about that. And right now my brain was very, very tired. I'd spent most of the time between two in the morning and right now on the phone with Father Corletti, talking to him and Marcus about the idea and all the practical aspects of getting my idea up and running.

"I don't know," I said honestly. "She's decent in the field, but I think she'd really rock at training to be an *alimentatore*. I mean, Laura rocks at research. Like mother, like daughter?"

"So the school would teach that stuff, too?" Stuart asked. "The history, the demonology, all of that?"

"Along with regular academic courses. Yeah." Though if this school turned out to be anything like my experience, there'd be more fighting and less academia, except for those on the *alimentatore* track.

"How are you going to recruit the academic instructors?"

I sighed. "Stuart, I came up with this idea yesterday. I haven't thought of everything yet. But you're right. We'll need to recruit. We'll need accreditations. And I'm really hoping my organized and resourceful husband will jump all over that."

"I've got back-to-back meetings today, but I'll give it some thought. I promise."

"Yeah?" He got up, then kissed me on the cheek before taking his coffee mug to the sink. "Anything for you. You know that right?"

"What are you doing for Mom?" Allie asked, padding into the kitchen in her bare feet and bunny-covered pajamas.

"Stuart's looking into some legal aspects of an idea I have." I couldn't help the fact that I was practically bouncing in my seat.

Allie glanced at Stuart, her brows raised. "Mom's dying to tell me what it is. Is it okay? Can you tell me? Is it a secret?"

I laughed. "No, I think it's okay for you to know, but you need to also understand that it may not happen. A million things have to fall into place to make it a sure thing."

"What?" Now she looked really interested. She pulled out a chair and sat at the table, then took one of the pieces of buttered toast I'd made for myself. "What's going on?"

"We're thinking about making the Greatwater mansion into a training center. *Forza West*. A full-on boarding school for training hunters."

"Whoa. That is so cool." Her eyes were wide, and she looked as giddy as I felt.

"While you two hash it all out all over again, I'm going to go to the office."

"Thanks, sweetheart. And Father Corletti said for you to go ahead and draw up the paperwork so *Forza* can purchase the building."

"I'm on it," he said.

"Then this is really happening?" Allie said.

"The purchase of the property, yes. But whether we can create a boarding school ... well, that's a bigger deal. But you'd like that?"

"Are you kidding? Of course."

"You understand it would be your actual school. Coronado High would be off the agenda."

"Oh."

"And?" I watched her carefully.

"I can get behind that," she said slowly. "But what about Mindy?"

"Well, that would be up to Mindy and Laura, wouldn't it? But even if she decided to stay at Coronado, you two would still be living next to each other."

"But you said it would be a boarding school."

I stumbled over that, because she was right, and yet I hadn't thought about that aspect at all. I wondered if Stuart had. Would we sell this house and move into the mansion? After all, staff and instructors usually lived on site, too.

Since I didn't know, I punted. "We'll figure it all out as it goes along," I said, probably more impatiently than I should have. "There's a million details to talk about."

"But—"

I held up my hand. "I've been up all night talking to

Father Corletti. Seriously, baby. We can talk about the details later."

"Whatever." But she didn't say it in an irritated-teenage way. Instead she said it in an *I'm bored of this conversation and ready to move on*-teenage way. I considered that a plus.

She got up and poured herself a cup of cream with a splash of coffee, then came back to the table. "I can go patrolling with Jared today, right?"

"You can. But you need to be careful. Be aware of your surroundings. Always alert."

"Mom. You don't have to say that every time I go patrolling. I'm not going to accidentally forget and then be all reckless and stupid because you didn't remind me that I'm supposed to be careful."

"Just being sure," I said, because she's a teenager and these things bear repeating.

She rolled her eyes, but she smiled. "He's picking me up in about fifteen minutes so I need to get dressed soon." She took another sip, then frowned. "It must be really weird to have to renew your driver's license every ten years or so because you look like you're exactly the same age as you were when you got it."

"Yes. That's something that I've always wondered about," I said dryly.

"I'm just trying to learn. That's what you said, right? I'm supposed to be learning all the time. This is my vocation now."

"Apparently you are better at studying when your vocation involves a boy."

She just smiled.

"Allie. He's too old for you."

"I know, Mother..."

And then she pushed back from the table and left the room, leaving me to smile into my coffee. He *was* too old for her, and she knew it. He also knew it, and I think he respected that. But I was definitely going to keep an eye on the two of them for the foreseeable future.

Once I'd had more coffee than a human being should consume in one morning, I started back on cleaning the house again since there was still much to be done before Saturday. I kept the TV on as I worked, as Timmy was already up and fed and camped out in front of *Sesame Street.*

He sang and I cleaned, and on the whole the morning felt about as average as you could get. Eventually, Eddie stumbled downstairs, made himself an Eggo waffle, then told me he was heading out to meet Rita for breakfast.

I glanced at the waffle and decided not to press the point.

"Is she coming on Saturday for You Know Who's p-a-r-t-y?" I asked, being cryptic since You Know Who was only a few feet away.

"As far as I know she is. Don't expect she'd want to miss it." He spoke casually, but I could tell that he was looking forward to having her here, playing host and showing off his great-grandson.

Once he was out the door, I turned my attention back to Timmy. "It's just you and me, kid. Want to help me clean?"

"Elmo," Timmy said pointing at the screen.

Isn't that always the way? Shoved aside by a monster. Albeit an adorably cute one.

By late afternoon, I'd done pretty much everything except vacuum the living room, which I was holding off on so as to not bother Timmy, who switched from television to quietly playing with his stuffed animals on the couch. Since the "quietly" was key, I didn't want to anger whatever benevolent gods had blessed me with this moment of peace.

I took a moment at the kitchen table to flip through a magazine, and looked up to see Mindy at the back door. I got up to let her in, expecting to see Laura trailing behind her, but it was just Mindy.

"Allie's not here. She went out patrolling with Jared."

Mindy bit her lower lip, cocked her head, crossed her arms over her chest. And me, with my keen ability to read body language, clued in that she was irritated.

"She told me she wanted to do nails stuff today. She was going to do mine this morning so they'd be polished and cool for the show."

"Maybe she got the times wrong," I said, knowing

full well that my daughter just forgot, her best friend pushed out of her mind by the power of a cute boy.

"I can't believe she went out patrolling again and didn't take me. It's not about getting hurt and having my understudy go on, I'm sure of it."

Since she was most likely right, I wisely stayed quiet.

"I've been training, Aunt Kate, and I'm good. I mean yeah, Allie's better, but she's practiced more. And she probably inherited some good stuff from you."

"I think she inherited more from her father," I said dryly.

Mindy shrugged. "Yeah, maybe." She looked back at me. "They really went patrolling together?"

"I'm sorry. They really did. Do you want to hang out? I'll pay you to babysit Timmy while I finish cleaning." She looked over at Timmy who was being the most well-behaved child ever.

"You'd pay me to watch that?"

I laughed. "I'm afraid if I move him so I can vacuum, all hell will break loose. I was hoping for a buffer."

"I'll watch him. You don't even have to pay me. Do you want me to take him over to our house?"

"Would you? That would be great."

As we started to gather up a few things to take with him, she paused and looked at me. "Can I tell you something, Aunt Kate?"

"Of course, you can."

"I don't know that I trust him. Jared, I mean."

I wasn't sure if it was warning bells going off in my head or irritation with my daughter, who clearly had still not yet told her best friend the full situation yet. "Why not?" I asked.

"It's probably just me. I just think he's—"

"What?"

She shook her head. "I just think he's not what he seems.

She was right about that. And I guess that also meant I'd been right—Mindy had the instincts to make a good *alimentatore*.

I considered telling her the full truth now, but I wanted to give Allie one more day to do the right thing. And honestly, I wasn't sure that this was the kind of thing Mindy needed in her head before she opened in one of the starring roles in the community musical.

I was no actress, but it seemed as if things like your best friend being part-demon and having a crush on a vampire were the kind of things that might distract you from your song and dance routines.

Or maybe I was just making excuses to stay quiet.

Whatever my reasons, all I said was, "I'll be honest, Mindy. We checked him out pretty well. You know that he goes to Coronado High, so Eric was able to dig into his records." Just saying Eric's name alleviated some of my guilt. Mindy might not know everything, but she did know the truth about Allie's father.

"Okay. Well, that's good. You guys are coming tonight night, right?"

She looked both excited and young. I went over and gave her a hug. "Of course, we are. I'm so proud of you. Allie is too." She grinned and didn't even argue with that.

Then she looked down at Timmy and took his hand. "You ready?"

"Ready!" he chimed.

She gave me one final smile, then led my little guy across the backyard to her home.

Suddenly, I was alone, my husband and my kids out of the house. Granted, Timmy was just across the way with my best friend's daughter. But Allie was out doing adult things, and one day soon, Timmy would be, too.

The more I thought about it, the more I realized that my role in the world was changing too. It was less about me being a mom or a Demon Hunter. Now, it was going to be about me training a new generation. Not my kids, but my students.

It was important work—maybe the most important —because there were things hidden out in the world. Evil things. I knew that well. And I needed to make sure that there were people around who could keep the world safe when my generation of Hunters stepped away from the job.

I looked around my home, feeling melancholy as I tried to decide what to do next. I was about to give it all up and go take a long bath when my phone rang.

I grabbed it up, pleased to see that it was Eliza. "Hey

cousin. What's your ETA for coming back to San Diablo? Do you have a date for the memorial yet?"

"Not yet. Do you need me up there? It's kind of crazy down here, to be honest."

"It's a little crazy up here too," I told her. "Apparently Allie is the only one who can defeat Lilith and there's a whole slew of demons trying to kill her."

"So, basically, things are rolling on as usual," she quipped.

I laughed. "Pretty much." I considered what she'd said a moment ago. "What do you mean things are crazy there?"

"I was in a car accident."

"What? Are you okay?"

"I'm fine. I promise I didn't die. I'm not a demon in an Eliza suit. But my leg is broken."

"Were you in the car?"

"No. I was in a crosswalk. Some guy ran me down. Honestly, if I hadn't been training, I would have probably been killed. Instead, I just landed wrong when I jumped out of the way. Broke my right tibia. It should heal clean, but I can't drive right now. I'm really bummed, because I thought I might go up to San Diablo for a night so I could do the birthday party after all. But I can't make it work."

"I'm so sorry. And Stuart doesn't have time to come get you. Mindy's show is tonight, and..."

"Don't worry about it. Seriously. It was just an idea that a reckless driver snuffed. You have enough to do.

And I still have things to box up. Speaking of, did you check out the box I sent back with Stuart?"

"I'm sorry," I said, glancing over to where I'd put it under the side table next to the couch. "I've been going a mile a minute."

"No worries. It's not like there's anything important in there. Wait for me and we can go through it together. Although I don't know when that'll be. Stupid leg. I'm moving so slowly now."

"I wish we could get you here easily."

"It's fine. And the truth is, Timmy won't even notice if I'm not at the party. Next week we'll figure it out, and I'll come back and give him a big hug. I really can't wait to get back. I miss you guys, Kate."

"I miss you, too. But I was going to call you today anyway." I gave her the rundown about my idea for a training center, hoping that she'd jump all over the idea of being on the faculty, then relieved when she did exactly that. So much so that she was practically squealing with glee.

"I would dance around my apartment if I could. Stupid cast. This is the best. This is such great news. And that's a perfect location."

"With all the occult weirdness in the past, it seems strangely perfect, too. It's like turning something bad into something good."

"Speaking of occult weirdness, one of the reasons I called is that I have this strange feeling."

"Strange how?"

"I don't know, like something bad is going to happen. And then you tell me that Allie is somehow earmarked as the only one who can defeat Lilith. Or the demons seem to think she can. I mean, that's big stuff, right?"

"Yeah. I'd say it qualifies as big."

"Well, it may sound crazy, but I had this sense that whoever hit me with that car was aiming for me. That it wasn't really an accident. And now I'm thinking— well, what if they're trying to pick off anybody who might be around to protect Allie?"

I suddenly felt cold all over. "I don't think that's silly at all," I said, thinking about the attacks on me and on Eric. On Jared, too. "I really don't."

"Oh, God. Then you need to be careful. Promise me?"

"We are," I assured her, although I wondered just how accurate that statement really was. My daughter was out patrolling with a vampire, after all.

I put Eliza on speaker so I could pull up the tracking app. They were still at the park. The same park that Eddie and Rita were at. I sent Eddie a quick text, asking him to go to the location and make sure all was well.

"Kate?"

"Sorry. Just taking your advice," I said, then told her what I'd just done.

She laughed. "Sorry to make you paranoid. Let me know what Eddie says."

Eddie's text came back immediately.

Already with the kid and the vamp. Both doing fine.

"I guess all is well."

"For now," Eliza said. "But I was listening to the news this morning. Did you know there's a daytime meteor shower this week. Arietids or arachnids or something like that. I don't know. But air and fire are Lilith's elements."

"How do you know that?"

"My mom used to do tarot cards, and she was into astrology and astronomy. I don't know if it really means anything, but I can't help but think that it's a sign that Lilith's up to something."

I thought about it. Air and fire. Meteors and the atmosphere.

And my daughter at the center of it all.

By four, both Allie and Timmy were back home safe and sound. In a normal family that wouldn't even be something to take notice of, but in my household, it was to be celebrated.

At five, I started to get ready to go to the community theater. By seven, Laura was in the living room sipping a glass of wine. I joined her, and we waited for Allie and Stuart, the latter having rushed in from the office only half an hour ago.

Eddie was staying to babysit, and Rita was going to

join him. They didn't intend to miss out on Mindy's show, but planned to skip the preview and just go to opening night.

"Are you nervous?" I asked Laura.

"Absolutely not," she said nodding her head in what was undoubtedly the true response.

I laughed. "She'll do great. She's got an incredible voice."

"But the question is, can she act?" Eddie asked, making Laura pale a bit. "It's not just about singing up on a stage like that." He chuckled, and pointed his finger at her. "Don't be a stage mom. She'll do what she can do, and she'll do her best."

"I know. I just hope her best is good enough to get a standing ovation."

I grinned. I had to admit I was a little jealous. I loved and was extremely proud of my girl, but I would never see her up on stage. Then again I don't know that anything could be better than the time I saw her execute a round kick to a demon's head, knock it flat on his back, and impale him through the eye in one single fluid motion. Honestly, it made a mother proud.

Speaking of the devil, my daughter pounded down the stairs in a casual summer dress and bare feet. I raised my brows, and she rolled her eyes in response. "My shoes are in the hall closet," she said. "I'm not going to go without them." I eyed Laura who grinned back at me.

"You look very nice. Mindy's thrilled you're coming."

"I was hoping Jared could come too," she said pointedly looking at me.

I held up my hands. "I did nothing to discourage him," I said. What I didn't add was that I was relieved when he had declined Allie's invitation, saying that there were things he had to take care of that night, but that he would happily join her Saturday for the public premiere.

Allie checked her watch and started to bounce. "We need to go. Where's Stuart?"

Soon enough the man in question appeared on the stairs, looking very dapper in one of his casual suits. He hurried down as well, checked his watch, and looked at all of us. "We really need to go."

Laura and I looked at each other, both fighting smiles. I shook my head, a signal not to say anything to him. Then we all bundled into the van and headed to the community center. Fortunately it was a short drive, and parking was easy since this was a preview night. And, as a bonus, because Mindy was playing one of the leads, we'd been given front row seats.

I sat between Laura and Allie with Stuart on the other side of our daughter. He leaned over her and looked at me, grinning as the curtain rose. I squeezed Laura's hand, then sat back to watch the show.

Into the Woods has always been one of my favorite musicals, but as I watched the fairy tale beginning followed by the story about what happens after happily ever after, I couldn't help but think about the parallels to my own life. To what Allie was going through, especially. She'd learned that her mother had a secret life, a special life. And she'd wanted desperately to be part of that.

She got that wish, but what came after was more difficult than she could have imagined. My baby girl was truly going into the woods herself, and I could only hope that at the end of the day, she would come out unscathed.

My deep, philosophical thoughts flittered away as the show really got underway. Mindy's voice filled the theater, clear and strong and beautiful. She and the boy who played the baker were perfect together, singing and dancing and looking so professional I almost forgot she was only fifteen.

More than once I leaned over to Laura and whispered how impressed I was, and Allie squealed and clapped at the end of every one of Mindy's songs. When the curtain fell, we jumped to our feet applauding the entire cast for their incredible performance, though I knew the four of us were mostly applauding Mindy.

When the curtain closed again, Allie turned to me enthusiastically throwing her arms around me and giving me a tight hug. "She was amazing. I had no idea she could do that. Oh my God, I would be mortified up there. And I would sound like a strangled hamster."

"But a cute strangled hamster."

"Yeah. Not sure that would be good enough. Oh my God, I can't believe how good she was."

"You need to go tell her," I said. "That's what previews are for."

As if to underscore my words, the curtain rose again and the cast came onstage, with the director stepping out and telling the audience that we could come up and talk to the cast. Allie literally leaped onto the stage, making me cringe, since that really wasn't the designated route to get up there. But since she pulled Mindy into a huge hug, I decided to let it go.

At first, Mindy looked completely freaked out by this massive show of attention, then she burst into laughter herself. Even from where I sat, I could tell that Allie was gushing and gushing.

They went through another round of hugs, then another and another. Finally, I saw my daughter's expression change, going darker, her brow furrowing. I went cold inside, then leaned over to Laura. "Right now, I really wish we had that voice amplifier."

"Right there with you." But this wasn't a moment that we could navigate for our girls, and as Mindy cocked her head and led Allie off into the wings where we couldn't see them. I could only sit, my stomach churning, as I wondered about their conversation, and about how their friendship would survive it.

CHAPTER 20

"My party, my party, my party!"
Fresh from his bath, a naked
Timmy raced around his room, waving his hands
above his head like the kid from *Home Alone* and
giggling like a fiend.

"Not quite your party yet, kiddo," I said. "Just a few
more hours. How old are you today?"

He held up three fingers. "Three! I'm three,
Momma!"

"That's right, little man. You've grown up so fast.
How did that happen?" I held the towel open and he
raced into it. I finished drying him with the soft
terrycloth, then wrapped his little body in the towel
and held him close. "Promise me you won't grow up
too fast, okay?"

"Okay, Momma. I'm big enough today," he said,
then tilted his head back and grinned at me. I pulled

him close, then bent my head to his, breathing in that clean baby scent, wishing I could store memories in boxes the way I stored old photographs.

"Are you big enough to get yourself dressed?" I asked when I broke our hug.

"Aye-aye, Momma!" He whipped off an impressive salute, then held his hand out for a high-five, that I enthusiastically met.

"Okay, kiddo. You get dressed while mommy goes and makes the house pretty for your party. You come down when you're ready, but no touching the party stuff, okay? We want it to stay pretty for your friends. Got it?"

He saluted again, and I left him to it, figuring I could send Stuart or Allie up if our little guy took too long.

"Love you, baby."

"I love you, too, Momma."

With those wonderful words lingering in the air, I headed down the stairs to find Allie pouring pretzels and Goldfish crackers into bowls for the guests. "What else should I do?" she asked.

I looked around, assessing what was left. Over the last few days, I'd cleaned the place to within an inch of its life. At this point, you could eat off our floor. And I dared anyone to find even a single dust bunny, at least downstairs.

I'd even pulled the stove out and cleaned behind it, revealing a dark, and grease-filled environment even more terrifying than some demonic lairs. Trust me on that.

In addition to all the cleaning, I'd covered the entire downstairs in an explosion of party decorations. I'm sure Laura—or any of my Mom Friends—could have done it with more finesse, but the end result was an eye-splitting array of color and cartoons that should make any toddler giddy.

Slowly, I turned in a circle. I still needed to put out the Nemo-themed cups, plates, and table cloth. Laura was bringing the cake. I had a plethora of juice boxes.

In other words, it was miraculously all coming together.

The kids' goodie bags were still on the list, and so I put Allie on that task. While she filled Pixar-themed bags with candy, small coloring books, and silly toys, I put up a few more streamers and fish-themed window clings on the glass squares of our French doors.

Then I looked back at the room. On the whole, I was impressed. I was also exhausted. Truth be told, I'd probably put more work into this than necessary for our relatively small guest list. Just the kids from Timmy's play group, the children of the moms in my self-defense class, and the kids who played in the day care during Mass rather than risk disrupting the service. (A life-saving feature of the Cathedral that, to my shock, was not offered at every cathedral around the globe.)

Bottom line, this would be a birthday party with

plenty of time for the adults to mingle—with Mimosas, too!—and very few organized activities for the kids. It was really about the fun.

The only thing specific I had planned was to sing Happy Birthday and eat cake at three, since Timmy was turning three. Otherwise, I was giving the kids free rein. They had options, sure—a station to throw bean-bags, a sand box, and lots of outdoor trucks and balls—but mostly I wanted them to be kids, something that I'm sure would shock my arch-nemesis, Marissa, who scheduled every event with precision timing.

All in all, I expected a low-key afternoon. Honestly, I should know better than to tempt Fate.

Once the decorations were complete and Allie had filled all the bags and put them out of reach of little hands, I called her into the kitchen. "So?" I asked as I spread the tablecloth and put out the paper plates and utensils. "When are you going to tell me?"

She blinked at me, apparently not having a clue what I was talking about.

"Mindy? You two talked at the theater. It's been two days and you haven't said a thing."

Granted, I'd been crazy busy yesterday getting ready for the party and handling mansion-related tasks. But I also hadn't wanted to push her.

Now, though...

Well, whether it was the right thing to do or not, I couldn't take it anymore. My curiosity was killing me. I assumed the girls were back on track considering the hugging and squealing that had happened on that stage, but I desperately wanted confirmation.

"It's all good, Mom," Allie said.

"Really?"

She sighed. "I told her it was all on me. That I'd been acting like a bitch." She cast her eyes down to the table, then back up at me with a shrug.

I forced myself not to comment on the language and just said, "Go on."

"I told her I hadn't meant to cut her out, and it wasn't about Jared. Not really." She drew in a breath. "And then I told her about the demon stuff inside me, and the golden light in Rome. And how we think that's why I'm faster now. Stronger." She shrugged again. "She already knew what happened to Daddy, so she gets it. And so I told her all of it. What had been in my head, I mean."

"Will you tell me?" I asked gently. "Will you tell me what *all of it* means to you?"

She took a Nemo napkin and started ripping it into tiny pieces. I almost said something—we didn't have that many extras, and I didn't want to vacuum again—but I bit my tongue.

"I don't know. I guess I got caught up in this whole I'm the Coolest Demon Hunter thing. But then when I realized that made me a target, too, I got scared. For me, but mostly for Mindy."

"I get that."

"I told myself I was better at this than she was—

fighting, I mean. And I am. But that's just one thing, you know? But I got it all mixed up in my head. I wanted to protect her, but at the same time I thought I wasn't like her. And then…"

She trailed off with a shrug.

And then what?" I pressed.

"And then I heard her sing. I mean *really* sing. Not like choir or how we sing to the radio."

"Her singing?" I could hear the incredulity in my voice. I had no idea where she was going with this.

She looked shocked that I didn't understand. "Come on, Mom. You were there. Her voice was like—I don't know. Like really something amazing, right?"

"It was," I said. "Mindy could have a real career in music if she wants, I think."

"I could never do that."

"Do you want to?"

"No. Not at all. But that's not the point. It's what I realized. About me being a bitch, I mean. "

That time I knew was goading me.

"Watch it," I said mildly. "And tell me what you realized."

"That I am special. But so what? She is, too. And that doesn't make either one of us better than the other. It just makes us different."

"Yeah," I said softly. "You're right."

"I'm still going to worry about her because … well, I really am stronger than her, and faster, too. But Mom, I'm getting stronger and faster than you, too."

"I've noticed. Does that scare you?"

"A little. I told Mindy that, too."

"What did she say? "

"She said she'd be there for me whenever I needed her." She brushed a tear off her cheek. "And I told her I was so sorry that I haven't been there for her." She smiled at me, then. "So I guess we're okay now. *No*," she corrected, "I know we are. Because she forgave me for being a—"

"Bitch," we both said at the same time, then laughed.

"Yeah," Allie said. "Pretty much."

"You know what I think?" I asked.

She shook her head.

"I think I'm incredibly proud of you both."

"Really?"

"Really," I said. "I love you, Al. I love Mindy, too. I'm glad you worked it out."

Her smile lit up her entire face. "I love you, too, Mom. Should I go see if he's dressed?"

I was about to suggest that she do just that when I heard another, "I love you." This one was coming from the living room, and as I stood up, Timmy trotted toward us.

"Love you, Allie!" he said, snuggling against her as she pulled him up into her lap, then flashed me a grin.

"We've got a weird family," she said, "but I think it's a pretty good one."

"Yeah," I agreed. "I think we're doing just fine."

CHAPTER 21

"Hey there, birthday boy," Eric said, scooping Timmy up as soon as he stepped into the entrance hall. He hung my kiddo upside down from his ankles the same way he'd done with Allie when she was little. And Timmy loved it just as much as his big sister had.

"Swing me, Unca David! Swing me!"

Eric was doing just that and Timmy was shrieking with glee when Stuart emerged from his office where he'd been wrangling with some sort of forms he needed for some regulation having to do with something about the *Forza West* plans.

"Wow," Stuart said, grinning at Eric. "Looks like you caught a very big fish."

"I'm a *boy*, Daddy. And I'm three!"

"Yes, you are. Good to see you, Eric. Careful, or you'll be carrying him around upside down all day."

"We could handle that, couldn't we, Timster?"

"Higher! Swing higher!"

As Eric chuckled, I beamed. I was getting used to the civil chatter between these men of mine, but I wasn't about to let myself hope that it would continue. That would be too good to be true.

"Daddy!" Allie bounded into the room, then stopped short. "Timmy! You stole my hug," she teased. "How is Uncle Eric supposed to hug me if he's dangling you?"

"*My* birthday. *My* Unca David."

"Okey-dokey. I'll get a hug from Stuart."

She sidled up to him for a hug, which he returned with a half-hearted squeeze. I don't know if Allie noticed, but I did. I met Stuart's eyes, saw the guilt there, and excused myself back to the kitchen.

"What's wrong?" Laura asked, the moment I rounded the corner. She was standing by the sink, sipping a Mimosa and chatting with Cutter.

I stopped short, not realizing they'd arrived from the back while the rest of us had been gathered by the front door. "Nothing. I'll tell you later. I'll be fine."

I closed my eyes, exhaled, and when I opened them again, she was holding a Mimosa out to me. "And see? I'm better already."

She tilted her head in question, but I waved it away. "Seriously. I'm fine." I glanced around. "Where's Mindy?"

"Bringing the cake," she said. "She'll be here in a few."

"Great. I think we're ready." I glanced at the clock. A quarter-to-one, and the party started at two with cake in the middle and a loosey-goosey end time of four. I could make it. I'd be exhausted at the end, but I could make it.

I turned in a circle, taking in the house, trying to think of what I might have forgotten. That's when I spied the box. Not that there was anything wrong with having a cardboard box under a side table, but I didn't want an eager toddler using whatever family documents Eliza had gathered as drawing paper.

I headed that way, tugged the box out, then hefted it, intending to take it to Stuart's study for safe keeping.

Naturally, I took one step and tripped over my own feet, dropping the box and sending papers tumbling. *Well, hell.*

Cutter and Laura dropped down by me, and Allie hurried over to help, too. With the exception of a few photos, the box was filled with nothing but paper, and we scooped it up and tossed it in the box.

I wasn't really even paying attention to what what I was gathering, so I'm not sure how it caught my eye, but I stopped short when I saw Eliza's family tree. A tree that shot off in one direction to my mother, Amanda, but had another familiar name up near the top.

Donnelly.

I pulled the paper closer and studied it, getting lost

in the ancestry lines. A Donnelly was one of my great-uncles? I wasn't sure.

But though I'd seen nothing specific on the paper, something buried deep inside me was certain that Father Donnelly's name was penned in somewhere on that tree. Just as I was.

If that was true, though, what did it mean?

"Mom?"

I jumped. "Sorry. Distracted." I shoved the family tree into the box and pushed it toward Allie. "Put this in the closet. I need to make a phone call."

"Sure. No problem. I just wanted to tell you that Jared's here. He came on this really cool vintage motorcycle and Daddy and I are going out front to see it. Stuart's got Timmy. They're getting the ice cream out of the freezer in the garage."

"Fine. Great. Sounds fun." I barely heard her. My mind was too full of questions, and as Allie flew toward the front door, I hurried into Stuart's study. I slammed the door behind me, and snatched up the phone. Then I tapped a pencil impatiently on Stuart's desk as I got routed through the switchboard to Father Corletti.

"Katherine, *mia cara*, thank goodness you are returning my messages."

"Father, I—wait. What? You called me?" I said a silent curse, then crossed myself, all the while wondering where I'd left my mobile phone. "Father, what's going on?"

"My child. Things are not as they seem."

297

"Wait. What? Which things?"

"The reports you have made. The reason the demons are protecting Allie ... Kate, it has all been horribly twisted."

"I don't understand."

"The demons do not want to keep Allie alive because she is the only one who can defeat Lilith."

"Then why—"

"They wish to keep her alive because she is the only human who can contain Lilith's energy without consent."

I sat down in Stuart's chair. Lilith was ridiculously powerful, so of course she would burn through a human body in an instant. She'd manifested only one time in the last millennium that I was aware of, and that had been when she'd moved into Nadia's body. Nadia, however, was a power-hungry ex-Demon Hunter who'd known the score and had traded her body for power.

She'd consented, and Lilith had hitched a ride into this dimension.

But there weren't very many Nadia's in the world, thank God.

Which meant that now we knew for certain—the baddest bitch in the demon realm was once again coming after my family. And this time, she wanted my daughter.

No. Way.

No. Freaking. Way.

I stood up, needing to tell Allie right away, only then processing what she'd just told me—she and Eric had gone outside to look at Jared's bike.

Jared.

The boy who supposedly wanted to protect my little girl so she could kill Lilith.

The lousy son-of-a-bitch.

"Father, hang on. I'll be right back."

I didn't wait for him to answer. Just shoved the handset into my back pocket as I raced out of the study and toward the front door, taking one of Stuart's pencils with me. I barely noticed Laura standing with Mindy and Cutter, all three of whom looked completely perplexed. Stuart was at the top of the stairs, calling my name.

I ignored them all.

I'd just reached the hallway when the front door burst open, and Jared raced in, the skin on his face raw from what looked like lash marks. "Kate! Kate! They took Allie and Eric! A van. They stopped, and they ripped off Allie's necklace, and—"

I didn't let him finish. Instead, I leaped on him, knocking him to the ground as I straddled him, the sharp end of the pencil over his heart. "Believe me when I say I can get this through your clothes and your skin and right into that cold, dead heart. I am highly, *highly* motivated."

"Kate—I didn't do anything. What the hell? What's going on?"

"You bastard. You unimaginable bastard. I *trusted* you. I thought you wanted to protect Allie, not hurt her."

"Hurt her?" That was Mindy's voice, but I ignored her as well.

"What are you talking about?" Jared asked. "I don't want to hurt Allie."

"She can defeat Lilith? Bullshit. You want her because she can *be* Lilith."

"No." He shook his head. "No, no, no. I don't want any of that. I want Lilith gone."

"Bullshit."

I heard a strange buzzing, and realized it was coming from my back pocket. The unpleasant beeping sound of a call that had been disconnected. "Stuart. Can you—"

Thankfully, he understood and took the phone from my jeans, then ended the call. I needed to call Father back, but first I needed to deal with this traitor.

"He's telling the truth," Mindy said, stepping into my line of sight. "At least, he mostly is. At least about wanting Lilith gone."

I looked between her and Stuart, then over to Laura, who shook her head as if to say she didn't know what Mindy was talking about.

"Stuart, can you find something solid and wooden and pointy. And a mallet. I want you to babysit this guy."

"On it," he said, then headed toward the garage.

"Okay, Mindy. What are you talking about?"

She took a tentative step closer to Jared. "They're blackmailing you, aren't they? You really do hate Lilith, but they're blackmailing you."

Jared stayed silent, so I jabbed the pencil down until he nodded. "Yes." He turned his head away, not meeting my eyes. And he didn't say another word.

I considered torturing it out of him—it was tempting, that was for sure—but I turned to Mindy instead. Right then, I needed information. "What do you know, Mindy? And how on earth do you know it?"

"I—well, when I was pissed at Allie I started researching him." She nodded to the vampire on the floor. "I told you I didn't trust him."

"You researched a vampire?"

"Well, he moves in the world like a human, right? So I checked what I could find. Addresses, driver's licenses, his parent's information. Which was really him, right? So I just kept going backward. It was kind of fun, actually, and I—"

"Mindy, sweetheart," Laura said. "What did you learn?"

"He's got a sister. Three generations back, there was always a sister. So I figure she's a vamp, too. But where is she now?"

"Staked?" Cutter asked, but I shook my head.

"Blackmail. That's what you said, right?" I directed the question to Mindy, who nodded.

"Blackmail?" Stuart repeated, as he came back in with a garden stake and a rubber mallet.

I nodded to Cutter. "Can you two keep that stake at his heart and get him in a chair. And if he lies, pound it home."

They did, with Stuart holding Jared in place by the shoulders, and Cutter keeping him in place with a well-placed stake and a clear willingness to use the mallet.

"Are you sure?" I asked Mindy.

"No. Except it makes sense. His sister suddenly doesn't seem to exist. But now he's interested in Allie? If Lilith was such a big deal to him, why didn't he come help us the last time Lilith blew into town? He showed up now because Lilith needed him. That's what I think, anyway."

"It's a good theory," I admitted, remembering that in addition to singing, Mindy worked on the school paper.

Laura looked at Mindy. "So you think that Lilith took his sister, and is forcing Jared to do what she says. Deliver Allie or his sister dies."

In the chair, Jared closed his eyes, then whispered something.

"Speak up," I snapped.

"Not dies," he whispered. "They'll just keep torturing her." His voice sounded strangled. "She's only ten years old. Do you know how long you can torture a vampire before they die? Try forever."

He lifted his chin, his expression as full of pain as

any I'd ever seen. "I've always looked after Celia," he said. "Since I was seven years old. How could I stop after we both got turned? How could I give up on her or force her to make her own way in the world, like some precocious child?"

I didn't want to believe him. But, damn me, I did. "How do you know she's being tortured? They've shown you? Telepathy?"

"Both. They took me to her once. A room, a long way from here. Dark, but with crystal walls. They had her chained. They cut her. Beat her. They made me talk to her, and then they pulled me out. They left her completely alone screaming for me to come back. To come rescue her. They could leave her for a hundred years. A thousand. She'd go mad. She'd grow weak. But she wouldn't die."

As he spoke, Stuart took his hands off Jared's shoulders, leaving it to Cutter to control the vampire. I wasn't too worried, but I was curious as to what Stuart was doing, especially when he dialed the phone he'd taken from me earlier.

I pushed down my curiosity, though, focusing instead on how Jared could help us now. Because as far as I was concerned, this vampire was only worthwhile if he provided a way to my daughter and Eric.

"So why can't you find her?" Laura asked. "You said they showed her to you telepathically, right? So why not use that to find her? Or at least to talk to her and let her know she's not alone."

"Crystal walls," I said. "He can't talk to her. Can't find her. Right?"

Jared nodded miserably. "They must open a door when they torture her. The only times I get flashes are when she's in pain."

"Help us," I said, bending down so I was looking straight in his eyes. "Help us find Allie and Eric. If you really care for Allie—and I think you do, Jared—then please, please help us."

He seemed to fall into himself. "I do care. For her. For you. For Mindy and Eliza." Behind me, Mindy scoffed. "I swear. But it's my sister. Can't you understand that? They'll destroy her."

"They'll destroy Allie, too. And who knows what they want with Eric."

"Lilith wants a mate," he said flatly. "Odayne's gone, but I guess Lilith liked Eric. She wants to park one of her consorts in his human body."

I cringed at that.

"Where have they taken them?"

He shook his head. "I don't know."

"I don't believe you," Cutter said, pressing the point so that it indented his shirt. "I stake you, your sister is all alone."

Jared closed his eyes. "I can't."

"Listen to me," I said. "Do you really want to be on their side? Allie's special. Help her. Help her and we will find your sister."

He shook his head. "There's no way. You'd never

find her. And, yeah, Allie's special. But that doesn't mean she'll win."

I felt the cold truth of those words, and forced myself not to think about it. "We will win. And we'll find your sister."

But Jared just shook his head, repeating, "I can't. I can't. I'm sorry, but I can't."

Behind Jared, Stuart held up the phone, and I heard Father Corletti's voice over the speaker. "He speaks the truth of his sister, *mia cara*. We received intel that the vampire Celia had been imprisoned by Lilith. Jared, help us and you will have the full power of *Forza Scura* behind you."

"How can you find something Lilith doesn't want found?" His voice shook. "I'm sorry. I can't let down my sister."

"So you'll let down the world instead?" I snapped. "Jared, if Lilith makes her way into Allie's body, what do you think will happen to this realm? In a year—or maybe just a day—Earth will be the real hell dimension."

But all he did was dip his head and mutter, "I'm sorry, I'm sorry, I promised her. I promised my parents. I swore I would always take care of Celia."

From the speaker, I heard Father Corletti sigh. "The boy must do what he believes is right. In a vampire, that is a rare thing. On that, at least, I do not condemn him."

"Well, I do," I said. "He's sacrificing my daughter

and the world. Come on, Jared. Think of the big picture."

"*Katherine.*" Father Corletti's sharp tone caught my attention. "There is still a hope. You must find them, and you must prevent the ceremony."

"How? Allie's phone is here and Jared ripped off her necklace." That was a guess, but from the way he winced, I knew I was right. "My phone isn't set to track Eric, and we don't know where they're going."

"Lilith intends to move into this world, Kate. I think you do know where she will go. Where she needs to go."

Of course. The ruins of the Stone Table. An old ritual site that predated the town itself, it had recently become a favorite location for demonic ceremonies. Not only that, it's where Lilith had tried this trick before.

"How do we stop her? We barely survived last time. Father, I don't have any weapon to use against a High Demon."

"There is a way," he said. "But you must listen carefully. Lilith will need to make the transfer into Allie's body —once in, she would only need to place her hand on Eric's flesh to open him up to a demonic entity. You must stop her before she enters Allie or all will indeed be lost."

"But how?"

"She will need Eric's blood. Prevent her from bleeding him, and you will stop the ceremony. Once he has shed even a drop, the door is open and she will attempt to come through."

"Attempt?"

"This is the second point at which you can stop her, though the cost is high. But child, there is not a third."

I swallowed, then met Laura's eyes. She looked as scared as I felt, and I saw the way she clung to Cutter's hand, her other arm around Mindy's shoulder. In front of me, Jared's head hung dejected. I was sorry for his sister's torment—I was—but not enough to sacrifice my daughter or this world.

As he held the phone, Stuart looked at me. Then he mouthed, *You can do this.*

I closed my eyes, bolstered by his faith in me. I *could* do it. More than that, I had to.

"I understand," I told Father. "Just tell me what to do."

CHAPTER 22

"*Here, here, here,*" I shouted, pointing at the turn-off to get to the Stone Table, a road down which I'd been many times. So many that I was beginning to think someone needed to pave it. For that matter, someone needed to haul the ruins away. Bury them at sea, or at least deep in a landfill.

Because honestly? I'd had enough of this place.

Cutter was behind the wheel and we bounced along. I'd conceded my driver's seat because I wanted to think and plan with this ragtag team that consisted of me, Cutter, Stuart, Eddie, and Jared.

Jared because we might need him. Cutter because he's got bad ass skills. Eddie, because he has the experience and has surprisingly sharp fighting skills for a guy his age. That, and he'd arrived home just as we were heading out, and when we told him the situation, he refused to stay behind, not even to help

Laura and Mindy play host to the entire birthday party.

And, of course, there was Stuart, who was only along because I didn't have time to argue, and he was determined. *"If you think I'm not going to be there for my daughter, you are so wrong,"* he'd said.

They were the right words, and I'd caved. With any luck, though, I could convince him to stay in the van. I really didn't want to split my focus looking out for him. Even more, I didn't want him to end up dead.

We parked, then tumbled out. I knew from experience that we had to walk the rest of the way. And as I looked up at the sky and saw four white streaks above us, I also knew we had to hurry. *A meteor shower. Fire and ice.*

Eliza's warning rang in my head.

Lilith.

I took off at a run,

It won't matter Kate.

The voice, cold and feminine, seemed to fill my head. I slowed long enough to glance at the men, and could tell from their expressions that it wasn't just me. I caught Stuart's eyes, his full of fear, and took off at a run again. Whatever was happening, the time was now. And oh, dear God, I hoped we weren't too late.

But you are too late, Kate. It's okay, though. I won't hurt you. In the end, you'll be my mother, too.

"You stay away from her, you bitch," I snarled, just before I burst through the final clump of brush and

309

into the open area around the battered Stone Table. I paused to get my bearings, noting the perimeter of demonic guards surrounding the ceremonial site.

"Mommy!"

"I'm here, baby," I called, searching the area and finding her bound to polished stone pillar I'd never seen here before. "It's going to be okay," I told her, even though I wasn't at all sure it would be.

I heard the grass rustle behind me and knew the men had caught up. But I didn't turn to look at them. I was too horrified by what I saw to my left—Eric tied naked to another pillar, his entire body covered with small cuts so that thin trails of blood crisscrossed his body.

No.

I meant to scream the word, but somehow it ended up only in my head.

Eric had already been bled. That meant there was only one chance left.

The chalice stone.

But where was it and what did it look like? For that matter, where was Lilith?

The second one was easy—all around us in the ether. But as for the other...

I met Allie's eyes. "A ceremonial stone. Have you seen it?"

She shook her head, struggling against her bindings, but it was no use. I doubted I would do better, so I didn't go over and try. There was no point. Until I destroyed the stone, she wasn't safe at all.

"Jared," I called. "What does it look like?"

He opened his mouth, then closed it when the air filled with the screams of a child in pain, as if trapped in a never ending nightmare.

It will never stop. Not if you help our Kate. But be my right hand, and you will have your sister back. Your sweet Celia who screams when the fire of my breath touches her. Your little sister who is slowly going mad because you've failed her. Who hates you because you haven't rescued her. You can free her now. Help me, and I will let her go. I might even give you her sanity back.

"She's lying," I called to him, as the demons who'd been standing like statues around the perimeter rushed the men.

"Don't worry about us," Cutter shouted, nailing one in the eye with his knife, and proving that his skills were just as extensive as advertised. Stuart and Eddie fought together, and I searched desperately for the chalice stone. But I saw nothing at all.

I had to find it. I *had* to.

"The chalice stone is the key," Father Corletti had said. "If she has already begun the ritual of the blood, then the next step will be for her to enter the chalice stone. It is an intermediary location between her realm and ours. She will go there, gather her strength and almost immediately leave again."

My head spun with the memory—and the importance of Father Corletti's words that he'd shared with all of us, speaking over the Odyssey's audio system as we'd raced toward the Stone Table.

I had to find the chalice stone.

"You must destroy the chalice while she is inside it. If you do, then you will have destroyed Lilith in her true form, and she will be no more. If you do not, then she will enter Allie and there will be no stopping her.

I'd told him I understood. What I hadn't told him was that his words had terrified me.

I hadn't realized they would get even worse.

"There is a price, mia cara. The one who destroys the stone—there is no coming back. You must understand this. The ancient texts are clear. There is only death or insanity, should the destroyer be unfortunate enough to survive. Stopping Lilith comes with a price. You need to understand.

"I need to save my daughter."

"In that case, you must know. The weapon is blood."

I'd said those words then, and I said them again now. We'd talked about finding another way in the car, but I knew there was no other way. Allie was the one who mattered, and not just because of her newfound abilities. She was my baby girl, and I wasn't going to sentence her to an eternity of torture trapped with a demon. I'd make the sacrifice willingly.

Too bad I couldn't find the damn stone.

"Mom! Something's happening."

Sure enough, the air around us seemed to shimmer. I felt a pull, as if all the air was gathering, and I heard

Eric cry out, as if this strange vortex was pulling the life from him, too.

Allie screamed, and as she did, I saw it—*The entire stone table, broken and battered, began to glow.*

The *table* was the chalice, and that glow was Lilith. It was now or never.

"I love you, Allie," I said, then sliced my palm with my knife as I raced forward, terrified but determined.

I didn't make it.

Instead, I was knocked on my ass by Stuart. "She needs you," he said. "And the world needs her. I love you, Allie," he said more loudly. "You and your mother are the best thing that every happened to me."

"Stuart!" Allie cried in tandem with me. "No!"

But it was too late. "I know what I'm doing," he called to us as he sliced his palm, then pressed it to the table, and the entire earth began to rumble.

Then I head Jared's voice over the din. "Celia!" he shouted. "I'm sorry." And in one crazy move, he tackled Stuart, knocking him free of the table and slapping his own bloody palm down.

Immediately, he was thrown backward, and I could only assume that vampire blood didn't work.

But had Jared saved Stuart? Or had he opened a door for Lilith to escape again?

I glanced back at Cutter and Eddie, neither of whom looked as if they had any more idea than I did. Then I ran to Stuart who was sprawled motionless on the ground. I bent over him, then exhaled with relief when I realized he was breathing. But although I shook him and spoke to him, he didn't wake up.

"Lilith?" Allie said.

"Do you feel her?"

She bit her lower lip, then shook her head. "I think she's gone."

Tentatively, I touched the table, expecting ... something. But it was just cool stone.

"She was expelled," Eric murmured, barely audible. "I felt it."

"Gone for good?"

"Don't know. Hope so." Exhaustion colored his voice.

"I'll get him down," Eddie said, hurrying to Eric.

"I've got Allie," Cutter said, glancing my direction. "You take care of Stuart."

I did, hurrying to him and trying to revive him, but it was no use. He was out. Completely unconscious. And I had no idea how long he would stay that way.

Behind me, Jared climbed to his feet and came over.

"Thank you," I said.

He just shook his head. "Too little, too late." He nodded to Stuart. "I'm sorry. I wanted to save him."

"I believe you," I told him. "And I'm sorry about your sister." She was lost, of course. The chances of finding the poor, tortured girl were next to none. "We'll help you look, I promise you that."

"I know. It won't matter."

"Maybe it will," I said, hoping to save her, but knowing the odds weren't in our favor.

A moment later, Cutter led Allie to me, and I clung tight to her.

"We won," she said, tears streaming down her face as she pressed a hand to Stuart's shoulder. "But it doesn't feel like it."

"It was too high a cost," I said. "It might be a victory, but we can't call it a win?"

"He'll be okay, Kate," Eric said, pulling me close as the EMTs loaded Stuart's stretcher onto the ambulance where Allie and Eddie were already settled with the paramedics. "He's alive. We'll figure this out. He'll be okay."

I nodded, fighting tears as I thought of my husband, cursed into insanity because he'd survived the blast from the stone. "He saved Allie," I said. "He doesn't deserve to fall into madness."

"Maybe he won't. Those records are ancient. Before decent medical care. Before drugs." He pressed his hand to my cheek. "He'll be okay, Katie-kins. Stuart's going to be fine."

I took a deep breath, intending to say that he couldn't know that. Instead, I asked, "Is that what you want?"

The question came out harsher than I intended, and I saw the flash of pain reflected in Eric's eyes.

"Do you love him?"

I nodded, tears stinging my cheeks as I wondered how such a simple question could be so fraught. "You know I do."

"And that's why I want him to be fine," Eric said.

I swallowed, only then realizing that my throat was thick with tears.

"Mom! Come on!" Allie's voice bellowed out from the back of the ambulance.

"Go," Eric said, and I sprinted that way, climbing in as the EMT started to shut the doors.

I had one last glimpse of Eddie, Cutter and Eric standing beside Jared. I whispered *thank you,* the words meant for all of them.

Then the doors closed and the ambulance started to bounce down the rocky trail, leaving one man I loved behind as I leaned forward and took the hand of the other.

He'll be okay, Eric had said. And though he had no mystical ability to make it so, the mere fact that he'd said it gave me hope. Not just for Stuart, but for our strange, messy extended family.

There were questions ahead, not the least of which was the bloodline that lead from Father Donnelly all the way down to my daughter. And God knew this family harbored secrets and demons and a strangely tainted bloodline. But we also had each other.

And despite everything, I had faith that would be enough.

THE END ... for now

Be sure to order book 8 in the Demon-Hunting Soccer Mom Series:

How to Train Your Demon

The Redemption Chronicles

A sexy apocalyptic urban fantasy trilogy with romance!

Born in Darkness

Lost in Shadows

Surrender to Dawn

Extraordinarily Yours

Writing as Julie Kenner

Sexy paranormal rom-com romps!

So (Very!) Much More than the Girl Next Door

Mayhem, Matchmakers, and a Bit of Bewitching

The Charmed Affair of an Invisible Bodyguard

The "Super" Secret Life of an Accidental Daddy

Never Trust a Rogue on a Magical Mission

How a Sexy Hero and a Marvelous Makeover (Sorta!) Saved
the World

The Seductive Charm of a Sexy Shifter

Other Paranormal Reads

Short and Sexy

His Wicked Touch

Seducing Sin

Tempting Fate

Stark International Novellas:

Meet Jamie & Ryan-so hot it sizzles.

Tame Me

Tempt Me

Tease Me

S.I.N. Trilogy:

It was wrong for them to be together...

...but harder to stay apart.

Dirtiest Secret

Hottest Mess

Sweetest Taboo

Most Wanted:

Three powerful, dangerous men.

Three sensual, seductive women.

Wanted

Heated

Ignited

Stark World Stories:

Set in the Stark universe.

Wicked Grind

Wicked Dirty

Wicked Torture

Justify Me

The following series have occasional

Stark World Easter eggs

Man of the Month

Who's your man of the month ...?

Down On Me

Hold On Tight

Need You Now

Start Me Up

Get It On

In Your Eyes

Turn Me On

Shake It Up

All Night Long

In Too Deep

Light My Fire

Walk The Line

Royal Cocktail (bonus book)

*Bar Bites: A Man of the Month Cookbook

(by J. Kenner & Suzanne M. Johnson)

Blackwell-Lyon:

Heat, humor & a hint of danger

Lovely Little Liar

Pretty Little Player

Sexy Little Sinner

Tempting Little Tease

Even more from JK:

The Fallen Saint Series

His touch is her sin. Her love is his salvation

My Fallen Saint

My Beautiful Sin

My Cruel Salvation

Rising Storm:

Writing as Julie Kenner

Small town drama

Rising Storm: Tempest Rising

Rising Storm: Quiet Storm

ABOUT THE AUTHOR

J. Kenner (aka Julie Kenner) is the *New York Times, USA Today, Publishers Weekly, Wall Street Journal* and #1 International bestselling author of over one hundred novels, novellas and short stories in a variety of genres.

JK has been praised by *Publishers Weekly* as an author with a "flair for dialogue and eccentric characterizations" and by *RT Bookclub* for having "cornered the market on sinfully attractive, dominant antiheroes and the women who swoon for them." A six-time finalist for Romance Writers of America's prestigious RITA award, JK took home the first RITA trophy awarded in the category of erotic romance in 2014 for her novel, *Claim Me* (book 2 of her Stark Saga) and another RITA trophy for *Wicked Dirty* in the same category in 2017.

In her previous career as an attorney, JK worked as a lawyer in Southern California and Texas. She currently lives in Central Texas, with her husband, two daughters, and two rather spastic cats.

Stay in touch! Text JKenner to 21000 to subscribe to JK's text alerts. Visit www.jkenner.com for more and to subscribe to her newsletter!

Printed in the USA
CPSIA information can be obtained
at www.ICGtesting.com
LVHW010046050923
757228LV00009B/390